Getting Dirty
with the CEO

Getting Dirty with the CEO

MIA SOSA

New York Boston

Copyright © 2016 by Mia Sosa
Excerpt from *Unbuttoning the CEO* copyright © 2015 by Mia Sosa

Cover design by name. [insert cover photo/art credits if applicable or delete this line.] Cover copyright © year by Hachette Book Group, Inc.

Forever Yours
Hachette Book Group
1290 Avenue of the Americas, New York, NY 10104
forever-romance.com
twitter.com/foreverromance

First published as an ebook and as a print on demand: October 2016

Forever Yours is an imprint of Grand Central Publishing. The Forever Yours name and logo are trademarks of Hachette Book Group, Inc.

The publisher is not responsible for websites (or their content) that are not owned by the publisher.

The Hachette Speakers Bureau provides a wide range of authors for speaking events. To find out more, go to www.hachettespeakersbureau.com or call (866) 376-6591

ISBNs: 978-1-4555-6847-5 (ebook), 978-1-4555-6845-1 (print on demand)

This book is dedicated to Olivia Dade.
We started this journey together, and we'll
continue to stumble along together, too.
Thank you for always being there for me.
And yes, you're right, your milkshake *is* better
than mine.
Sending you heart-eyes emojis for days.

Acknowledgments

This is my third published book, and the number of people who deserve my thanks continues to grow. If I don't do justice to those people here, I'm screwed. Okay, here I go:

Everything I do begins and ends with my hubby and girls. Thank you for cheering me on, making me smile, and being proud of my accomplishments. I love you always and in all ways.

My family has continued to champion me and my career, and I can't thank them enough for pimping my books. Now if my mother could just work on the women at her beauty salon, I'd be all set.

I'm so fortunate to be able to call Sarah Younger my agent. She's always available for me, gives me sound advice, and encourages my dreams. She sends fantastic GIFs, too. Thanks for everything, Sarah.

My new editor, Madeleine Colavita, helped me write a better book. She says doing so is her job, but that's only half the story. She *cares* about the manuscripts she edits, and her love for words shines through in everything she does. It may be your job, Madeleine, but you do it exceptionally well, and I've grown as an author as a result of working with you.

To the rest of the Grand Central Publishing/Forever Yours family: Thank you for everything you've done on my behalf.

My friend and cackle partner Soni Wolf has beta read most of the books in The Suits Undone series, and I'm so grateful for her insights and feedback. A home-cooked empanada is definitely in your future, woman.

A special shout-out to Tiffany Winters, Stephanie Taylor, Sofia Tate, and Kennedy Ryan, because sometimes writers just need to talk with people who "get" them.

And as always, I must recognize The Dragonflies, The Cackle Corner, my *Hermanas*, The Binders, my law school tribe, and Team Sarah. These folks are my jam.

Finally, to the people who purchase my books: Thank you for giving a relatively new author a chance to enter your reading worlds. I hope you enjoy my books as much as I enjoy writing them.

Getting Dirty
with the CEO

PROLOGUE

San Juan, Puerto Rico

The sounds of the salsa band irritated the hell out of Daniel Vargas, but as he rounded the outskirts of the ballroom, he pasted on a "life couldn't get any better" smile, hoping everyone would believe he was having a great time at Graciela and Ethan's wedding.

What he wouldn't do for a little air and space. A reprieve from the what-ifs that kept urging him toward a dismal place in his head. He snuck a glance at his parents, who sat with their good friends, the mother and father of the bride. Their wooden expressions didn't surprise him. These days, life happened around them, and they simply watched like bystanders to an event they hadn't expected to attend. His parents had never learned how to hide their pain behind a cheerful exterior. Daniel, on the other hand, had perfected the skill.

He needed a distraction. His gaze floated over the faces of the wedding guests until it settled on a familiar face.

Mimi Pennington.

The bride's best friend—and distraction in the flesh.

Bull's-eye.

She stood by the open bar and typed on her phone, giving him a minute to watch her undetected. The bridesmaid dress she wore skimmed her delicate ankles and hugged her generous curves. She'd pinned her blond hair on top of her head, her bangs and a few runaway strands framing her face. Though she was petite, Mimi's larger-than-life personality made her appear six feet tall to him. And *damn*, that mouth. It was an entity unto itself, and for reasons he had yet to decipher, its barbs had recently begun landing on him. Still, like a moth to a six-alarm fire, he was drawn to her anyway.

Didn't matter that she would skewer him. He'd much rather focus on Mimi's sharp tongue than the sadness in his parents' eyes. So he strolled over to the bar and rested his elbows on the counter. "Hey, Fireworks."

She stopped typing and raised her head—but she didn't bother looking at him. "What do you want, Vargas?"

"I'm flattered. Do you have a sixth sense when it comes to me?"

She turned to face him then, her blue eyes sparkling. "You know how dogs have this supernatural ability to hear sounds at high decibels? Well, I have a similar talent for detecting pompous men. I could sense you from across the room. Watching. Plotting. Arroganting."

He chuckled, the brief exchange already lifting his mood. *This* was why he chose to engage with her: A conversation with Mimi never traveled along a straight path, and the journey was just as enjoyable as the destination. "Arroganting?"

"Being arrogant. It comes so naturally to you, the word deserves to be a verb."

Well, as to her, other more interesting actions came to mind: kissing, licking, sucking, fu— He stopped himself. *Bad, Daniel. Pay attention to what she's telling you.* "But you don't know me very well. How'd you come to that conclusion?"

She gave him a full once-over before responding in a flat tone. "I know enough."

He raised a brow as though he were mildly interested in her answer. In truth, the need to uncover the source of her disdain had occupied more of his time than he cared to admit. She'd erected a wall between them, and he couldn't help wondering what would happen if he scaled it. And since he was a man who thrived on being likable, her ire made him uncomfortable. He'd always played off his confusion well enough—a smirk being his go-to move—but the question remained: What the hell had he done to piss her off? "Care to clue me in?"

She swiped at her phone while she spoke. "Do you remember when I tried to pitch you for your business at the Blakely Awards Dinner?"

He recalled speaking with her at the event, sure. He'd been there in his role as a board member of her best friend's community service organization. But he'd talked to Mimi only briefly, and he couldn't recall what they'd talked about. "I'm sorry. I'm drawing a blank."

"Yes, well, I'm not surprised." She jabbed at her phone. "You were more interested in having a conversation with my breasts."

That wasn't *entirely* out of the realm of possibility. She had a magnificent rack. But he was usually smoother than her memory indicated, and certainly less boorish when admiring a woman's body.

Still, his gut told him that her resentment came from another source. Even before the Blakely Awards Dinner, she'd made it clear he didn't impress her. Now he had no idea how to propel himself out of the sinkhole he'd apparently fallen into. He'd try, though. "I'm not saying this is what happened, but I do wear contacts, and it's *possible* I might have been having an issue with them."

Her eyes narrowed and she curled her upper lip. "You're the butter knife in the drawer, Daniel."

Well, damn. Sparring with Mimi required a full night's rest and a clear head; he had neither. Maybe it was time to disengage and find a less lethal form of entertainment for tonight. He raised his elbows off the bar and opened his mouth to apologize and make a hasty exit, but before he could do that, a woman holding a small bouquet of flowers rushed to Mimi's side and whispered in her ear.

Mimi's eyes bulged and she nodded. "I'm so there. Give me a sec." She faced him and smiled. Given that her smile was directed at him, he suspected it was fake as hell. If she invited him to kiss her lips, they'd probably be laced with arsenic.

"Do you speak Spanish?" she asked him.

"I do."

"Great. So apparently there's another party going on in the hotel. We're planning to crash for a few minutes." She pointed to the woman by her side. "This is Rosa, by the way. Gracie's cousin."

"Good to meet you, Rosa."

Rosa gave him a shy smile. Now *that* smile seemed genuine. "Hi." She placed the bouquet on the bar counter and tugged on Mimi's arm. "Mimi, we should go."

"Okay," Mimi told her. To him, she said, "Want to join us?"

Rosa covered her mouth with her hand and gave Mimi a questioning look.

Mimi's face looked hopeful, which made him suspicious, of course. Oddly, though, he was hopeful himself. Maybe he could use this as an opportunity to begin scaling that wall. "Why would you want me there?"

She raised her eyebrows as though the answer were obvious. "Because we're crashing a party, and if anything goes down, it might be helpful to have you around. You know, to intercede on my behalf, particularly because I don't speak Spanish." She stuffed her phone in her clutch. "I can see the idea doesn't appeal to you. No worries. I'm just going to pop out and come back in before Gracie and Ethan leave for their honeymoon."

She spun around.

Despite his reservations, he touched the back of her arm to stop her and she froze. So did he, since the softness of her skin scrambled his brain for several seconds.

She twisted her head and glanced at his hand on her arm before pinning him with a heated gaze. "What is it?"

His brain cleared enough to register that her words came out choppy. Ah, she wasn't immune to him after all. That morsel of information opened up so many possibilities. He'd always been attracted to Mimi's crackle and pop, eager to stoke her fire simply because her taunts kept him grounded in the present, far away from his unpleasant past. But what if he were the object of Mimi's desire? What if she channeled all her passion in a different direction? To his bed, for instance.

After clearing her throat, she repeated her question and flicked her gaze to his fingers on her skin.

He dropped his hand as though he'd touched a flame, which, in a way, he had. "I'll come. I need a distraction anyway."

"Excellent. It's just a floor below this one, in Salon C."

The women whispered to each other as he followed them out of the ballroom. After a few false turns, they found the sign for Salon C. Rosa descended the stairs beside him while Mimi led the way.

"So, Daniel, do you live in Washington, D.C., like Mimi?" she asked.

"I do."

"Do you have family on the island?"

"Plenty. You—"

Mimi laid a finger against her mouth and shushed them. "Let's try to be discreet." She cracked open the door and peeked inside. The steady thump of dance music and flashes of light told him they'd found the right ballroom. Mimi and Rosa scurried through the door.

He followed them inside and stopped short to survey the room. And after his eyes adjusted to the strobe lighting and focused on the scene, his jaw dropped.

There were men. Everywhere. *Half-naked men everywhere.* Okay, maybe not everywhere, but certainly a dozen of them, and *fuck*, they wore thongs. Pink thongs. Blue thongs. Even leopard print thongs. Chests flexed and asses out, they gyrated around the room, competing with each other in an epic battle of the bulges. And he couldn't un-see any of it.

Mimi whooped. "Now this is the kind of cock fight I can get down with."

With his mouth still hanging open, Daniel spied a woman in a short red dress, her long hair covered by a cheap wedding veil. She was sitting in a chair of honor in the center of the room and waving dollar bills in the air. One of the men straddled her and she inserted the money between his ass cheeks.

For the love of...

By his side, Mimi held her stomach as she took in Daniel's dumbfounded expression.

Damn her.

She'd tricked him into crashing a bachelorette party.

Mimi: 1. Daniel: 0.

* * *

Mimi debated whether to break out her iPhone and take a picture of Daniel's face. It. Was. Priceless. Ha. Mr. Perfection looked less than perfect at the moment. He'd scrunched his face so that his brows almost touched, and he was running his hands through his hair as he backed up.

She laughed. "Where you going, Daniel?"

He stopped mid-step. "You knew this was a bachelorette party?"

"I did."

"Why didn't you tell me that?"

"I didn't think it mattered," she said with a shrug of her shoulders. "Does it?"

"Do *you* think I want to stare at a bunch of men in thongs?"

"I don't know. Do you?"

He smirked. "Even if I wanted to stare at a man in a thong, I assure you a leopard print would not be my first choice."

Oh, good. He had a sense of humor lurking under that polished veneer. "Point taken. You're free to leave, Daniel." She waggled her eyebrows. "I'm going to hang out for a bit and watch the show. Make sure Rosa doesn't get into any trouble."

She glanced around the room searching for her fellow party crasher, but Rosa had disappeared into the throng. *Go, Rosa.* One of the male strippers was leading the bride-to-be back to her table while another fully clothed stripper crooked a finger at a woman in the audience. That woman nearly upended the chair in the center of the dance floor in her rush to sit on it. The emcee, meanwhile, pumped his hands in the air, inciting the crowd even more.

Beside her, Daniel made no move to leave and instead put two fingers to his mouth and whistled. *What the hell?*

Daniel motioned for the emcee's attention and pulled the man to the side, speaking rapid-fire Spanish to him. Dammit. If only she'd paid attention to Señora Colon in high school. Mimi strained to hear what Daniel was saying, though the exercise was pointless. She did appreciate the sound of his voice, however, each roll of his *r*'s making him more attractive in her eyes. *No, no, no.* This was Daniel. An arrogant, self-centered ladies' man if ever there was one.

The emcee exchanged words with one of the dancers, and before she knew what was happening, the dancer pulled Mimi to the center of the room and guided her to sit in the chair.

Daniel clapped and whistled from his spot in the audience.

She pretended to protest her situation, shaking her head and covering her face in feigned embarrassment. In reality, however, she mentally licked her lips in anticipation. The stripper was cute, a little young for her taste, yet attractive enough for a one-night stand.

But then he sauntered away, and Daniel took his place.

Her mouth went dry, and her face burned. *What is happening? I cannot compute. I cannot compute.*

In an unexpectedly suave move, Daniel spun around to face the crowd of women and loosened his tie. A collective cheer erupted from the audience, and playing to the masses, Mimi fanned herself.

He wouldn't strip. No way. Right?

The music changed tempo, slowing to a sinewy Reggaeton beat that made her think of the slip and slide of limbs between silk sheets. Daniel rocked his hips as he flicked the top button of his dress shirt. The man had rhythm in spades, and his movements made her think of *his body* slipping and sliding with hers between silk sheets. Given that his smoky gaze had zeroed in on her face, she guessed that had been his objective.

Any minute now he'd laugh and pull her from the chair, bowing to the ladies who'd expected a lot more skin. Except he flicked another button. And another. And yet another. And then he slipped off his suit jacket and let it fall to the floor.

"More, more, more," the women behind him chanted.

Mimi caught a glimpse of his defined pecs through his open shirt, and her breath hitched. *No. Absolutely not.* She closed her eyes and clamped her legs shut. *Stand down, lady bits. Stand the fuck down.*

The crowd roared. The floor shook. Her own sense of self-preservation forced her to open one eye. He'd taken off his shirt, and she blinked several times to make sure she hadn't been transported to the set of *Magic Mike*. Nope. That was Daniel. Daniel with the six-pack abs. Daniel with the broad shoulders. Daniel with the so freaking happy trail.

In a trance, she watched him stalk across the dance floor and face her with his legs apart. Then he winked at her and held out his hand. "Had enough?"

Mimi had never been one to suffer bullshit, so she told him the truth. "Quite the opposite. I want more." Just in case that hadn't been clear enough, she trailed a single finger from his Adam's apple to his navel. "*A lot more.*"

He bent at the waist and whispered in her ear. "You have ten minutes to head upstairs and say your good-byes."

She leaned toward him and breathed in his scent. *All male. All yummy.* "Where are we going after that?"

He lifted her out of the chair and pulled her flush against his naked chest. "To your bed."

* * *

As soon as Mimi hit the button for her floor, Daniel used his body to push her against the elevator wall. Her perfume, a tropical scent with a hint of citrus, drifted over him. With their bodies pressed together, her ample breasts touching his chest, he stared at her for a few seconds cataloging her features. They'd never been this close, her heat penetrating his shirt and warming him from the outside in. From this new vantage point, he could see that her eyes were blue-gray rather than true blue, and her pupils were dilated.

Instinctively, he tightened his hold on her hips, adjusting her body so she could feel his erection against her stomach. Her eyes fluttered closed as she lowered her head. "Yes," she moaned against his neck, and then she grabbed his ass and pulled him closer, grinding herself against him. He mentally cursed the elevator that would take them to the hotel's fourth floor. The mechanical cock blocker ascended at a leisurely place, its cables creaking and rumbling, and Daniel wondered if he and Mimi would be its last riders. Ever.

Mimi didn't seem concerned about impending death as she escalated her exploration of his body. She slipped her hand between them and coasted her fingers over his crotch. Every muscle in his body reacted, tightening in anticipation of getting the same attention. His mind was already steps ahead of the present, picturing the moment when he would plunge into her, and he mimicked the motion by rocking his pelvis against her. Now he finally understood the appeal of sex in public places.

"Kiss me," she said in a breathy voice as she continued to stroke him through his slacks.

A shudder ran through him as his mouth brushed over hers. Once. Twice. Unreal. Her lips were softer than he'd imagined. Foreign, too, because nothing on his own body possessed that smooth texture. Once his tongue found hers, a cascade of frenzied movements followed. The kiss couldn't have been less choreographed. It was messy and all-consuming, more about getting all of their senses involved than about demonstrating their skill in this basic mating ritual. Finesse would come later. For now, they devoured each other.

His mouth never leaving hers, he skated his hands over her breasts, stopping at the hard peaks and rubbing them in slow circles. In answer, she moaned her approval and squeezed his erection. She established a rhythm with her hands: fast, fast, slow, fast, fast, slow. He deepened the kiss, hoping to interrupt her patterned assault. He'd come in his pants if she did that for more than a few seconds.

Finally, he drew back, inhaling much-needed air. When his breathing had slowed, he caressed the sides of her face. A dusting of freckles dotted the apples of her cheeks. "You're beautiful," he told her, his mouth inches from hers.

Mimi's eyes clouded over, not with passion but with boredom. "You don't have to whisper sweet nothings to me, Daniel. That's not what this is about."

She'd delivered the pronouncement in a matter-of-fact tone, her flat affect pulling him out of the moment. The elevator dinged as though she'd orchestrated the sound to serve as the period to her sentence.

He pulled her through the parted doors and faced her. "What's this about then?"

With a wicked gleam in her eyes, she clasped her hands around his neck and drew him to her. "It's lust. Plain and simple. It won't change anything."

He kept his face relaxed, her words never altering his demeanor, but inside an alarm went off in his brain, warning him to reconsider his plans for the evening. Taking the night to its logical conclusion was exactly what Mimi wanted—shit, he wanted it so badly he was hard as granite—but he also suspected she'd vote him off the island as soon as they were done. Today's lust. Tomorrow's old news.

Which would have been fine if this were anyone but Mimi.

Mimi engaged him in a way no other woman had. Who else would get him to channel his inner male stripper like he'd done this evening? And he wanted more of her, not less. Their chemistry hadn't started in the bedroom, and he didn't want it to end there, either. But convincing her to consider him as more than the guy she loved to hate wouldn't be easy. To do that, he needed time. As much as it would kill him to walk away, he knew this with certainty: If he wanted her in his bed for more than one night, he had to stay out of her bed today.

I'm fucking insane.

He snaked a shaky hand around her and hit the elevator button. "Let's pick this up again when we're in the States."

With her eyelids at half-mast, she dropped her arms and shook her head in confusion. "You're leaving?"

"I am."

She narrowed her gaze. "This is payback for the bachelorette party, isn't it?"

Standing there with her flushed skin and languid gaze, she unknowingly tempted him to revert to his initial plans, but he held firm. "I'm glad to hear you think my leaving is a punishment of sorts, but no, that's not the reason. I'm not interested in being your one-night stand, Mimi. I want more, and this just isn't the right time for what I have in mind."

She said nothing for several seconds, her furrowed brow and blinking eyes revealing that he'd stumped her. But she recovered quickly. "That's too bad, because this is the *only* time for what I have in mind."

If she thought that statement would make him second-guess himself, she was wrong. Now more than ever he knew he'd made the right call. "You don't mean that, Fireworks."

"Oh, Daniel, I assure you I do. What's your objective, Vargas?"

He stepped forward and rested his hand on her waist. She didn't pull back. An excellent sign, indeed. "It's called delayed gratification."

She puffed out a dismissive breath. "Someone's never heard of self-gratification, I see."

"I've heard of it, but it's a poor substitute for what I can give you."

The ding of the elevator caused her to jump back. When he

stepped on, her eyes turned stormy and she rubbed her temples. "God, you're the most conceited man I've ever met."

He pressed the button for the first floor. "And yet you still want me."

She dropped her hands to her sides. "That's it? Seriously?"

He left her with one word. "Seriously."

As the elevator doors closed, she let out a frustrated growl.

At least now he'd evened the score.

Mimi: 1. Daniel: 1.

CHAPTER ONE

Washington, D.C.
Four months later

A charitable bachelor auction? Seriously?

Mimi Pennington battled the urge to roll her eyes—and lost.

Her firm's fiercest competitor claimed to be the premier public relations strategist in the Washington, D.C., area. Judging by the spectacle onstage, however, the company's creative juices had been sopped by an extra-absorbent paper towel.

She stood in a corner of the large ballroom, processing the antics. Bachelor Number One, a tall, burly man with a Stetson, strutted across the stage, unbuttoned the jacket of his midnight blue suit, and gyrated his hips. *Nope, nope, nope.* As if that weren't bad enough, Mr. Stetson then turned around and lifted his jacket to give the audience a view of his ass. Mimi howled with laughter. *Oh, this is too much.*

After she'd regained her composure, she scanned the sea of

cream-clothed tables, noting that some of the guests wore wide-eyed expressions. When her best friend, Gracie, had offered her a ticket to this exclusive fund-raising gala, Mimi had snatched it up, recognizing the event as a plum networking opportunity. And because she never missed a chance to promote her services, she'd arranged to put up ten hours of her own consulting time for bidding in the silent auction. So the evening was about making connections and maybe snagging a new client. She hadn't expected to be entertained, too. *Bonus.*

Now that the fund-raising festivities had begun, Mimi made her way across the ballroom and found her and Gracie's table.

Gracie jumped up from her chair and hugged her. "Hey, sweetie. Had no idea you were already here."

"I've been mingling," she whispered in Gracie's ear. "These people are dry as fuck. Did someone spike the punch with a sedative?" She pointed at the stage. "Are they not seeing what I'm seeing?"

Gracie covered her grin, her dark brown eyes laughing for her. "There's no punch, wise ass. And please be good. I'm trying to raise some money for my charity here."

Mimi took the seat to Gracie's right, her gaze skating over the faces at the table. To her surprise, Gracie's husband wasn't one of them. "Where's Ethan?"

"He's traveling on business this week, so you get me all to yourself."

"Lucky me." Mimi angled her body toward the stage. "So how is this supposed to work?"

"Each nonprofit gets to put up a bachelor for bidding. The winning bid gets a date with the bachelor, but if the highest bidder wants to pass on the date, she—or he—can choose something else—like golf lessons with a retired PGA golfer. I'm really hoping we can make enough money to meet our renovation budget." Gracie turned her attention to the stage. "Oh, look, the next bachelor's up."

Mimi followed Gracie's gaze. A tall, wiry man with dirty blond hair dug his hands in the pants of his tuxedo pants and took center stage. He squinted his eyes against the bright lights that were trained on him, his face otherwise impassive—and *very* pale. Mimi scooted her chair closer to Gracie and spoke to her in a hushed tone. "Bachelor Number Three looks like he's going to puke. If that happens, I swear I'm breaking out the popcorn."

Gracie hiccupped on a laugh but didn't turn around.

"So you're just going to ignore me, huh?" Mimi asked.

"Yup."

"Killjoy."

Gracie turned around and pretended to scratch her nose with her middle finger. As usual, Mimi had brought out the ten-year-old in her best friend. She considered this one of her most noteworthy skills in life.

The emcee, a sprite of a woman with a saccharine-sweet smile, gave a rundown of Bachelor Number Three's bid-worthy credentials. "Our next single is here to support Kindred Center, a battered women's shelter in Southeast D.C."

Now that was a cause Mimi could support, even if she wasn't enamored of the idea of yet another bachelor auction. She glanced at the bidder card assigned to her place setting. Bids started at one thousand dollars. Offering any more than that would mean she'd either be dipping into her personal savings or eating tuna fish and crackers for the remainder of the year. Still, she reached for the card.

"Tell him to remove his jacket and turn around for us," a woman yelled from the audience.

Guests turned their heads and stretched their necks to see who had made the request, some of them no doubt thinking it was crass. *Now we're getting somewhere.* Mimi spotted the heckler on the other side of the ballroom. She was hard to miss. The glitter on the woman's gown served as a beacon under the dim lighting, making her appear as though she were a disco ball come to life—or a finalist in the World Figure Skating Championships.

"He's an attorney with Hillman and Greene," the emcee continued. "Alternatively, he's offering three hours of trust and estates counseling."

Wait. The guy drafts wills for a living? Mimi promptly dropped the bidding card on the table. She could send the shelter a check and avoid a date with him altogether. *Definitely a better option.*

Bored with Bachelor Number Three, Mimi turned away from the stage and scanned the room. Perhaps she could chat up an old client of the firm in the interim. A deep chuckle and several giggles snagged her attention and drew her gaze to a table several feet away.

Ugh. Daniel Vargas.

Player extraordinaire.

Man-on-her-shit-list since he'd left her hanging months ago.

With an arm curled around the chair next to his, he basked in the attention of the females at the table. One particular woman, in an admittedly lovely blue dress, seemed to be vying for a special place among his groupies. *Don't bother, sis. The only person who's special to Daniel is Daniel.*

She tapped Gracie on the shoulder and leaned in to whisper in her ear. "By the way, who'd you pick as your bachelor?"

Gracie turned her head to the side and winked. "You'll see."

* * *

"Bachelor Number Five is here on behalf of Learn to Net, an organization that serves D.C. residents who don't have Internet service in their homes. LTN provides access to research libraries, online job applications, and tutoring websites, and helps reduce the information gap between lower-income families and more affluent ones."

Mimi nearly stumbled out of her chair when she saw Daniel onstage. "You didn't."

"I most certainly did," Gracie said with a twinkle in her eye.

Mimi smirked. "I bet he was happy to do it, too."

Gracie shook her head. "Actually, he gave a good fight. Said the idea of being onstage, and I quote, *'parading his wares,'* would make him feel objectified."

"Coming from a man who objectifies women, that's rich. So how'd you get him to cave?"

Gracie winked. "I played the guilt card. Told him that as the only single male member on the board, it was his duty to help me raise money for LTN. When that didn't work, I threatened to complain to his parents."

"Very professional on your part, sweetie."

Gracie gave her a devilish grin. "A family connection has its privileges."

"Devious. I'm rubbing off on you. *Finally.*" She looked up to see Daniel smoothing his hair and brushing off imaginary lint on his shoulders. "A taste of his own medicine would be good for him, I think."

Gracie said nothing. Instead, she peered at Mimi like a detective ready to begin her interrogation.

Mimi fidgeted in her seat. "What?"

"Why don't you like him?" Gracie asked.

Even now Daniel thrived on being in the spotlight. He stood onstage wearing a grin that suggested there was nowhere else he'd prefer to be. "You mean apart from his bloated ego?"

"Yes, apart from that. He might be a tad too confident, I'll give you that, but he's not a bad guy. Is there something you're not telling me?"

"Okay, I'll tell you, but this stays between us. No sharing with your hubby. Promise."

Gracie frowned at her. "What the hell, Mimi? You've been keeping secrets? From me?"

"Promise," Mimi repeated in a firm and urgent voice.

Gracie blew out a breath, her version of a long-suffering sigh. "Fine. I promise not to tell Ethan."

"Okay. Remember your wedding?"

A crease appeared between Gracie's brows. "Um. Of course I remember my wedding."

"Daniel and I almost had sex that night."

Gracie gaped at her.

"Close your mouth, Gracie."

Gracie pressed her lips together. Then she turned to the stage and watched Daniel as though she'd discovered a scandalous secret about him. After a beat, she said, "What? When? Where? How?"

"It's a long story that we probably shouldn't get into here."

Gracie shook her head in confusion. "Okay, okay."

"I'll tell you this, though. The man is hung like a horse." She whinnied to emphasize her point. "Too bad I didn't get to ride him." She pretended to pull on a set of reins and whinnied again.

Gracie barked out a laugh and covered Mimi's mouth with her hand. "Be quiet."

Mimi swatted Gracie's hand away. "What? It's true."

"But none of this explains why you're not a fan." Gracie narrowed her eyes. "Wait. Did he act like a jerk when you rejected him? Because if he did, I'll—"

"*He* rejected *me*, Gracie."

Gracie tilted her head to the side, her lips pursed. "Excuse me?"

Mimi couldn't say the words again; they were entirely accurate and too painful an admission to repeat. "You heard me the first time."

"Did he give you a reason?" Gracie asked in a soft voice.

Uh-oh. She'd heard that voice before, usually when Gracie was in Mimi-handling mode, which meant they'd dissect the incident from all angles before Gracie was prepared to move on. Mimi refused to have that conversation now.

"Let's just say the night didn't turn out the way I'd expected it to and leave it at that, okay? Besides, the Marine I met on my flight to Puerto Rico took the edge off."

Gracie nodded. "Okay. But let me just say I'm sorry that happened. And I'll be sure to knee Daniel in the nuts for you."

Mimi groaned. "No, no. Please don't do or say anything to him. I don't want him to think he affected me in any way. I'm only telling you because I need to be able to skewer him in a safe place, and you're my safe place. The truth is, I wasn't prepared to go through with it, either. It just irks me that he beat me to the punch."

Gracie covered Mimi's hand with hers. "So no harm then."

Mimi nodded. "Right. No harm."

Well, maybe just a little. That night in Puerto Rico she'd experienced a different kind of chemistry with Daniel, one that didn't involve teasing on his part or taunting on hers. Now that she'd gotten a bite-sized sample of what it would be like to have sex with him, her brain didn't know whether to slap him or order a full-sized meal.

They'd communicated twice since that fateful night. A few weeks after the wedding, she'd arranged for a leopard print men's thong to be hand delivered to his office, not as a sign of a truce but to signal that his rejection hadn't affected her in the least. When he didn't respond, she'd decided to excise him from her brain—with a scalpel if necessary. But a few weeks later, he sent her a box of pocket-sized vibrators in a dozen different colors. The note inside read, *A self-care package to be used until you come to your senses. Fondly, Daniel.* He'd underlined the word *come.*

He truly was a jerk. But he also had a ridiculously sexy body, bedroom brown eyes, and a manaconda between his legs. *Well, hello there. Nice to meet you, Kryptonite.*

The buzz from the audience grew as the emcee completed her rundown of Daniel's attributes and announced that the bidding would begin. Gracie turned to the stage. "Wish me luck."

"Good luck, sweetie."

Mimi wanted to shut down any further musings about her encounters with Daniel, but the man in question—along with his sizable junk—was standing on the stage. *This is my life.*

The emcee tapped her mic. "Okay, ladies and gentleman, the bidding floor is one thousand dollars, and there is no ceiling. Who's ready to get us started at one thousand dollars?"

Dozens of women raised their bidder cards.

"What about fifteen hundred dollars? Can I get fifteen hundred dollars? Fifteen hundred dollars for Learn to Net."

The women's hands remained in the air.

"Wonderful. You're being generous tonight. Let's see if we can pick things up here. Anyone ready to give me two thousand dollars for a date with Mr. Vargas."

"Three thousand dollars," said the human disco ball.

Dozens of hands dropped.

"What about thirty-five hundred? Anyone prepared to give me thirty-five hundred?'

"Thirty-five hundred dollars," said another woman.

"Thirty-five hundred dollars from the woman in the blue dress."

Ah. The woman who'd been flirting with Daniel at his table. Had they planned this?

With one hand on her cocktail and another hand on her bidder card, the human disco ball stood up. "Five thousand dollars," she said in a raspy voice. "He's *mine*, ladies."

Human disco ball was definitely a smoker.

Gracie tapped her feet in excitement. "Oh, this is better than I expected."

Onstage, Daniel replaced his wide smile with a deep frown, and he knitted his brows.

So he doesn't want to go on a date with human disco ball, huh? Poor thing.

For the next minute human disco ball and the blue dress tried to outbid each other. Mimi, meanwhile, was rooting for the human disco ball, whose flushed skin and boisterous gestures signaled a serious hangover in her immediate future.

Each time someone other than human disco ball raised their bidder card, Daniel's eyes lifted, his expression brightening with hope. And each time his rowdy pursuer upped her bid, his face fell in defeat.

She loved the idea of making him squirm, so Mimi raised her bidder card. *Commencing Operation Get Rid Of the Blue Dress* in five, four, three, two… "Ten thousand dollars."

Daniel's gaze shot to hers. With his eyes wide, he mouthed, *What are you doing?*

Having fun, Mimi mouthed back with a saucy smile.

Just as she had hoped, the ten-thousand-dollar bid caused the woman in blue to tap out. Much to Mimi's delight, human disco ball was no quitter, however. "Eleven thousand dollars," she said with a wave of her cocktail.

"I need you to raise your bidder card, ma'am," the emcee told her.

"Oh, yes, here," she said.

"Do I have twelve thousand dollars? Is someone ready to give me twelve thousand dollars?"

Daniel's gaze whipped to Mimi's, and when she threw up her hands and shrugged her shoulders, his eyes narrowed in understanding.

Take that, Mr. Perfect.

With a feigned pout, Mimi dropped out of the bidding.

The emcee tapped her mic. "We have eleven thousand dollars on the table. Going once, going twice, going three times. Sold to the lady in silver. We have our winning bid for a date with Daniel Vargas. Eleven thousand dollars to LTN."

The human disco ball whooped and ran to the stage to collect her prize. Daniel grimaced when she tackle-hugged him and nearly brought him to the floor in the process.

Mimi burst out laughing. The evening had turned out much better than she'd anticipated. "Are you getting pictures of this, Gracie?"

Gracie's mouth gaped. "You're so evil."

"Me? What did I do?"

Her best friend stared at her in silence.

"Oh, c'mon, Gracie. That woman was going to win the bid no matter what. I was just having a little fun."

"How?"

"By taunting Daniel with the possibility that he'd escape her clutches."

"And what if she hadn't upped her bid?"

Yes, Mimi. What if?

She'd earmarked the money in her bank account for the down payment on her own condo, but in the moment, with Daniel's smug grin staring back at her, she'd risked her ability to pay for her future home simply to needle him. Mimi bristled at the realization that she'd abandoned her good judgment for such a stupid reason. She couldn't tell any of this to Gracie, though. Her friend would make too much of it. So she settled for a half-truth. "Then I would have happily dipped into my hard-earned savings in support of my best friend."

"*Right.* You know I'd never take your savings. And you could have gotten us in trouble. They could accuse me of planting someone in the audience to artificially inflate the winning bid."

"Gracie, relax. If anyone asks, I'll show them a bank statement proving I could have paid the winning bid if I'd had to."

"Okay, fine. Don't be surprised if you've made a frenemy, though."

Mimi scoffed at the idea. "Daniel doesn't scare me. And besides, he has nothing he can hold over my head."

She glanced at Daniel's face, and he pinned her with a "you are so going to regret this" stare.

Nope. There was definitely nothing significant he could hold over her head.

Thank goodness for that.

CHAPTER TWO

Daniel held his breath as the woman who'd won a date with him squeezed his waist as though it were that last bit of toothpaste in a nearly empty tube. If her grabby hands weren't enough, she reeked of alcohol. Desperate to find a reason not to honor the date, he made a mental note to ask the event organizers if her obvious inebriation nullified her bid. With his face averted, he pried her off him. "Lisa, is it?"

"Yes, yes, Lisa." The slur in her voice confirmed that she was flat-out drunk.

He guessed Lisa to be about his age, though he found it hard to tell since she was wearing more makeup than the entire cast of a Spanish telenovela. "Lisa, are you interested in architectural design services? That's another option."

She ran her hands down the lapels of his jacket. "No way, handsome. I'd like a date."

Of course she would. The easy route would have been to laugh off her advances, play up his charm, and get as far away from Lisa as he could. But a vision of his mother chastising him for not doing the right thing stopped him. "Lisa, I'm sure you're a lovely woman, but you're drunk, and I'm guessing you know some of the people here. Is there someone who could take you home?"

Lisa blinked several times, suddenly appearing a lot younger than he'd first thought.

Was she even processing his words?

She groaned. "Oh, God." Her voice quivered. "You're right. Can you walk me to my table? I came with a friend. She'll take me home."

Daniel gave her a reassuring smile. "Of course." He held out his arm, and Lisa hooked her own through it.

"Thank you," she said.

"No problem."

She swayed against him while he did his best to hold her up so she could walk across the ballroom without embarrassing herself any further.

A young woman, Lisa's friend presumably, was ready for the handoff. "I've got it from here," she told him.

She and Daniel nodded at each other, and then he spoke to Lisa. "Lisa, I'll be sure to get your contact information from the organizers. We'll schedule a date soon. In the meantime, take care of yourself."

With her gaze on the floor, Lisa mumbled her thanks before disappearing with her friend.

Out of the corner of his eye, he spied Mimi at the far end of the ballroom, heading toward one of the exit doors, the sway of her shoulder-length blond hair matching her clipped pace. *Not so fast, troublemaker.*

He strode toward the double doors at the north side of the ballroom, intent on finding Mimi and…what? What *would* he do when he found her? He needed a plan, preferably something in the way of an ambush.

He considered the possibilities as he made his way across the ballroom, until Gracie intercepted him.

"In a rush to get somewhere, Daniel?" she asked.

He muttered a curse, remembering that he was here as a board member of LTN and should have been working the room on its behalf rather than pursuing Mimi. The woman might as well be his personal railroad switch, because she diverted him off his usual track whenever she was near. "Gracie, hey. Congrats on the donation. Wish I would have gotten you more."

"More? Are you kidding me? I'm delighted with the result." Gracie peered at him. "So were you heading out?"

"No, I wanted to talk to Mimi about something."

Gracie raised a questioning brow. "You did?"

"Yes. Did she leave for the evening?"

"No, she's checking on whether anyone bid on her consulting package."

His ears perked up. *Did someone say ambush?* "What consulting package?"

"She put up some hours of consulting to benefit all of the participating charities. You know, publicity and PR services. Brand management."

An idea took shape, one involving Mimi at his disposal for several hours. He'd definitely have her attention then. "Did she now?"

Gracie gave him a sly smile. "She sure did."

"When does the bidding close?"

"At eight o'clock. Why?"

"Thought I'd take a look at the items up for bid. And anyone with auction experience knows the best time to bid is just before the end."

"Well, I won't keep you. But first, I have a bone to pick with you."

That sounded ominous. "What did I do now?"

"You haven't responded to my housewarming invitation. You coming next week?"

Shit. He'd hoped to dodge it, honestly. Before she married Ethan, and what seemed like ages ago to Daniel, he'd pursued Gracie like a Neanderthal. Then she'd made it clear nothing would ever happen between them, and he'd wisely stepped aside. But not before Gracie had convinced him to help her make Ethan jealous. "Not sure that's such a good idea. Does Ethan even want me there?"

Gracie patted his arm. "Ethan's over it, Daniel. You were at my wedding, for goodness' sake."

"So were my parents. I assumed it was a courtesy."

"I'm not *that* courteous. Anyway, Mimi will be there."

"And that's incentive how?"

Gracie watched him closely. "I see how you look at her."

"How? Like she's deranged. Because she is, you know."

"No, not like she's deranged. Like she intrigues you."

She does. But Gracie doesn't need to know how much. "What can I say? I'm easily intrigued."

"Fine. Who am I to argue? This act has been working for you so far. No reason to change a good thing, right?"

"I have no clue what you're talking about."

Gracie studied his face. "No, no, I suppose you don't. Anyway, the offer stands. If you're interested in joining us, just show up. No RSVP required."

"Thanks, Gracie. I'll think about it."

He turned to leave, but Gracie pulled him back by his jacket sleeve. "One more thing. Mimi's got thick skin, but she isn't always as tough as she seems. Bear that in mind the next time you talk to her, okay?"

Well, this is…strange. He had no idea what to make of Gracie's observation. Which now made him curious to discover the meaning behind it. "Sure. I'll bear that in mind."

The ballroom door closed behind him with a thud.

He spied Mimi engaged in conversation with a man who looked to be around Daniel's age. Though she wore a smile, it didn't reach her eyes. Perfectly professional. Perfectly polite. Minutes ago, she'd been fucking with Daniel, likely trying to annoy him for some unknown reason. Now, however, with her angelic face set in calm repose, one would never know she had such devilish tactics in her arsenal. Her ability to flip the switch on her sassy attitude fascinated him.

The man at her side bent at the waist and wrote something on a sheet of paper, presumably placing a bid on Mimi's consulting package. *A potential client then.*

When the man straightened to his full height, he stepped closer to Mimi, and Daniel wondered if he and Mimi knew each other. But what did it matter? Whether or not she knew the man well, Daniel wasn't above a little cock blocking of his own.

Just as he was about to approach them, the man moved even closer to Mimi and ran a finger down her bare arm. She stumbled backward, her face contorted and her hands outstretched as though he'd thrown a bucket of boiling water on her. *And her eyes.* Her gaze darted everywhere, searching for an escape. She had none of the fire he'd come to associate with her. Suddenly, Daniel experienced an overwhelming urge to protect her—and a raging need to crush the man's skull.

With his hands fisted at his sides, Daniel stomped toward them.

Mimi's eyes cleared when she saw his approach. She straightened, almost as though his arrival had galvanized her into action. "Hi, Daniel."

Daniel relaxed his hands. Whatever the man's touch had provoked in her had passed in seconds. And he doubted Mimi would appreciate him making a scene. He hoped his presence alone would deter the bastard from making another unwanted advance. If not, they'd have a problem. "Mimi. Always nice to see you."

"Likewise," she replied.

Her expression dulled, however, telling him the opposite was true.

"Daniel, this is... I'm sorry, I didn't catch your name."

The man scowled, though it was unclear whether he'd done so in response to Mimi's claimed failure to remember his name or Daniel's interruption. "James Mortimer."

Daniel held out his hand to Mortimer as he edged closer to Mimi. "I didn't mean to intrude, but I'd like to get my bid in before the auction closes."

"You're bidding on my consulting package?" Mimi asked, her voice high and tight.

Daniel read the bid description. Ten hours of her time. *Ah, payback's a bitch, isn't it?* He turned to Mimi and gave her a smirk—for her eyes only. "Wouldn't miss the opportunity to work with you for anything in the world. It'll be fun, don't you think?"

To his satisfaction, she gave him an equally charming sneer—for his eyes only. But she said nothing in response, and he was disappointed. Mimi was a slicer and dicer. That sharp tongue and witty brain had the capacity to shred lesser men into tiny pieces. Perhaps

Mortimer's presence caused her to tamp down on her usual feistiness. *What a shame.*

An attractive woman appeared at Mortimer's side and leaned into him. "Honey, I'm not feeling well. Can we go?" She gave Mimi a frosty smile but didn't ask for an introduction.

Mortimer frowned for a split second and then smiled for his audience. "Unfortunately, we have to cut our evening short." He directed a pointed look at Mimi, who turned away and studied the program in her hand. "It was lovely to meet you, Ms. Pennington."

"The same, Mr. Mortimer."

Mortimer turned and regarded Daniel with a snake's smile. "Mr. Vargas, was it?"

"Yes."

"Enjoy the rest of the evening."

Daniel jammed his hands in his pockets, stopping just short of puffing out his chest. "I intend to."

With Mortimer gone, Daniel scanned the bidding sheet. Mortimer's bid was nine thousand dollars, and the silent auction closed in two minutes. He scribbled in his bid, straightened to his full height, and gave Mimi a wink. "Wish me luck."

"Oh, I'll wish you something all right."

Everything about her turned him on. Pity she didn't feel the same. Yet. "You never intended to win a date with me, did you?"

"Why would I buy the cow when the milk's gone sour?"

"Because the cow has more fresh milk to produce, and it's yours for the drinking?"

"*Ew.* That's disgusting."

"*Ew.* You have a dirty mind. A word to the wise, Mimi. If you screw with somebody, be prepared for them to screw you right back."

"We tried that already, remember? Didn't quite work out that way."

"Oh, I definitely remember. Ready to finish what we started in Puerto Rico?"

"Hmmm. Let's see." She tapped her lips with two fingers. "Um. That would be a no."

"What is it about me that you find so unpleasant? Because I have to say methinks the lady doth protest too much."

"See there? *That* right there is what annoys me. You go around acting all suave and smooth and expecting everyone to fall at your feet. And I bet they do. Oh, I bet they do."

She laughed, though he failed to see what aspect of this conversation was funny. Her reaction wasn't just about him. Something had prompted her to feel this way about men, or about *men like him*. He wished he knew what.

"My guess is that you've gone through life flaunting your sexuality and throwing your fake-ass charm at everyone. It's gotten you laid. It's probably gotten you clients, too. But take away your good looks and sparkling personality, and what are you left with? I'll tell you. Not much. And *this lady* doth prefer way more than *not much*."

He simply stood there, taken aback by her rant. Her cheeks turned pink when he didn't immediately respond. Was she imagining someone else's face as she ripped into him, or was this really about him? Hell, it didn't matter. Either way, there was way too much to unpack here. "Ouch. Okay, well, if you need me, I'll just be sulking in a corner. Some pretty little lady is bound to come over and ask what's wrong. See you around, Mimi." He spun around and strode away. Over his shoulder, he called back, "Can't wait to find out if I've won the bid. I think we'd make an excellent team."

But proving that point was going to be a hell of a challenge.

CHAPTER THREE

Monday morning, Mimi trudged to the office break room with one thought on her mind: *Coffee, come to Mama.*

Okay, if she was being honest with herself, she also had Daniel Vargas on the brain. As he'd no doubt planned, he'd won her consulting package.

Nina, her closest friend at the firm, poked her head out from behind the open fridge door and greeted her with a warning. "Watch out. He's in a mood."

Shit. That's all Mimi needed. *He* referred to her boss, Ian Humphreys, also known as Sir Jerk-a-Lot or Sir-Jerk-Off-a-Lot depending on Mimi's mood. On a good day, Ian made her wish she were British so she could call him a wanker with a straight face. On a bad day, she seriously questioned whether she should look for another job.

Screw that. No way would she leave this job—not of her own volition, certainly. She'd worked too hard to move up the ranks, starting as an intern, moving on to associate, and now serving as a senior associate, which left her with just one rung left to climb. As a partner, she'd have her own team, and she'd no longer be Ian's subordinate. That day couldn't come soon enough.

Mimi riffled through the coffee selections and dropped a K-cup in the Keurig. She leaned against the counter and waited for the machine to brew her coffee. "What's up his ass this morning? Though it's so tight I can't imagine anything could get in there."

Nina's shoulders shook with laughter. "I wish you'd give him a taste of your sass. I hate the way you act around him."

Nina saw the side of Mimi—the *real* Mimi—that she'd never let any other member of the firm see, most of all Ian. Accustomed to her friend's continuing complaint, Mimi simply laughed it off. "Yes, I'm sure that would go over really well with Ian."

"One day I'd love to see you rip that man to shreds. I'd be standing behind you with a dust pan."

"All in due time, my dear. You know how this works. Play the role of the agreeable and dutiful employee until I make partner."

Nina brushed her shoulder-length hair off her shoulders. "Yeah, yeah. I've heard that before."

Mimi scanned Nina's features. Her friend's flawless brown skin couldn't hide the dark circles under her eyes. "Rough weekend?"

Nina stirred her cup of coffee and sighed. "Kevin's giving me a hard time again."

Nina's parents had been killed in a car accident when she was twenty-two, leaving her the sole guardian of her younger brother. That her parents had actually planned for the possibility of their deaths, and had asked Nina to shoulder the responsibility of raising Kevin if necessary, weighed on her heavily. "I tell myself I've just got to get him to eighteen, but I don't know if I'm going to be able to contain him. He doesn't want to follow my house rules, and I'm getting tired of it."

"Do you think he needs a male figure in his life? Someone he can talk to about the things he doesn't want to share with you?"

Nina cradled her coffee cup and took a sip. "Maybe. I don't know. I never imagined I'd have to raise someone else's child, not at my age. My parents always told me they'd want us to stay together if anything ever happened to them, but I never thought it was a scenario I had to worry about."

"Well, you're doing an incredible job. And the hard time Kevin's giving you just might be evidence of that."

Nina blew out a frustrated breath. "Thanks."

Mimi took in Nina's outfit: a fitted black jersey dress, a cropped red blazer, and a pair of black pumps. Sexy but professional. And yet still more leg than Mimi would dare to show in the office. "Quite a fetching outfit today, I must say."

Nina twirled and craned her neck to inspect her own backside. "Makes my ass look great, doesn't it?"

"You're a mess." Mimi grabbed her cup of coffee and hooked her arm through Nina's. "C'mon. I have to make a quick call before the Monday morning meeting, and we can't be late, of course. Wouldn't want to keep Lord Humphreys waiting."

With their arms linked, she and Nina walked down the hall.

"He might spank you," Nina whispered.

She separated herself from Nina with a playful push. "Thanks for putting that cringe-worthy visual in my head. See you in ten."

Back in her office, Mimi dropped onto her chair and jiggled her mouse to bring her computer to life. Her first objective was to get Daniel to relinquish his claim on her consulting package. She pulled up the e-mail that had popped into her in-box only a half hour ago. The message from the event organizers had thanked her for her contribution to the evening's success. It had also passed along Daniel's contact information so she could arrange to "deliver" his prize. Indeed.

She punched in Daniel's office number, imagining each jab as a poke in his eye.

A soft-spoken voice answered the line. "Good morning. This is the Cambridge Group. How may I help you?"

"This is Mimi Pennington of Baxter PR. I'm trying to reach Daniel Vargas."

"Yes, Ms. Pennington. Will he know what this is regarding?"

"He will."

A rustle and a few dings later, the man of the hour answered the line. "Mimi. So good to hear from you."

She hadn't expected him to sound so sexy over the phone. Maybe without a visual to associate with Daniel's voice, her brain simply responded to the pleasant sound. *Gah. Shut the fuck down, brain. Slice him into pieces, mouth.* "Cut the crap, Daniel. This isn't a social call."

He chuckled. "I'd never expect that from you. To what do I owe the pleasure of your call then?"

"I'm following up on the consulting package. I'm assuming it was a joke and you have no intention of asking me to honor it. I'm happy to transfer it to someone else—"

"You're wrong."

"Excuse me?"

"I intend for you to honor it, Mimi. In case you haven't noticed, I do own a business, and my company could use that consulting. We'd like to hire a new architect soon, so it would be a good time to work out a publicity plan."

Mimi's mouth moved, but no words emerged from it.

"Have I startled you into submission?" He coughed. "Silence. I meant silence."

The word *submission* had triggered her to imagine herself on her knees at his feet. Not her thing, she didn't think, but the picture in her head seemed strangely titillating. *And wait. Why am I not angry about this? Okay, this is a problem.* She shook her head. "Daniel, be serious for a minute. You and I both know that this is a bad idea."

"Is it? I don't know that at all. We're talking ten hours, Mimi. Hardly a lifetime. And I paid good money for the privilege of your expertise. You're not suggesting you can't stomach me for ten hours, most of which I'm guessing you won't even have to be in my presence?"

All true. At most she'd have to spend a couple of hours talking to him; the other hours would be spent doing research on the company and its industry. Fine. If he wanted her expertise, he'd get it. Ten hours wasted for a good cause. And then she could focus on her firm's *real* clients. "Okay, fine. I'll do some research on your company and prepare an initial analysis."

"Do you need anything from me?"

"Not right now. The point of this is to assess your current public image and presence. I can do that all by myself. Then we can meet and discuss my thoughts and suggestions. I assume your firm's on the interwebs?"

"It is."

Muttering to herself, Mimi pulled up a Google search on the

firm and clicked on its website. "Fine. Is there someone who handles your scheduling? I'll contact them about a meeting next week."

"Her info's on the site."

"Great."

"I'm looking forward to it, *Mimi*."

"I'm not, *Daniel*."

His laughter rang through her earpiece before she slammed the phone into its cradle. *Jerk.* Mimi blew a breath that ruffled her bangs. *Ten hours. I can handle that.*

Minutes later, when she joined her colleagues, everyone on their six-member team except Ian was sitting around the large glass conference table that dominated the sparsely decorated space. No under-the-table shenanigans possible in this room. "Morning, everyone," she said in a cheerful voice.

Her colleagues grumbled their replies. As usual, nervous energy radiated off the walls. Ian had that effect on his team.

As though summoned by her thoughts, her boss entered the room and took the seat next to her. She straightened her shoulders, instinctively sitting up now that he was near. As a young girl, she'd done the same when her father joined them for dinner, a rare event that required her to use her best manners. Not for the first time she marveled at the similarities between the two men. Not only did they share many of the same physical attributes, but they'd both mastered the role of domineering asshole. It was truly unfortunate that the job she loved came with a prick of a boss.

Ian stared at his legal pad. "Okay, folks. Talk to me, and be succinct. What's on your plate for the week?"

Each Monday, Ian called a team meeting to keep everyone updated on the various moving parts in the firm's work. Or so he claimed.

Geoffrey, a junior associate, piped in first. "I'm working on the executive news briefing for Derringer PC."

Ian nodded. "Right. The last one was too long and too detailed. Find a way to give them the essential information without glossing over it."

Geoffrey nodded. "Got it."

The silence that followed made the fine hairs on Mimi's arms rise. She lifted her head, her gaze moving from the legal pad in front of her to what she thought would be Ian's profile. Instead, her gaze landed on his face—and he was staring right at her.

"What about you, Mimi?"

She cleared her throat. "I have two press releases to draft and three press releases to edit. And I'm researching press coverage on Harmon industries."

"Whatever happened with the auction? That was this weekend, right?"

Mimi had hoped to bury the results of the auction, but Ian the micromanager was bound to ask about it. Plus, she'd mentioned it to him as further proof that she was a self-starter. Since the winning bid had been claimed by Daniel Vargas, all she'd managed to do was fuck herself. So now she was a self-fucker, too. *Nice.*

She went with a noncommittal response. "So someone bid on my consulting package."

Ian's nostrils flared. "Who's the prospective client then?"

"Someone I know."

Ian's beady eyes narrowed. "Does that *someone* own a business?"

"Yes, an architectural firm. The Cambridge Group."

"We've worked with architects before. Sounds promising."

"I'm not so sure about that."

Ian rubbed his chin as he considered that. "Oh?"

"It's just"—she licked her lips, suddenly feeling parched—"I seriously question whether they're looking to hire someone, that's all."

Ian narrowed his eyes. "But he bid on your consulting package, right? So hiring you isn't out of the question."

"No, no. It's just—"

Ian gave her a dismissive wave. "We'll discuss this more later." He leaned forward in his chair and gazed at the faces of the rest of the team's members. "Anyone else planning to work this week?"

While another member of the team discussed his to-do list, Mimi scrambled to think of a reason why the firm shouldn't court Daniel as a client, one that wouldn't reveal that she was letting her personal feelings take precedence over the firm's business. Ian would have questions, and if she wanted to avoid his wrath, she'd better have answers. But what could she say, really?

The truth?

The guy's an asshat, and I can't stand the idea of working with him. Ian himself was an asshat, so he'd neither understand nor care.

Or, *The guy's ridiculously hot, and if I were forced to work with him, I'm not sure I'd be able to keep things professional between us and we'd probably end up having hate sex?* Eh. Probably not something she should admit to her boss—especially since she'd spent the last five years portraying herself as his asexual colleague.

Ian had managed to call on everyone around the table, and still Mimi had nothing. He rose from his seat. "All right, people. That's all for now. Make sure you're billing your time precisely. We can't get paid if you don't record your time. And remember, whether you're sitting at your desk or on the toilet, if you're thinking about the client, it's billable."

Mimi scrunched her face while she gathered her pad, pen, and iPhone. *Did he really have to be so foul?*

She was poised to bolt out of the room, but Ian stopped her with a hand. "Let's chat," he said as he shut the conference room door. "I'd been meaning to talk to you about this, and I guess now is as good a time as any." He pinched his slacks before sitting at the edge of the conference room table.

Mimi sat back down and twisted her upper body to face him. "What is it?"

"The partners met last week to discuss your progress at the firm."

Mimi's ears buzzed, and her hands went clammy. "And?"

"Your evaluations have been good, and your contributions were noted. Still, it was pointed out that you have no real experience either bringing in a client or handling one on your own."

Dammit. Her ears were on fire. They were probably red, too. "It was pointed out *by whom?*"

Ian gave her a smug smile. "It doesn't matter. The point is, if you want the partners to admit you to their ranks, you're going to have to show us that you can attract business to the firm. Seems to me landing the Cambridge Group account would be the perfect opportunity to demonstrate your readiness for partnership."

"Seems a little unfair to hinge my advancement on getting work from someone who I suspect isn't looking to hire. Plus, he and I don't get along very well."

"Mimi, we're a business, not a sorority. Who gives a shit if we like our clients? If they can pay the bills, nothing else matters. Besides, life isn't about fairness. You know who gets rewarded, whether it's deserved or not?"

She waited for him to continue, knowing it was a rhetorical question. When Ian had a point to make, it benefitted no one to disrupt him.

"People who get the job done, that's who," he continued. "So get the job done, and then we'll talk about partnership."

"By any means necessary, huh?"

"By whatever means you choose, Mimi."

Wait. This couldn't be happening. She'd almost had sex with Daniel—before he'd rejected her, that is. And when she remembered her tirade at the charitable auction, she mentally aimed a gun at her head. Now he was the key to her promotion? Someday she'd have a great laugh about it. But today?

Shoot. Me. Now.

CHAPTER FOUR

Mimi banged her head on the restaurant table—repeatedly. Maybe having lunch with Gracie wasn't such a great idea in her current state.

"Mimi, people are starting to stare," Gracie said. "Chin up, *chica*. It's going to be okay."

"No, it's not," Mimi said from under the veil of her hair. "This is my job we're talking about, Gracie. If I fuck this up, I can kiss partnership good-bye. Ian all but told me as much."

"Well, don't fuck it up then."

Gracie's stern voice got her attention. Plus, unlike Mimi, Gracie almost never cursed. Mimi raised her head and flicked her bangs. "If I can't whine with you, who can I whine with?"

Gracie grinned. "Stop pouting. You can *always* whine with me. My point is, don't let your feelings about Daniel stand in the way of your promotion. This might even be a good thing."

"How so? Please. Enlighten me."

"Well, for one thing, you know the man. You're not starting from scratch."

"But that's just it. I'm not his biggest fan, and the thought of having to kiss his ass to get his business makes me want to retch."

"Since when have you ever kissed a man's butt to get his business?"

"Never."

"Exactly. Why would Daniel be different?"

"Because I've called the man an egotistical asshat to his face?"

Gracie's mouth twitched. "Well, yeah, there's that."

"Oh, and how could I forget? I sent the man a leopard print thong—to his office, no less."

Gracie leaned forward and waggled her eyebrows. "I'll admit that's a unique client gift."

Mimi threw up her hands. "See what I mean? I'm doomed."

"You're not doomed. It's a challenge. You thrive on challenges."

In the workplace, yes. In her personal life, no. The situation with Daniel was a mix of both, and it was freaking her out. She forced her thoughts about it aside. "Okay, enough about me. How's the house coming along?"

Gracie's eyes brightened. "Wonderfully. You haven't been around since our interior decorator worked her magic, so I can't wait for you to see it on Saturday. The yard isn't finished, though. We'll get to it eventually."

She couldn't help envying Gracie's excitement about her new home. Mimi herself desperately wanted to own her own place, and for two years now, she'd set her mind to purchasing a new condo in Capitol Hill or Penn Quarter. Her own place. *Hers alone.* But her savings wouldn't be enough. She'd need the significant bonus and pay raise that came with partnership to pay her mortgage each month. And now partnership itself depended on her ability to get Daniel and his colleagues to hire her. *What a shit fest.*

She pictured a familiar scene from her adolescence: her mother sitting at the dining room table, pretending to be happy, while her dad pretended to be working late at the office. Her mother, who'd once been content in her role as arm candy, had never worked a day in her life after she'd married. But soon after, Mimi's mother learned that her husband had a very sweet tooth—and she alone would never satisfy his cravings. At least that's what Mimi had gathered from the screaming matches she'd overheard when she was supposed to be asleep.

Gayle Pennington rarely let the façade slip, but when Mimi came home for a visit during college, Gayle had been uncharacteristically frank with her. She'd held Mimi's hand in her own, her face as serious as her words were urgent. "Never let a man control your entire well-being. Independence will be your freedom." Her mother had said so little and yet spoke volumes, and Mimi knew that the advice was as much a criticism of her mother's own choices as it was of her father's philandering.

Freedom required a woman to be successful in her own right and to own a place of her own. Gayle should have left Mimi's father, but with nowhere else to go, and more than two decades of playing the role of the happily married socialite as her only vocation, she'd resigned herself to a loveless marriage.

Mimi refused to let that happen to her. Having a place that was hers alone was a big part of her protection plan.

"Are you serving real food at least?" she asked.

Gracie narrowed her eyes. "*Real* food?"

"You know, something that'll actually stick to my bones. It's okay if you're not. I'll just be sure to scarf down something before I get there."

"Yes, I'm serving *real food*. And I'm planning some adult games, too."

Oh, boy. Knowing Gracie, they'd spend the evening playing charades. "Um, Gracie, do you want me to handle the games?"

"No," Gracie said with a self-satisfied smile. "I'm all set. I think we've had enough of your party games to last a lifetime."

"Are you kidding me? Look me in the eye and tell me Pin the Cock on the Donkey wasn't hilarious. And preparing it wasn't easy, you know. It's hard finding cutout dicks in all shapes, colors, and sizes."

Gracie snorted. "Okay, I'll have to admit that was fun, but no I'll handle it. Besides, you'll be busy."

"Doing what, pray tell?"

"Making nice with Daniel."

Mimi's eyes bulged. "*He's coming to your housewarming?*"

"He is. And this will be a great opportunity for you to smooth things over with him."

Mimi groaned and dropped her forehead to the table. Not only was he messing with her work life, now he was mucking up her social life, too.

Damn you, Daniel.

* * *

Daniel peered at Gracie and Ethan's new home through the windshield of his car. It was a nice house, some might call it charming, with a wraparound porch and plantation-style shutters. Sandwiched between two similar homes on a cozy street in Chevy Chase, turning leaves scattered across its lawn, the house screamed domesticity. They'd moved to the burbs. Expensive burbs, but the burbs nonetheless. Daniel shuddered at the thought of living outside the city.

A few guests mingled on the porch, wineglasses in hand. His gut churned, warning him that being here was a mistake. Ethan didn't like him. Mimi did nothing but tease him. And Gracie tolerated him because he was a member of LTN's board and their parents were longtime friends. So coming here was like going into the lion's den, getting mauled, and then being passed around to the remaining dens in the vicinity.

So *why* was he here? Much to his annoyance, the thought materialized before he could deny it: *Because Mimi will be here, you idiot.*

And there it was. The truth. The sad, pathetic truth.

Sure, he could live without being Ethan's best friend. He had three men at Cambridge who would always have his back. But Mimi? Mimi's disdain affected him in a way he couldn't begin to explain. He refused to believe her dislike of him sprang solely from her deep-seated belief that he was an egotistical bastard. But if it did, his behavior in Puerto Rico would have done little to change her opinion of him. So what he needed was a second chance. Hence, his arrival at the lion's den.

When he walked in, Gracie greeted him with a smile. "I'm so glad you came, Daniel." She carried a wineglass in one hand. With the other, she linked arms with him. "Come, we'll find you some liquid courage."

He grinned. "Do I need it?"

"I suspect you do."

"Why? Is Ethan planning to kick my ass?"

"Ethan is the least of your worries." She drew him close so she could whisper in his ear. "She's in the living room."

He pretended not to hear the heads-up.

Gracie gave him a tour of the main level of the house, picking up a glass of wine for him along the way. She never lost her step or broke her concentration as she picked up discarded plates and smiled at guests who'd already made themselves comfortable. All the while, she treated him to random information about each room like a parent who couldn't help sharing pictures of her newborn. It wasn't a large crowd, but there were enough people in various parts of the house that energy flowed through it.

Eventually she directed him to the kitchen. They'd spared no expense there, appointing the room with a stainless steel refrigerator the size of a small car and counter appliances he'd never seen before. If he'd had any foodie tendencies, the professional chef's kitchen would have made him salivate. But he had no such inclinations, preferring to enjoy the experience of eating food rather than cooking it.

Gracie heaped various hors d'oeuvres on a plate. "Here. If you'd like more, help yourself."

He popped a bite-sized crab cake into his mouth. "Thanks for sheltering me, Gracie, but you don't have to babysit me for the duration of your party. I'll be fine."

"Is that what I was doing?" she asked with an innocent smile.

"I think so," he replied.

Gracie's husband appeared at her side and cleared his throat. "There's my lovely wife." Ethan kissed Gracie's forehead and drew her close. She basked in his attention, her adoration mirroring Ethan's.

Daniel placed his plate on the kitchen counter. "Ethan."

"Daniel. Thanks for coming. A friend of Gracie's is a friend of mine."

"I'm glad to hear it. I'd wondered if you'd be okay with my being here."

Gracie's eyes widened and she peered over his shoulder. "Excuse me, gentlemen. There's someone I should say hello to."

With Gracie gone, both men laughed at her obvious ploy to get them to talk, and the tension between them eased.

Daniel spoke first. "I'm happy for you. You two are obviously meant for each other."

"Thanks for saying that. I agree one hundred percent."

Daniel held out his hand. "Are we cool?"

Ethan took it. "Yeah, we're cool."

A voice behind them broke the moment before it became awkward. "What the hell are you doing in the kitchen, E?"

"Came to replenish my plate, Mark. Didn't know you were keeping tabs on me."

Mark Lansing had been the best man at Gracie and Ethan's wedding. Daniel had met him the night before the couple got married.

"Oh, hey. Daniel, right? We met in Puerto Rico." He stuck out his hand. "Mark Lansing."

"Yeah, nice to see you again."

Mark smiled to himself as though he were remembering a private joke. "Good times in Puerto Rico. Good times."

"Don't let Gracie see that smug look on your face, Mark. She'd like to believe Karen is a real-life *Jane the Virgin*."

Daniel had no idea what they were talking about.

Mark saluted Ethan. "Duly noted. Just hurry up and give me

backup. Individually, those women are fine, but get them together and it's like someone dropped me in the middle of a *Mad Max* reboot. And if that's not enough, Mimi's gearing up for the games portion of the evening."

Ethan's eyebrows shot up. "Now this should be entertaining."

The men walked single file into the living room, where Mimi stood behind a sofa table shuffling index cards.

Mark joined Karen, Gracie's sister, and wrapped his arms around her. Ah. So that's what they'd been alluding to. He hadn't known they were together. And judging from Mark's possessive hold on her, and the way Karen melted into him, it wasn't casual or new.

He turned his attention to the far more interesting person in the room. Mimi wore skintight jeans and a fitted white shirt. The deep V of her top taunted him. Each time she moved, he caught a glimpse of the lacy white bra underneath. She'd done something different with her hair, too. Her usual bangs were gone, held away from her face by a fancy hair clip. Without her bangs to frame her face, her features stood out prominently. Her lips, painted bright red, obliterated his ability to do much more than stare at them.

She motioned for everyone to join her. "Gather around, ladies and gentlemen. Gather around."

A few guests who'd been chatting on the porch entered the living room and settled on the comfy chairs that filled the room.

"As I'd suspected she would, Gracie wanted to play charades. Using my supernatural powers of persuasion, however, I've convinced her to let me handle the games. So we're going to play Two Truths and a Lie instead." Not surprisingly, Mimi captivated the audience with her dynamic personality.

Although a few guests groaned at the announcement, Mimi

didn't let their lack of enthusiasm deter her. "Ah, ah, ah, don't despair, ladies and gents. It'll be fun, or enlightening, at the very least. I promise. Now, this won't be your typical Two Truths and a Lie. Your index card will give you the required topic, and I'll be monitoring your cards to make sure you're playing along." Mimi pointed two fingers at her eyes and then directed them to the crowd, letting everyone know she'd be watching them. "You get one opportunity to pass on a topic. You'll share two truths and a lie. Other guests can ask you questions to try to trip you up. The person who figures out the lie wins a small prize and goes next. Got it?"

"Got it," some of the guests responded. Others chatted with their neighbors, either smiling or grimacing at the prospect of having to share personal information about themselves.

"Anyone want to volunteer to go first?"

Gracie separated from Ethan and jumped up from the sofa. "I do."

Mimi rubbed her hands together. "Excellent. My first victim."

Gracie wagged a finger at her. "Be nice." She wove her way through the few guests standing between her and Mimi. With a playful flourish, she drew one of Mimi's index cards and read it. Her eyes went round as saucers, and then she looked at Mimi and shook her head. "Pass."

Mimi read the card over Gracie's shoulder and laughed. "Oral is such a broad topic. I thought for sure you'd be okay with it."

Gracie shook her head. "Another, please."

Mimi handed her friend a different card, and they shared knowing smiles.

"Okay, I can work with that one," Gracie said. "The topic is the future." She cleared her throat and tapped her lips as though she were thinking about her three statements, but Mimi's anxious face told him Gracie knew exactly what she would say. "Okay. Statement number one. I'm expecting."

Ethan leaned forward and his gaze roved over Gracie's face and body. A few guests gasped.

"Statement number two. I don't love my husband."

Mark burst out laughing. "Well, hell, Gracie. We all know that's not true."

Karen jostled him with her shoulder and placed a finger over his lips.

Gracie rolled her eyes at Mark and continued. "Statement number three. I'm pregnant."

Ethan shot up from the couch and reached her in seconds. The other people in the room might as well have not been there for all the attention he paid them. "Graciela, sweetheart, we're going to have a baby?"

Gracie's eyes glistened, and she nodded. "Yes, Ethan, I'm pregnant."

With a look of awe on his face, Ethan smoothed the hair at Gracie's temples and leaned in to kiss her.

The guests erupted into applause, and a collective *aww* filled the room.

Mimi threw the remaining cards in her hand in the air, and they came down like confetti. "So much for the game. This calls for champagne."

She walked toward the kitchen, and Daniel figured this was his shot to speak with her alone. "I'll help you."

She narrowed her eyes. "Fine."

"So I'm guessing you were in on that back there?" he said behind her.

With brisk movements, Mimi readied a tray of champagne. "I was."

Beside her, he removed the foil over the neck of the champagne bottle. "That was really sweet."

Mimi stopped fussing with the glasses and straightened her shoulders. "It really was. I'm so freakin' happy for them." She wiped her eyes. "Eyelash."

He laughed as he unwrapped another bottle. "Right. Can't have anyone thinking Mimi has a heart."

"What's that supposed to mean?"

"Oh, c'mon. You pretend you're this hard-ass, but I'm starting to suspect you're really a softy inside."

"You're an expert at pretending, so you should know, huh?"

"Pretending? What do you mean?"

"Look at you, Daniel. Your hair's never out of place, your clothes are never wrinkled. I mean, I've never seen anything but a smile or a sly grin on your face."

"You say all that like it's a bad thing."

"It is. It's unnerving. No one can be happy one hundred percent of the time."

"I'm not. I just don't shit on other people's days because I'm having a bad one myself. So, listen, I've been meaning to talk to you about what we started in Puerto Rico…"

"Oh no, Daniel. That ship has sailed." Pointing to her crotch, she continued, "The porthole is closed." Then she pointed to his crotch. "There she does *not* blow."

Daniel barked out a laugh. Did she just make a joke about *not* giving him a blow job? That did it: She was his dream woman. "Are you done with the maritime references?"

"The last one was a literary reference."

"Wait. Are you saying I have a *Moby Dick?* Dating me sounds like a no-brainer then." He popped the champagne bottle, smiling inwardly at his impeccable timing.

"It's. Never. Going. To. Happen."

He focused on her plump lips as she enunciated each word. *Ah, this woman.* He loved playing in the sandbox with her. "Why. The. Hell. Not?"

"Because it's against the rules."

Rules? What the hell is she talking about?

CHAPTER FIVE

In the span of a few seconds, Daniel's expression went from mild amusement to confusion.

Mimi loved catching him off guard. She filled the champagne glasses as he shadowed her. "Let me break this down for you so we can move past it. I have three rules for dating. One, I don't date people I've met through my friends."

He scrunched his eyebrows. "Why not?"

"Because when shit gets ugly, I need an easy exit."

He leaned against the counter and crossed his arms over his chest. "That's a cynical way of looking at a relationship."

"I don't recall asking for your opinion of my dating rules."

He waved a hand in front of himself. "Do continue then. This is fascinating."

She placed the champagne bottle on the counter and held up two fingers. "Two, I never date men with personalities similar to my father's."

"Let me guess. I remind you of your father."

"Ding, ding, ding."

He beamed at her. "Tall? Charming? Irresistible?"

"Yes, yes, and yes. To most women. *Too many women*, unfortunately."

She hadn't meant to be so candid, but she couldn't retreat now.

His playful smile slipped. "I'm starting to feel like I never had a chance here."

"That's what I've been trying to tell you. My dad's also egotistical and dismissive of women."

"That's not me."

"I'm not surprised you think so. He's delusional, too."

He pressed his lips into a firm line and clenched his jaw. "You think you've got me figured out, don't you? That's your thing, I suppose. Slot everyone into your preconceived boxes, so you don't have to do the heavy lifting of actually getting to know someone."

Though he'd hit a nerve, she donned a bored expression and waited for him to continue.

"Well, I don't date judgmental women, so I guess we'll never know what could have been. Out of curiosity, though, what's the third rule?"

She held up three fingers and waved them in front of his face. "I never mix business with pleasure."

Because her father had screwed with her head on this point, encouraging her to do the exact opposite. "If you insist on having your own career, then use your assets to your advantage," he'd said. Just the kind of advice a young girl always dreamed of getting from her daddy. "Men are idiots that way," he'd explained when her face had twisted in disgust. So, yeah, the idea of blurring the lines between her personal and professional lives terrified her.

The man who'd made a pass at her during her first internship out of college had taught her a related lesson: If she wanted to avoid harassment in the workplace, she would always have to downplay her femininity. Nothing like a work colleague's hand slipping under your skirt to get that point across.

"What does your 'no mixing business with pleasure' rule have to do with me?"

"Did you forget about the consulting package, Daniel? You're a potential client now."

"Oh, c'mon, Mimi. Ten hours of your time hardly qualifies as a *long-term* client relationship."

"Because the notion that I'd be able to get your *long-term* business is laughable? Is that what I'm hearing? Dismissive of women much?"

"I didn't say that. I didn't think you'd *want* my business. And if you'd like me as a client, you have a funny way of showing it."

"You're a lost cause. I'll work on the rest of the architects at your firm."

He pushed himself off the counter and faced her. "Good luck with that. I'm the CEO. If you want our business, you'll have to woo me, too. And I have to say, so far you're doing a terrible job."

Then he picked up the tray of champagne-filled flutes and left the kitchen. And he had the nerve to whistle on his way out.

She finished the glass of bubbly in her hand in one gulp. Holding the stem in a death grip, she imagined it was Daniel's neck. Screw yoga. When she was pissed, her imagination calmed her just fine.

Gracie's sister, Karen, rushed through the swing door with an empty champagne flute in her hand. She dropped her head and blew out a breath.

Did Karen even realize she wasn't alone?

"You okay?" Mimi asked.

Karen whipped up her head, straightened, and gave Mimi a tremulous smile. "I'm fine." She looked around the kitchen. "Any more champagne?"

Mimi slid to the left to reveal the two bottles on the counter behind her.

After a nod, Karen grabbed one of the bottles, removed the foil, and popped the cork. She placed the tip to her lips and drank straight from the bottle.

"Whoa, woman. What's wrong?"

"Nothing's wrong. Just thirsty."

"Right. And guzzling champagne made more sense than drinking a glass of water?"

Karen raised the bottle. "We're celebrating."

"And you're hiding." She surveyed Karen, noting her skin was uncharacteristically pale. "From Mark?"

Karen dropped her head. "Yeah. I guess I am."

Mimi lifted herself and sat on the counter. "Come. Tell Mimi your problems."

Karen joined her, close enough that their thighs touched. "He asked me to give up my apartment. Before we got here. And when Gracie made her announcement, he leaned over and said, 'That could be us.'"

"Let me guess. You're not ready for that?"

"No way. The baby part, I mean. The giving up my apartment part, I'm not sure about. I'm practically living with him as it is, and he renovated his loft to add an office for me. And he's right that financially it doesn't make sense for me to be paying rent but..."

"But it scares you?"

Karen took a long breath, as though she were relieved that Mimi understood the problem without her having to say more. "Yes. I'm not sure why, but it does."

"You want my advice?"

"I'm sure you'll give it to me anyway."

Mimi bumped Karen's shoulder with her own. "True. Keep the apartment."

"You think?"

"I do and here's why. Let's say you and Mark have an argument, or you're pissed off with him about something. Or worse. What if you find out he's been with someone else?"

Karen shook her head in dismay. "Goodness, Mimi, you're a bundle of optimism."

"I'm a bundle of realism. In any of those situations, you have no place of your own to go to. You're stuck. Sure, you can call up Gracie, but Ethan is Mark's best friend. That might cause tension for them. So you come to me, and of course I'll let you stay, but is that really ideal? There's something empowering about having your own backup plan."

Karen looked at her with pleading eyes. "I love him, though."

"You're whipped, my dear."

"And so what if I am?"

"Nothing wrong with it, just as long as you don't lose your head and start making bad decisions. There are many ex-boyfriends and ex-husbands out there. Someone loved them once, too. Breakups happen."

"I'm not sure I'd want to live my life waiting for the other shoe to drop, but you're right that a backup plan never hurts. And sometimes I just want to get away, you know? Med school is kicking my ass, and it's comforting to know there's always a place where I can cut myself off from the rest of the world."

"Well, there you go. Explain that to him. Problem solved. He might not like it, but eventually he'll come to understand. If he loves you, that is." She gave Karen a reassuring hug. "And I'm sure he does."

Karen rested her head on Mimi's shoulder. "How'd you get to be such a smart lady?"

"I think it's more accurate to say I'm cautious."

"You *can* be both, you know."

Thinking of her own exchange with Daniel minutes earlier, Mimi agreed. Going forward, she'd need to be both smart and cautious when dealing with him. Otherwise, the man would interfere with her career aspirations, and no way in hell was she letting him do that.

CHAPTER SIX

With a steaming cup of coffee in his hand, Daniel strode into the conference room and plopped into a chair. One of his legs bounced in anticipation of this morning's meeting with Ms. Mimi Pennington. Damn. Her name alone excited him. As he doodled on his legal pad, he chuckled to himself, picturing Mimi's horror-stricken face when he'd told her she would have to woo him, too.

He looked up, and three sets of eyes stared back at him.

Jason scrunched his face into a "what gives?" expression. "So what's the deal with this publicist?"

Daniel feigned a dismissive wave. "It's nothing. A joke, really. She gave me a hard time at that bachelor auction a couple of weekends ago, so I bid on her consulting package. We get ten hours of her time. Figured I'd waste some of it for a good cause. Just do me a favor. Listen to what she has to say, and then we're done. Fifteen minutes, tops."

Amar, the most thoughtful of the bunch, peered at him. "How much did you pay for this little joke?"

"Ten thousand dollars."

He whistled. "That's an expensive joke."

"Not so expensive when you consider it benefits charity."

"Still, that's a lot of money," Amar noted.

"It is," Daniel replied.

Amar wouldn't let it go. "Which one?"

Daniel dropped his head in exasperation. "Which one what?"

"Which charity?"

"All of them. It went into a pool to be divided among them. What does it matter?" The irritation in Daniel's voice caused those three sets of eyes to refocus on him.

Jason grinned at Amar.

Amar widened his eyes and smirked.

And Spencer lifted a single perfect brow. Jesus, did he *tweeze* them?

These men knew very little bothered him. He'd learned to look at life's everyday problems as minor irritations in the grand scheme of things, so his annoyance was bound to make them curious. Well, this was just perfect. If he'd revealed too much, they would hound him about his connection to Mimi. Not that there was a connection. He'd wanted one, but after his run-in with her last weekend, he doubted whether that would happen. She'd essentially told him not to fuck with her—literally and figuratively—and now that she'd educated him about her "rules," he'd have to be a masochist to continue pursuing her.

The voice of their receptionist, Felicia, intruded on the charged moment. "Mimi Pennington is here for her appointment."

Jason hit the intercom. "Send her in, Felicia."

Daniel tapped the table with his pen as he waited for Mimi to arrive.

"Stop that," Spencer said. "It's annoying as shit."

"Drink your coffee and stop worrying about me," Daniel countered. "And sit up."

Spencer shook his head. "What am I? Twelve? What's got you so weird, D?"

"I'm not being weird. It's Monday."

As though that somehow explained anything. He dropped his head and whipped it back up when he heard the click of Mimi's shoes outside the door.

He blinked several times, failing to recognize the version of Mimi Pennington who walked into the room.

The form-fitting clothing that emphasized the delicious curve of her breasts and her wisp of a waist? Gone.

The trademark ruby red lipstick she wore on her pouty lips? Gone.

The sassy smirk that made him feel as though he were the butt of every joke she'd ever made? Gone.

Her clothing and demeanor matched the color of the conference room's walls: gray.

She intended to do business today. The change in her appearance made that clear. This woman wouldn't engage in verbal sparring or tell off-color jokes. Her transformation intrigued him, because it confirmed what he'd already suspected: He had a lot to learn about Mimi Pennington. And given the chameleon who'd joined them, he would start with the most pressing question: *Why did she feel the need to change?*

She cleared her throat, and Daniel blinked. *Right. Introductions.*

He rose and met her at the head of the conference table. If he hadn't been so focused on the absence of color on her lips, he would have missed her small intake of breath as he strode toward her. *Ah, Mimi. I feel it, too.*

But he wouldn't show it. Not in front of the guys. "Hello, Ms. Pennington. Thanks for taking the time to meet with us."

She smiled at the guys, but when she returned her attention to him, she adopted a neutral expression. The fact that she'd visibly arranged her face to greet him told him he affected her. Whether he could capitalize on that fact still remained unclear, however.

She held out a hand and offered him a firm handshake. "You're welcome. And no need to be so formal. Mimi's fine. It's good to see you again, Daniel."

Bullshit. She didn't want to be here, and for the first time since he'd made the bid at the silent auction, he regretted having forced her hand. Messing with her at a party was one thing; toying with her job was quite another. But it would only raise everyone's suspicions if he turned her away now. So he'd stick to the original plan: let her talk and then release her from any further obligation to consult for them.

He turned to his partners. "Gentlemen, this is Mimi Pennington of Baxter PR."

Jason, Amar, and Spencer stood, and she greeted each with a handshake and a friendly smile. "May I sit here?" she asked.

Daniel focused on the slender finger pointing at the seat beside him. "Sure. Here's fine."

After she'd settled in, Amar took the reins. "So Mimi, Daniel tells us that you're here to consult with us. What exactly do you do, and what can you do for us?"

She glanced at the papers in front of her and set them aside. "Baxter PR has three areas of concentration: brand development, publicity, and crisis management. Or as I describe them: show, tell, and bury. I wear different hats depending on my client's needs. If clients want to manage their publicity—good or bad—they hire a publicist. If they're going for total image management, a public relations relationship is more appropriate. You with me so far?"

The men nodded in unison.

"Great. I reviewed your website and checked to see what press you've received in the past six months. Tell me this: Are you working at full capacity?"

"Our plates are full, if that's what you're asking," Spencer offered.

"It's not. Are you turning away new clients because you have no time to take on their projects?"

Amar spoke up then. "Not at all. We take on every new client if the project's the right fit."

"Then you're likely not realizing your full potential."

Daniel sighed and the men turned their attention to him. "Care to be less cryptic, Ms. Pennington?"

She narrowed her eyes. He got the distinct feeling that if they'd been alone, she would have stuck out her tongue at him. *Too bad we're not alone.*

"Sure. It's clear your business is doing well, but you could be doing better. You want demand to outpace your supply. You do excellent work. The client testimonials on your website attest to that, but there are hundreds of architects in the DMV area that do excellent work, too. What makes your firm different? What are you offering that clients can't get anywhere else? Or if they can get it somewhere else, *why* should clients get it from *you?* In short, gentlemen, you need to manage your brand."

"What does managing our brand entail?" Spencer asked.

"It means looking at your business from top to bottom and figuring out why a client should hire you. It requires me devising a compelling story for you based on those attributes of your business that are unique to you. It means giving your potential clients a sense of who you are as individuals, beyond the degrees, apprenticeships, and awards. Your website provides information about your services and that's it."

"Am I missing something? We're an architectural firm, not YouTube, Mimi. Isn't that what our website is supposed to provide: information?" Daniel asked.

For a minute, the sparks in her eyes threatened to singe him. *Fireworks had reentered the building.* And he welcomed her return.

"Yes, information is one piece of the puzzle. But this isn't an assembly line, gentlemen." She locked eyes with him when she said the word *gentlemen,* stressing the word in a way that suggested she didn't include him in that category. "You're highly skilled individuals who each contribute something to the firm's persona. That's what attracts clients: the people behind the business."

Daniel trailed his index finger over his bottom lip as he considered her. She glanced at him then and paused as though her thoughts had scattered around her. If only he could get her to acknowledge her attraction to him.

"Each of you has a story," she continued. "Tell the world your story, and make it a good one."

Daniel wanted to ask her about her story. She'd impressed him with her knowledge and insights. He was familiar with her ever-present smirk, but he'd never encountered her in a professional setting. Seeing her in business mode added a delicious layer to a cake he already wanted to eat. Apparently he was a masochist.

So where did that leave him? He had a feeling he could overcome her concerns about dating someone she'd met through her friends. In fact, he could point to Mark and Karen as a successful example. Hell, he'd even be willing to date her in secret for a short time if that would ease her concerns. And her ridiculous assertion that he reminded her of her father was based on a host of assumptions she'd made about him. Over time, he could show her how faulty those assumptions were. So as he saw it, if they weren't working together, he might have half a chance of convincing her to date him.

Daniel glanced around the table, eager to wrap up the meeting.

Spencer stared at the legal pad in front of him and twirled a pen in one hand. From experience, Daniel knew the movement meant Spencer was going over Mimi's words and wanted to ask more questions.

"Let's say we were interested in hiring you to help us with brand management, what would you do for us?" Spencer asked.

Mimi gave Spencer a warm smile, and Spencer returned his own—at full wattage.

Wait. What the hell? Spencer's interested in hiring her?

Daniel leaned forward. "Well, I know you likely don't have time for us, Mimi, so the ten hours of consulting should suffice, and I'm guessing you've already used most of them reviewing information about the firm, so—"

"Ms. Pennington probably has a handle on her own schedule, Daniel," Amar said.

Daniel wanted to smack the smug grin off his face. This was what happened when you went into business with your roommates from grad school: They fucked with you any chance they got. Once they'd seen each other in their skivvies, the dynamic had changed forever.

Daniel resigned himself to continuing this farce a few minutes longer. He sat back and smoothed his tie. "You're right. Sorry for the interruption, Mimi. Feel free to continue."

Mimi licked her lips and addressed his friends. "Well, because you all provide a personal service, I'd want to get personal with you. I'd like to know a little more about each of you. How did you start the business? What drives your designs? How do you work together? Get underneath the gloss, so to speak. And I'd need access to your past work, you know, the stuff that isn't reflected on the website. Using that info, I'd present you with a brand strategy. Suggest a redesign for the website. Discuss ways to get your name out to media outlets. Perhaps a business development event for past and prospective clients."

Jason's head bobbed up and down. Yeah, this was going to be a problem. The guys were hooked, and Daniel couldn't blame them. She knew her shit.

Hell.

Unless he did something soon, he'd be forced to work with her.

A woman who didn't like him.

A woman he couldn't stop thinking about.

A woman who'd made it clear that she wouldn't entertain the idea of dating him if they worked together.

Mimi gathered her papers and placed them in her leather portfolio. "Any questions, gentlemen?"

Jason, who rarely spoke in firm meetings, chose this moment to channel his oratorical gifts. "Mimi, this has been very helpful. I'm sure I speak for all of the partners when I say that you've presented a compelling case for us to hire you. We'll discuss your services and get back to you. Do you have a retention agreement with your company's hourly rates?"

"I do. I can send that to you as soon as I return to the office."

"Wonderful. Anyone else have anything to add?" Jason didn't wait for an answer and rose from his seat. "I'll walk you out."

Mimi smiled. "Thank you, gentlemen. I appreciate your time."

Spencer and Amar voiced their thanks like she was a foreign dignitary visiting their country for the first time. *Damn.* These men needed to chill.

Before she walked out the door, Daniel stopped her. "Thanks for the time you spent on us. You obviously took this seriously, and I appreciate it."

She cocked her head and regarded him with a frown. "Well, of course I took this seriously. I'm a professional."

"Right. Of course."

"Have a great day, Daniel."

"You do the same, Mimi."

He could have sworn he glimpsed a smirk as she turned toward the door.

Minutes later, Jason returned, his huge grin setting off alarm bells in Daniel's brain.

Had he and Mimi exchanged words while she waited for the elevator? Daniel had to know. "What the fuck are you grinning for?"

Jason cocked his head and glared at him. "What the fuck is your problem?"

Daniel threw his pen on the table and jumped up from his seat. "Never mind. I'm just a bit jumpy today. Didn't get much sleep."

Spencer cleared his throat. "Let's just finish this up. To me, it's an easy decision. We're doing well, but we could be doing better, and Mimi will help us. I say we hire her."

"Agreed," Amar said.

"Same," Jason said.

Daniel dropped back onto his chair. "Wait, wait, wait, guys. This is not how we operate. We don't know her hourly rates. We haven't seen an engagement letter. We have no idea what she's going to recommend for a brand strategy. Let's not jump into this."

"Fine," Jason said. "I'll e-mail her this afternoon to follow up. Let's authorize her to come up with a proposal, and then we can hire her."

Daniel gnashed his teeth. Mimi had delivered an excellent presentation, but the possibility that they were thinking with their dicks pissed him off. "Does your enthusiasm for hiring her have anything to do with the fact that she's gorgeous?"

Amar leaned forward. "Are you serious?"

"I am."

His lips twitched. "Yeah, she's gorgeous—"

"She's got that repressed librarian thing down pat," Spencer added.

Daniel wanted to snarl at them, but he kept his temper in check.

Amar scanned his face. "Are you suggesting that we shouldn't hire her because she's gorgeous? Because that would be ludicrous. She's smart as hell, and she can take us to the next level. We know fuck all about branding ourselves."

Spencer stood, ambled to Daniel's seat, and placed his hands on Daniel's shoulders. Leaning over, he asked, "Does your lack of enthusiasm for hiring her have anything to do with the fact that she looks at you like you're a wad of gum stuck to the bottom of her shoe?"

Daniel shook Spencer's hands off him. "No."

He could mention that he'd almost had sex with Mimi. Not a blow-by-blow account, but a factual statement that would hint at the cause for his resistance. Except that wasn't the real reason he didn't want to hire her. No, he worried that if they did hire her, she'd shut him down forever, and that possibility didn't sit well with him. Plus, telling the guys his and Mimi's personal business would have been a dick move, and she didn't deserve to have her professional image affected by what she did in her private life.

They waited. He seethed. Lacking any good ideas for derailing their desire to hire Mimi, he relented—for the time being. "Fine. We'll have her present her proposal."

"Excellent," Jason said as he rose from his chair. "I have a client meeting in ten minutes. Later, gentlemen."

The others followed suit, leaving Daniel alone with a million and one thoughts.

Amar knocked on the conference door and stuck his head back into the room. "So how'd that expensive joke work out for you?"

Daniel gritted his teeth. "Very funny, asshole."

Amar laughed and tipped an imaginary hat. "That's what I thought."

CHAPTER SEVEN

After her meeting with the Cambridge Group, Mimi floated to work. Other than Daniel, the firm's principals expressed enthusiasm about hiring her, and if they did, she'd be one step closer to demonstrating her readiness for partnership.

Once back in her office, she rested her head against her chair and stared out the window. Though it was too early to tell for sure, she suspected Daniel would pose a problem. He didn't seem keen on having her around, probably because he had trouble adjusting to the idea that she was anything other than an empty head with big boobs. Her toned-down appearance at today's meeting wouldn't immediately change his opinion of her, not after their encounter in Puerto Rico and the silly antics since. But maybe over time, she could convince him to think of her as a professional and nothing more.

First, though, she needed to make some adjustments herself. When she'd first walked into the conference room that morning, she'd set her sights on sitting as far away from Daniel as she could. But after considering the possibility that he'd stare at her from across the table—probably remembering her breathy voice as she'd all but begged him to have sex with her—she'd convinced herself that sitting next to him would lessen the potential for eye contact. *Big mistake.* The chemistry between them threatened to set the room on fire, and she'd tried to deflect it by going into über-professional mode. So yes, her brain had no problem resisting Daniel, but her body was a different story. Even now, her brain and body warred with each other, tugging on the sensual images that kept replaying in her head.

Mimi squeezed her eyes shut and let out an undignified groan.

When she heard a throat clear, she snapped her eyes open.

Nina was peeking into her office. "I heard a moan," she whispered from the door. "Damn, woman, are you masturbating in here?"

Mimi scrambled to straighten herself in the chair and waved her hands frantically. "Shut the door, Nina."

If she hadn't been so concerned about someone overhearing Nina's question, Mimi would have doubled over in laughter. Nina's brain matched hers. In fact, Nina had once described them as personality twins. Which was the very reason Nina complained when Mimi didn't stand up for herself in the workplace.

Nina stepped into the office and swung the door closed. "You're flushed. What have you been doing in here?"

"Nothing. Jesus. Listen, this doesn't leave this room."

"Oooo. Juicy gossip." Eyes wide, Nina strode to one of the chairs facing Mimi's desk and dropped into it.

Mimi loved this woman. The minute Nina had walked into the firm, Mimi could tell she'd found her partner in crime. "Okay, that account I'm supposed to land, the one with the guy I don't get along with?"

Nina jiggled her foot as she listened. "The one you mentioned at the Monday meeting last week?"

"Yeah. That one."

Nina gave her a knowing grin. "He's hot, isn't he? I could tell something was going on with you. I saw the way you practically slid under the table to avoid talking about him with Ian."

"Yes, he's hot. He's a bit of a jerk, too. Well, maybe not so much a jerk. Maybe just a bit full of himself."

"Goodness, I've never seen you this flustered about anything. So what's the problem? You're so attracted to him that you want to jump his bones."

"More like I don't want to be attracted to him, but I almost jumped his bones anyway."

Nina's lips moved as she worked out what Mimi had told her. Then she jerked forward, her eyes bulging. "Shut. Up. You made a move on the guy already?"

Mimi fell back against her chair and stared at the ceiling. "Yes."

"Where and when?"

She kept her eye trained on the ceiling fixture. "Not important. It was a one-time thing. Several months ago. And it didn't end with us in bed, thanks to him. But now I have to try to get the guy's business."

"Wait. He turned you down?"

"Yep."

"Did he give you a reason?"

Mimi pursed her lips. "Yeah. Some bullshit about not wanting to be another notch on my belt. Said he'd only pursue me when I was ready to give him a real chance."

"And now you've got to work with him. Any possibility you'd give him the chance he wants?"

Mimi lowered her chin and glared at Nina. "Hell no. My personal and professional lives do not belong in the same room together."

"Um, I hate to tell you this, but your personal and professional lives are so in the same room together they're practically shacking up. Brings a whole new meaning to the phrase *debriefing your client.*"

"You plan to take that bit on the road?"

"Hmmm. Let me think about it. I'm sure there's more. *Ooooh*, I know. You should make it your job to unlock your client's *fullest* potential."

Against her will, the corners of Mimi's mouth quirked up. "Get out of my office."

"Oh, c'mon. You know I'm just kidding. Seriously, what's your plan?"

"My plan is simple. I'm going to forget that I ever fondled his dick and treat him like I'd treat any other client of the firm."

"You almost had sex with him?"

"Yes, I just told you that."

"And he's a tad arrogant, you say?"

"Yes."

"And he wants you?"

"He claims to be interested, yes."

Nina shook her head in disbelief. "Right. Okay then. Can I help you with this account, because I really need a front row seat to the hilarity that's about to ensue?"

"Thanks for the vote of confidence."

Nina stood. "Oh, sweetie. Don't get me wrong. I have the utmost confidence in you. It's this guy who's going to be the problem."

Mimi hung her head. Nina was right. But she had no clue how to control Daniel.

"Lunch?" Nina asked from the door.

"Can't. I'm meeting my realtor. Checking out a new space in Penn Quarter."

"Have fun with that," Nina said before she walked out the door.

Mimi's cell phone buzzed in her purse, cutting off any further thoughts about Daniel and what trouble he might make for her. She fished through her bag for her phone and stared at her mother's image. With a sigh, she accepted the call. "Hi, Mother."

"Hi, Mimi. How are you?"

Her mother could have been talking to one of her book club members for all the familiarity she demonstrated in that sterile greeting. Come to think of it, her own greeting hadn't been overly affectionate, either. *How sad.* "I'm fine, Mother. Is everything okay? With you? Dad?"

"Yes, yes, everything's fine. I have news. Your dad's receiving an award from the Austin Chamber of Commerce next month, and he'd like you to join us at the awards ceremony."

Mimi waited for her mother to say more.

"It's for his positive impact on family-style entertainment and tourism in the city," she continued.

Right. Before his death, Mimi's grandfather had given her father the reins of several amusement centers in Central Texas. Wanting to expand the family business to fit Austin's active lifestyle, Mimi's father had opened three trampoline parks. She'd always found it odd that her father had spent his professional life working in the business of entertaining families when he couldn't be bothered to spend much time with his own.

"Let me guess. Having his daughter there plays into the 'family man' persona he'd like to convey."

"I suppose so, yes. But apart from that, I'd like to see you, Mimi. We don't see each other often enough, and I'm getting on in years."

"Mother, you're fifty-five. I think it's a little too early to be writing your eulogy."

Mimi shook her head when she heard her mother's lighthearted laughter; she hadn't heard the sound in a long time.

"Yes, dear, I know. But we haven't seen you in months and…And I miss you."

"Well, when you put it that way, how can I refuse? I'll make the time to be there." She jotted the details in her planner. "Got it."

"Thanks for coming, dear."

"No problem. And thanks for calling, Mom."

"I think that's the first time you've called me 'Mom' in years. I like it."

She pictured her mother's elusive smile. Like her mother's laughter, Mimi hadn't seen that smile in a long time. "I like it, too."

She rarely spent time with her mother. If she could manage to be cordial to her father for the duration of the event, the trip would be a worth it. But from her experience, being cordial to her father would take a miracle.

* * *

"It's a beautiful space," Mimi said as she toured the condominium Beth, her realtor, had said "she just had to see." The model boasted a large kitchen with stainless steel appliances and a wall of exposed brick in the living room. The juxtaposition of old and new had been one of the features she'd told her realtor she was looking for. "It's over budget, though."

"I know," Beth said. "But it ticks off all the must-haves on your list, and you won't close on the property for another six months. You have enough for the earnest money deposit?"

"I do, but I'd like to be sure I'm going to be able to close on the home six months from now."

"We can still look elsewhere. I just thought this place would be perfect for you, so I had to show it to you. There's a community rooftop terrace, too."

"Don't get me wrong, I appreciate it. And you're right, a unit like this one would be perfect. But I don't want to be impulsive about this."

"I understand," Beth said.

"Can I have a few minutes to walk around some more?"

"Of course. I have some calls to return. I'll wait for you in the dining room."

Mimi nodded, her mind already picturing the way she'd decorate the interior. An overstuffed couch would be the living room's centerpiece. She'd fill the space with plants, her only nod to domesticity that didn't end in disaster. And she'd need another large bookshelf for all the books she'd collected over the years.

She was getting ahead of herself, of course. The deposit would sink her savings, and without a promotion, she'd be stuck with a property she couldn't afford. Which meant if she wanted a place like this one, she'd have to secure a few new clients for the firm. So she'd bust her ass to get the Cambridge Group's account, and if that didn't work, she'd be disappointed but she'd be fine, too. Sure, Ian had suggested that getting the Cambridge Group's business would be key, but he'd forget about that account if she brought in several other clients. With a renewed sense of purpose, she found Beth in the living room.

"So what do you think?" Beth asked.

"I'm going to crunch some numbers tonight. Assuming those numbers look decent, I'd like to make an offer."

"Excellent. I had a feeling you would say that."

Now she had to convince the Cambridge Group to hire her. Doable.

And maintain a professional and platonic relationship with Daniel. Doable.

And forget that she was desperately attracted to him.

Impossible.

CHAPTER EIGHT

Daniel sailed into the office after lunch. Ms. Mimi Pennington would be visiting him this afternoon, and that alone was enough to make him whistle.

"Someone have a good lunch?" asked Felicia from behind the reception desk.

Daniel stopped at the desk and sifted through the day's mail. "Yes."

"Your mail is in your in-box already," Felicia noted.

He dropped the stack and saluted her. "Efficient as usual. Thank you."

Felicia giggled. "You're welcome."

He heard more giggling. Except it wasn't coming from Felicia. He turned his head in the direction of the conference room and muttered under his breath at the scene playing out behind the glass wall. Jason and Mimi talking over a take-out lunch. "How long have they been in there?" he asked Felicia.

"Oh, not long. Half hour maybe? She's due to see you next."

From his perspective, they appeared to be getting along very well. Jason was demonstrating something with his hands and Mimi threw back her head and laughed in response. Jason joined in her laughter and then dug into the sandwich on his plate. As he chewed, he looked up and spotted Daniel. Of course, he waved.

Daniel pulled open the conference door. "Hey, Mimi. I'm on a tight schedule. Do you think we might be able to move up our meeting? Maybe start in five minutes or so? Assuming you're done here, that is."

Jason's enthusiastic chewing slowed. "Yeah. We're almost done."

Mimi looked between him and Jason and gathered the remains of her lunch. "Sure, not a problem." Her professional smile reappeared. "I'll stop by your office in five, okay?"

"Thanks. I appreciate that." He nodded at Jason. "See you later."

He lumbered to his office, unsure why he'd just made that power move. It had been juvenile, yes, but when it came to Mimi, he lost his ability to think clearly. Unfortunately, he'd accomplished nothing other than being a jerk to one of his closest friends.

He raked a hand through his hair and collapsed into his chair. When Mimi knocked on his open office door minutes later, he straightened and beckoned her to come in.

She glanced at him and dropped her gaze to the floor, slipping her oversized purse off her shoulder and taking a seat in silence. The bag was the size of his travel luggage. From it, she pulled out a pad and pen. "I'm just going to ask you a few questions, try to get a flavor for who you are as an individual and as a colleague."

He tapped a single finger on his desk, and her gaze followed the rhythmic movement. "Ask away," he told her.

"Okay, so tell me a little about yourself. Something that's not on the website."

"I like taking long walks in the park, cuddling puppies—"

She raised her head to the ceiling and huffed. "You know what, if you're not going to give me a chance, I can just stick with the information on the website." She rose to leave. "I'll show myself out."

He stood and reached out to touch her forearm. When she drew back, his hand hovered awkwardly in the air. "I apologize." He motioned for her to sit. "Please. I won't waste any more of your time."

She sat back down, her big blue eyes wide and wary.

"I'm a twin."

Her eyes grew even wider, a phenomenon he hadn't thought possible. "There are *two* of you?" she asked.

"Was."

"I'm sorry. That's more than I need to know for my purposes. We can move on to something else."

He fiddled with his cuffs. "Yes, let's move on to something else. I'm not sure why I brought it up anyway."

In fact, in the five years since his sister's death, he'd never volunteered that information. But this was what Mimi did to him. Around her—*because* of her, really—he acted out of character, like it or not.

"I went to Harvard for undergrad and grad school," he continued.

"Yes, I know that. I'm impressed. What else?"

"Let me finish, Ms. Pennington."

She pretended to zip her mouth shut. "Sorry. Continue."

"I went to Harvard on a scholarship. My parents didn't have much money, but I'd demonstrated proficiency in standardized tests early on, and I was given the chance to attend a grade school for academically gifted children. This was in the age when New York public schools still had money for special programs like that."

"What was Harvard like?"

"I experienced culture shock. In my neighborhood, I'd met very few white people, so when I went to Harvard, I had to adjust to a new world that was different from what I was used to. I couldn't speak as much Spanish as I had at home, the foods were unfamiliar, even the music I heard in the dorms sounded strange to me."

"Was it a good experience?"

"It was, mostly. That is, once I got the chip off my shoulder and realized I deserved to be there just like everybody else. Talking to my sister helped. She was at Georgetown then."

"When did you discover that you wanted to be an architect?"

"I don't know that I had that one 'aha' moment. I think in college I was content to just get through it. I felt like graduating from college would be enough of an accomplishment. But I had a political science professor who took it upon herself to push me."

Mimi stopped taking notes and sat back in her chair. "She changed you."

"I'd say she guided me. She said she saw my potential but worried that I wasn't prepared to do the work. I took that to heart and started studying all the time. Anyplace I could find. The library. The student center. The lawn. And that's when I started to notice the buildings on campus. How they were designed. What made them interesting. How they fit into the environment. I took out a few books on architecture. A year later, I decided to apply to the grad school. Had no idea what I was doing, but I was interested enough to take on the challenge."

"And that worked out very well for you, I take it."

"It did. And I met Jason, Amar, and Spencer there. We took the same class our first year. Architecture and the Environment. By the second year, we'd found an off-campus apartment together."

She grinned, a twinkle in her eye suggesting that she was remembering a funny moment. He wished that expression were meant for him.

"What?" he asked.

"Jason told me about one of your epic pranks."

"Which one?"

"The Oreos."

He relaxed in his chair, enjoying their conversation. "That was Spencer's idea. To be fair, Jason's obsession with those cookies was out of control. Can you imagine two grown men in their boxers switching out the cream for toothpaste in an entire package of Oreos? But Jason's face when he bit into one was worth the effort."

Her throaty laugh filled the room. "I can picture it, too."

They smiled at each other while she absently toyed with her necklace. His gaze, initially drawn to the movement, moved to her neck, a place he'd volunteer to nibble on all day. He could easily imagine her meeting him in his office after a rough day at work and falling into his lap. Without a word between them, he'd nuzzle her neck and swoop in for a soft kiss. The thought made him smile even wider. But when he glanced at her face, she'd set her mouth in a firm line.

He straightened. "Sorry. Where were we?"

Mimi turned the page in her pad and positioned her pen to continue her note taking. "How'd you start the firm?"

"We went off to internships and first jobs elsewhere. Jason and I found ourselves in D.C., Spencer was in California, and Amar was living it up in New York. But we never lost touch, and when we saw each other at a reunion a few years later, I planted a seed in their heads about working together. Two years after that, the Cambridge Group was born."

"So fast-forward to now. Is there anything you'd like to change about the firm?"

"A couple of things. We need focus, just like you said. I'd like a client to come to us because we're the best at doing something no one else does or very few other firms do. And I'd like to increase our gender diversity. Right now we look a bit like an old boys' network. It's time for a change. We've even gotten flack from a women's group at Harvard, and to be frank, I can't really say they're wrong."

Mimi cocked her head and regarded him with a bemused expression.

"What?" he asked.

"You're throwing me off here."

"I'm not as arrogant as you'd assumed, huh?"

"No, you're still arrogant. But you've got other layers, too."

She tapped her pen on her mouth and stared at a point behind him. His gaze zeroed in on the movement, and he forgot what he was about to say. Her lips—whether painted or not—were like the neutralizer in *Men in Black*: capable of wiping his memories clean in seconds.

Abruptly, she threw the pen in her purse, shoved the legal pad under her arm, and stood with an outstretched hand. She didn't look him in the eyes, though. "Thanks for sharing. This has been super helpful." She cringed as though she regretted her phrasing.

If she'd avoided his gaze like this weeks ago, he would have been offended. But slowly he was learning that Mimi's lack of engagement meant he'd rattled her composure—and that was a great develop-ment in his opinion. After rounding his desk, he grinned and took her small hand in his. "I'm super glad it was super helpful."

Her gaze whipped to his face, and she blushed. Christ. Rosy cheeks had never turned him on, but this was Mimi. How the hell could they work together without him getting his hands on her body again?

She cleared her throat. "So I've talked to the guys, and I have all the info on your projects in my drop box. I should have a proposal ready sometime next week. Would that work?"

"Yes. That would be fine. Send me a few dates and times. I'll co-ordinate on this end and ask Felicia to confirm with you."

"Great. Okay."

She strode to the door.

"Mimi."

She spun to face him. "Yes?"

He motioned to the floor. "Don't forget your purse."

She rolled her eyes. "Right." Then she grabbed the bag and scram-bled out of his office.

I know what you're feeling, Ms. Pennington. Believe me, I know.

* * *

A week later, Daniel approached Mimi's pitch meeting with an im-pending sense of doom. On the one hand, he believed she would help the firm boost its public image. On the other hand, he worried that if the firm hired her, she would forever be out of his reach.

Tough shit, he told himself.

But you're attracted to her, the devil on his shoulder taunted.

Maybe she'd made the rule for this precise reason. For men like him—men who couldn't see the forest for their dicks. With a resigned sigh, he plodded down the hall, preparing himself to play the role of the professional executive attending an ordinary business meeting when all he really wanted to do was spend an entire weekend convincing Mimi to let him into her life. Preferably in her bed.

Listen to what she has to say. Ask a few questions. Let the guys do the rest. The only problem? The woman running the meeting consumed his thoughts, the memory of their interlude in Puerto Rico replaying in his head and tempting him to imagine its logical conclusion. And really, if he could forget about it as she was apparently trying to do, he'd welcome the amnesia. But he knew it wasn't going to happen. No, he and Mimi had unfinished business to attend to. Whether or not she wanted to admit it.

But first, he needed coffee.

Minutes later, he entered the conference room and found Mimi placing folders on the table. He stopped short when she gave him a big smile. It unsettled him, frankly. The guys could have her smiles. He wanted her to shiver at the sight of him. Hell, even a sneer would be better than this sanitized greeting. "Good morning, Mimi."

"Good morning, Daniel." She set the last folder down and stood at the front of the room.

He relaxed his shoulders and widened his stance, trying to look casual as he took a sip of his coffee. "Where would you like us to sit?"

"Wherever's comfortable for you. I didn't think a PowerPoint was necessary. I've got screenshots of my ideas for the website in the folders."

He nodded and walked to the back of the room, pulling out the chair directly across from the head of the table. From here, he could watch her without the guys being aware of it.

Jason, Amar, and Spencer filed into the room, and a chorus of "good mornings" followed. After everyone settled into their chairs, Mimi opened her own folder.

"So after talking with all of you and looking over your past projects, I've come up with a common thread I think you could use to brand yourselves effectively. Environmentally-friendly design. Take a look at the projects in your folder. Every single one of them incorporates ideas about sustainability, renewable resources, and reducing the negative impact of the design on the environment. And it's no surprise this is the case, given how all of you met in a class on this very subject."

The others shook their heads. Now that she'd pointed out this commonality, he guessed they were connecting the dots.

"Your personal and professional stories are intertwined, and I think you could really sell that aspect of your relationship. You learned together, you work together, and you produce excellent results together. I'm aware of your concern about this being a closed boys' network, so we'd have to make clear that how you came to work together is just the beginning of the story and that there's room for expansion. I've included some mockups of the website redesign. And you'll see a list of suggested action items."

Spencer furrowed his eyebrows. "What's this about new headshots?"

Mimi pursed her lips in an "I hate to be the messenger of obvious news here" look that made Daniel grin.

"To put it bluntly, your photos on the website look like driver's licenses," Mimi said. "So new headshots for all. I wouldn't need all day. In fact, I'll bring the photographer's studio to you. Just give me an hour of your time. I'll work with Felicia to set that up." A blush crept along her collarbone, ascended to her neck, and spread to her cheeks. "If you hire me, of course. I don't mean to be presumptuous."

Amar waved away her apology. "Don't worry about it. What else do you have in mind?"

"Spencer and Daniel, we need to get some buzz for your work on the Whitmore. I'd like to get *Architectural Digest* to cover the ribbon-cutting ceremony. Ideally, we'd get some press that discusses how you met the museum's vision. And for all of you, we'll definitely want coverage of the panel you're doing at Harvard next month. It shows that even the graduate school recognizes your contribution to innovative design."

She'd shared several solid ideas, no question. And if they didn't have this unfinished history, he'd jump at the chance to hire her. But damn if he didn't worry about what that would mean for them. Could he *choose* to work with someone he desperately wanted when he didn't have to?

He glanced at her, noticing her hand gestures as she talked. The way her eyes lit up when she was excited about a topic. The way she flicked the tip of her tongue to the corner of her mouth after she'd made a point. *Fuck.* The tiny movement conjured images of her doing the same thing in his bed. She'd be under him, her lithe body pressed against the mattress as he moved over her. He'd look into her eyes, and when he filled her, she'd flick her tongue at the corner of her mouth and close her eyes.

When Daniel refocused on the meeting, Amar was waving his hand in front of Daniel's face.

"You with us?" he asked.

Mimi laughed. "I think he's worried about his headshot."

All this talk about her plans for the firm might as well have been a dozen doors slamming in his face. And he wasn't ready to let her go. Daniel stood on shaky legs. "Gentlemen, I need to speak with Mimi for a minute. Excuse us."

Mimi nodded, her eyes round from the interruption.

She walked behind him, her shoes clacking against the floors, but he didn't turn around, because he didn't know if he could acknowledge her without pushing her against the nearest wall and kissing the ever-loving shit out of her.

When they reached his office, he ushered her in and closed the door behind them. He strode to his desk and hit the remote that controlled the blinds, darkening the room into shades of brown and gold.

He faced her and tried to gather his thoughts, unsure why he'd brought her here in the first place.

Standing by the door, she shook her head in confusion. "What's going on, Daniel? Is something wrong?"

He closed the distance between them and blurted out the first thing that came to mind. "I've been thinking about your rules."

She gave him a blank look. "What?"

"No, not your rules. Given where we are, just one rule in particular. The one about not mixing business with pleasure."

Her eyes widened. "Is this the Twilight Zone? Why are you thinking about that *now*? I'm presenting my brand strategy to you and your partners. And I can't…" Her head dropped. "Oh."

"Yes, oh. How important is it to you that you get our business? Because I've just decided to abstain from the vote, but I know they're going to hire you. And if they do, that means…"

She brought her fingers to her temples. "No, no, no. You're not doing this to me now. Absolutely not." Then she jerked her thumb behind her. "I'm going back in there. And we'll just pretend this conversation never happened. Okay?"

"Okay."

She turned and placed her hand on the doorknob, and he dropped his shoulders in defeat. Before his common sense could kick in, though, he reached above her head and placed his hand on the door, stopping her from swinging it open. "Wait."

She didn't turn around.

Is she composing herself?

Slowly, she faced him, half of her body hidden by the fabric of his open jacket. "What, Daniel?" she said with a tremor in her voice.

He lowered his head and inched his mouth closer to hers, so close that he felt her soft breath skate over his chin. With his eyes, he tried to will her to meet his lips. Unless she initiated it, the kiss wouldn't happen.

"I want you to be sure about this," he prompted.

Her eyelids fluttered closed. Then she pushed him away. Hard. So hard that he stumbled. When he righted himself, he met her cold gaze.

"You're unbelievable, you know that? I think I'm smart enough to know what I want, and It's. Not. You."

"Okay, I could respect that if I thought it was true, but—"

She balled her hands into fists. "Daniel, *listen* to me."

He stepped in front of her. "I'm listening."

"I *need* you to take me seriously as a professional colleague. If we're going to work together, you'll have to put aside your attraction to me and treat me like your PR person. Nothing more. Can you do that?"

Fuck. When she said it like that, how could he deny her? "Sorry. I'm trying."

"*Try harder.*"

"I will. But—"

"But what?"

Her voice rose, no doubt in frustration.

Well, he was frustrated, too. "Listen, you've got to cut me some slack here. I can't forget that night, okay? And the idea that we're just going to pretend it never happened seems wrong somehow."

"Oh, I haven't forgotten, Daniel. Something's corrupted your memory, though. *You* walked away from me, so I'm not inclined to feel sorry for you." She dropped her head in frustration and raised it again. "Look, I realize I'm asking a lot of you, but let's just be content to be colleagues."

"Friends."

"Acquaintances."

"Maybe we could become acquaintances who flirt with each other."

She pushed him away from her. "God, will you cut it out? This is important to me. And I'm not your plaything. Go rut elsewhere."

She was right. He was acting like a dick. But he'd never considered her his plaything.

Contrary to Mimi's belief, he knew how to be in a relationship, preferring to focus on one woman at a time. Being an attentive boyfriend had never been a problem for him. But as several of his ex-girlfriends had pointed out, he didn't share much about himself. One woman had said dating him was like being on a perpetual first date. Ouch.

He had his reasons, though. Some parents handed down secret

recipes. His parents, on the other hand, had passed on their ability to avoid any discussion of their feelings whatsoever. At his sister's funeral, a single tear had rolled down his father's face, and the grumpy old man had clawed the tear away as though its appearance had disgusted him. Knowing his father, Daniel was sure it had.

He wanted to be different with Mimi. He could tell her that he'd lain in bed the past few days thinking up excuses to call her. Could confess that even the memory of the jokes she'd made at his expense brightened his day. But what would be the point? Clearly they had different views about the situation: He wanted to be with her, and she wanted his firm's account. "I'm sorry if I made you uncomfortable. Acquaintances it is, then."

For a brief moment, he swore her eyes dimmed. But that wouldn't make sense, so he dismissed the possibility that maintaining a professional wall between them was as hard for her as it was for him.

He opened the door for her.

Before slipping out of his office, she gave him a weak smile. "Thank you."

He nodded.

As he followed her back to the conference room, he resisted the urge to notice the way her slacks revealed just a hint of the fine ass underneath. *Okay, not really.*

Try harder, she'd said. Of course he'd pretend he didn't care. That part came easy to him. The hard part? Working with a woman who was off-limits to him, one he suspected was his perfect match.

CHAPTER NINE

Mimi picked at her nails as she returned to the conference room. Before opening the glass door, she closed her eyes and took a calming breath, well aware that Daniel wasn't far behind her. She pasted on a confident smile and waltzed into the conference room as though Daniel hadn't just interrupted her pitch and damn near kissed her in his office. "Sorry about that, gentlemen. Now where were we?"

As Daniel took his seat, Amar saved her, continuing the meeting seamlessly. "We have potential clients coming in a few weeks. What's your time frame for getting the website revamped?"

She tapped her pen on the table. "We work closely with a website designer who can turn it around quickly. If your goal is to get it up and running before then, we'd need those new headshots as soon as possible."

Spencer drummed his fingers on the table. "If we retain you, what's your best estimate of how much time you'd be spending on our firm's PR?"

"That depends on your needs. I'd say twenty hours in the next two weeks, and it would taper off dramatically after that. Also, we'll be monitoring your publicity, but that's something we'll do on our dime, as a measure of our results, and that can be done remotely."

She risked a glance at Daniel, expecting to see him watching her, but he was staring out the window, his hands folded on the table. "Any other questions?"

Daniel turned his head and pinned her with a clear gaze. "I have one question."

Her heart thudded in her chest. Was he about to make his objections known? "What's that?"

His smile injected a jolt of life into his flat expression. "When can we begin?"

She swept her gaze around the table and registered the smiles of the others. "As soon as you'd like," was her stunned answer. Expecting a sense of relief to flood her senses, Mimi furrowed her brows when a knot formed in the pit of her stomach instead.

Wow. She'd gotten the gig. *So why I am not as excited as I thought I'd be?*

Daniel stood. "I have a meeting at eleven o'clock. I'll leave you to work out the arrangements with Jason." He picked up his legal pad and left the room without so much as a nod in her direction.

There. That was the answer. Now she'd have to work with Daniel, but obviously he wasn't happy about it. She had to figure out a way around the awkwardness. *I can do this. I will do this.*

But how?

* * *

What she'd needed was perspective—and a couple of days out of Daniel's presence. In that time, Mimi had come up with a plan. While she generally avoided treating her clients with any kind of familiarity, her history with Daniel called for a different approach as to him. He'd gotten to know the version of her she shared with friends and people outside work. Interacting with him as though he were no different than the other men in his firm now seemed horribly unfair. She'd almost had sex with the man. So going forward, she'd relax a little around him. Maybe in turn he'd relax, too, and then they'd be able to work together without suffocating from the thick tension between them.

Though she now had a plan, she wasn't quite ready to implement it. And she refused to dwell on the reasons why. Still, she had a job to do, so she traveled to the Cambridge Group's offices Wednesday morning to check on the photography session she'd arranged for the men.

Mimi stopped at Felicia's desk on her way in.

"Are the men being tortured yet?"

The receptionist gave her a mischievous grin. "They are. The photographer's using the main conference room."

"Great. I'm going to take a look."

Mimi's heels clicked across the marble floor. She mentally reminded herself to suggest an area rug for the reception area. "Felicia, who's up now?"

"Daniel."

Mimi's stride slowed. As usual, her timing was perfect. *Dammit.* "Anyone else left to go?"

"They're all done, I think."

Great. If she turned around and left, Felicia would wonder why.

And she did not need Felicia wondering anything. She continued down the hall and braced herself for the impact of seeing him again.

She pulled open the double doors of the conference room and tiptoed inside.

The photographer had transformed the room into his personal studio, complete with the ubiquitous blue backdrop she'd seen in a thousand-and-one other headshots. Daniel sat on a stool with one foot on the floor and the other resting on the stool's crossbar.

He acknowledged her with a curt nod and turned his attention to the scene outside the conference room window.

Well, it's nice to see you, too.

The photographer positioned himself in front of his digital camera, which rested on a steel tripod that probably cost more than Mimi's entire outfit. "Turn your body at a slight angle facing me," the photographer told Daniel.

"Like this?" Daniel asked.

"Yes, that's great. Now give me a warm smile."

Daniel complied, giving them the charming, arresting smile Mimi had seen him use in social settings, the one that said, *I'm the life of the party, and you should want to get to know me.* It matched his perfectly combed hair and the flawless fit of his navy blue two-piece suit. Even the tie, blood red and slim, rested in the middle of his chest as though it were ironed into place. And it was all wrong. In fact, nothing about the shot worked.

Several clicks of the camera later, Mimi stepped in. "Can I have a word with you?" she asked the photographer.

The photographer ambled over to her. "What's up?"

"First, let me make clear that you're giving me exactly what I asked of you."

"Why do I get the feeling that's not a good thing?"

"It's not, unfortunately. But it's also not your fault. It's mine. Seeing the setup made me realize that I'm looking for something a little different for these guys. One of the points we're working on for branding is their commitment to environmentally friendly design. So now it occurs to me that a headshot won't do. Any chance we could take a few photos outside? In the park across the street?"

The photographer shrugged. "I get paid by the hour, Ms. Pennington. If you want photos outside, you can have photos outside. But I've got another appointment at three, so we'd have to be done before then."

Mimi clapped her hands together. "Great." She jerked a thumb in Daniel's direction. "Now let me get the honcho's okay."

She straightened her shoulders and took a deep breath. *Is it strange that I want to wish myself good luck?*

Daniel watched her approach, his face impassive in a way that was at odds with his usual happy-go-lucky shtick.

"Hi, Daniel."

"Mimi."

Not going to make this easy, huh? "So I have an idea about the photos."

"Yeah?"

"Yes. I'm thinking we should try a few shots outside. It'll be a good way to play up the firm's environmental spin."

"Is that what we're calling it? A spin?"

"The firm's track record for creating environmentally friendly designs is part of its branding, yes, but if calling it a spin troubles you, we don't have to call it that."

"You're so accommodating."

"Look, can we not do this here?" she said as she gestured around her. "Let's get these new shots. I'll round up the rest of the gang, and the photographer will get started with you. Game?"

He said nothing for a moment. Simply watched her. She wanted to fidget, but she willed herself not to. And she realized then that his brown eyes held the key to his true mood. Whatever he showed on the outside, if his eyes didn't match it, it wasn't true. To anyone who hadn't made that connection, he would have looked at ease and unaffected by her presence. But his eyes told a different story; they were focused so intently on her that the chirping birds and blaring car horns faded out of her consciousness until all she saw or heard revolved around him.

He broke eye contact first. "Fine. I'm doing a poor job of showing it, but I do trust your expertise."

In the breathless moment before he'd called that silent truce, she'd wondered whether working together was asking too much of both of them. But he'd indicated a willingness to try, and she certainly had more reasons than he to make the effort. She smiled. "Okay, then. I'll gather the rest of the troops and meet you outside."

Minutes later, Mimi ran across the four-lane street, and joined Daniel and the photographer in the park. "The rest of the guys went to lunch," she told them. "We'll have to do theirs another time." This was a good thing, actually. If the photos didn't work, she'd only inconvenience Daniel, and since they weren't on such great terms to begin with, she could live with that.

The photographer tested a few shots with Daniel seated on a bench. Mimi peeked at the photos filling the digital screen. *Much better.* The natural lighting and outdoor setting gave the image the relaxed feel she'd been looking for. But something was still off. She bit her lip in contemplation.

"Are you itching to say something, Mimi?" Daniel asked.

The sun's rays hit his face, causing him to squint as he looked up at her.

"I'm thinking." With her head tilted, she paced behind the photographer. "I've got it. Let's make a few adjustments."

"Like what?"

"Unbutton your jacket."

He used his hand to shade his face as he peered at her. *Dammit.* The command had seemed harmless in her head, but it conjured images of him stripping for her in Puerto Rico. Slowly, he unbuttoned his jacket, his gaze never leaving hers.

"Anything else I can do for you? Should I ditch the tie, too?" he asked.

Mimi swallowed, her throat dry and tight, as he raised his hands to his collar. Suddenly, a dozen images flashed through her brain: his striptease, the way he'd used his body to push her against the elevator wall, the press of his impressive erection against her stomach, and the jolt of electricity that had coursed through her when she'd stroked him.

"No," she told him once her brain's synapses had begun firing again. "The shirt and tie stay on."

He settled his hand on his stomach. "As you wish. What else?"

Mimi eyed the photographer.

"This is your vision," he said. "Go for it."

"Can you sit on the bench back with your feet on the seat?" Mimi asked Daniel. She leaned over to demonstrate. "Maybe rest your elbows on your legs and cross your hands together under your chin?"

For a few seconds, Daniel said nothing, his eyes skating over her body as she showed him what she meant. "You're quite the bossy one, aren't you?"

This was exactly the progress she'd hoped for, and because they had history, she'd allow him some leeway. "Quit it."

"Yes, ma'am."

With a half smile on his face, Daniel followed her instructions as the photographer captured each pose. Mimi rounded the tripod and looked at the recent set of photos. Definitely an improvement. They were close, but not quite there. She went over to Daniel and ruffled his hair. She was so immersed in getting the perfect shot that she breached his personal space, the intimacy of having her hands on him freezing her on the spot.

He stood, his eyes narrowing as he surveyed her face. "This isn't fair, Mimi. You've got to give me a break here."

She jumped back at his words. "I was just trying to make you look less pristine. We need to make you approachable, less starchy."

He pinned her with a narrow-eyed stare.

"Can you put one foot on the bench? Be casual but authoritative?"

"I'll do my best." Then he adjusted his body as she'd suggested.

Mimi turned to the photographer. "Can you grab this shot?"

The photographer nodded and clicked his camera. Mimi glanced at the digital screen again and gave Daniel a thumbs-up. "We've got it."

The photographer packed up his equipment while Mimi checked her phone for recent e-mail messages.

Daniel slipped back into his jacket as he sauntered over to her. "You know your comments about my so-called perfect appearance are starting to offend me."

Mimi quirked her lips. "You? Offended? I figured that was impossible given you're coated in a protective barrier of ego no single barb could ever hope to penetrate."

Daniel jumped back, jerking with each step as though her words had physically struck him. "I'm wounded," he said in a strained voice.

"Acting is not your strong suit," she said in a flat tone. "Anyway, you can't argue with the facts. I've seen you numerous times, in different settings, from a gala to a housewarming, and I've never seen a single hair on your head out of place."

He inched closer and stopped just short of her. "Are you suggesting I can't get dirty? Because I assure you I can be *very dirty* when necessary."

Well, shit. She should have seen that one coming. The sound of his voice was a physical caress, and as effective as any foreplay she'd ever experienced. Mimi couldn't think of a quip fast enough, not when she was focused on suppressing any outward sign of the tremor that ran through her. Instead, she breathed him in, registering the heat of his body and the scent of him—sunny, salty, and too much for her senses. "Prove it, then."

His pupils dilated before his eyelids fell to half-mast. "God, I've wanted you to say that for so long."

Before he could advance any further, Mimi scrambled out of his reach. "Wait. What are you doing?"

"I'm going to show you how dirty I can be—"

"I didn't mean *right now*, Daniel. I have something else in mind."

He pursed his lips and blew out a long breath. "Oh?"

"I was thinking we could run a race together. It's called the Dirty Thirty."

He scrunched his brows. "What's that?"

"The Dirty Thirty is an annual mud run at National Harbor. Two miles, thirty obstacles, and *lots* of mud. By the end of it, you'll be caked in dirt. In fact, that mud will find its way into crevices you didn't even know you had."

"Sounds delightful."

"Sounds *dirty*. Think you're up for the challenge?"

"How strenuous is the course? Does it require training?"

"Daniel, before my first race, I'd run to the bathroom and get winded. So no, no training required. It's a charity event, to benefit kids with leukemia. I tried to convince Gracie to do it with me, but she passed. You can sign up online."

"Hang on. I'm still wrapping my head around the fact that you compete in mud runs."

She scrunched her nose. "*Compete* is a bit of an overstatement. I did my first run as part of a work retreat. Under protest, I might add. But I happened to love it, so here we are."

"When is it?"

"Saturday."

"*This* Saturday."

"Yup."

"That's not a lot of time."

"Time for what?"

He tugged on his lip and considered her. "Never mind." After a few seconds, he grinned. "What's in it for me?"

"Other than proving me wrong about your need for perfection? Nothing."

"Eh. Proving you wrong on that point isn't worth it. But..."

"But what?"

"But I'd do it for a chance to spend an evening with you. Dinner, dancing, whatever."

The man was relentless. But she'd opened herself up to the suggestion, hadn't she? "C'mon, Daniel. That's not fair. We've been over this before."

"*As friends*, Mimi. Dinner, dancing, and whatever *as friends*. You don't doubt your ability to resist me under those circumstances, right?"

Of course she did. To him, though, she said, "Absolutely not. I don't doubt my ability to resist you under *any* circumstances."

"Then wouldn't it be worth it to you? To see me covered in dirt from head to toe. I'd even let you take a gloating selfie with my filthy body in the background."

Was it? Was it worth it? Oh, yes, dinner with Daniel was definitely worth seeing him covered in mud—so long as the dinner remained professional, *which it would*. "You're on. Dinner only. No dancing. And *definitely* no *whatever*."

"Dinner this Saturday then."

"*This* Saturday?"

"Yes, *this* Saturday."

She nodded as though the prospect of having dinner with him were no big deal. But it was. "Fine."

"Great."

Yeah. Great.

What had she gotten herself into?

CHAPTER TEN

Saturday morning, Mimi drove from D.C. to National Harbor, an area just south of the district that ran along the Potomac River in Maryland. To Mimi, the outlet mall and a small restaurant on the main street were its best attractions. The latter served the most delicious margarita she'd ever tasted, and she'd tasted *lots* of them in her lifetime.

The crisp October air heightened her senses and energized her for the race to come. As she waited in line to check in, she scanned the crowd for Daniel. Though she'd invited him as a challenge, she secretly hoped he'd have fun. If he whined about his hair being dirty—even once—she'd consider it his loss. As far as she was concerned, someone who couldn't have fun at a mud run was *not* her kind of people.

She rose on her toes and searched the throng of runners. *Where is he?*

Behind her, a body came too close, brushing against her backside. Mimi whipped around, ready to berate the stranger for invading her personal space. She groaned when she discovered the body was Daniel's.

"Looking for me?" he said.

Now that she realized he wasn't a creeper trying to cop a feel, she missed the warmth of his body against her back. But she wasn't supposed to be having these feelings about Daniel. *Dammit to hell.* Okay, maybe he wasn't a stranger-danger-type threat, but yeah, he was still a threat.

She couldn't see his eyes behind the designer sunglasses he wore, but she could just imagine that his eyes were twinkling, a perfect match to his playful grin. "You almost scored yourself a knee to the nuts."

"Now's not the time to share your kinks with me, Mimi. We agreed to keep this professional, remember?"

She sucked her teeth and waved his comment away like a pesky fly. "Glad to see you showed up. For a minute there, I wondered if you'd chickened out."

"And forfeit a chance to take you to dinner? Never."

He considered dinner with her a prize? That was kind of sweet, actually—assuming he didn't have an ulterior motive. But who was she kidding? With men like Daniel, dinner always came with an ulterior motive. Guarding herself against his disarming nature, she refocused on the reason for her invitation: to get him dirty.

Suddenly, her brain registered that Daniel wasn't wearing a suit, or even a dress shirt and slacks. "Daniel in casual clothes. Give me a minute to take this in." She stepped back, nearly bumping into the person in front of her.

Daniel, meanwhile, removed his sunglasses and waited for her inspection.

Daniel in athletic shorts and a tank top.

Oh.

Oh, shit.

Mimi coughed to cover her reaction. Her brain, meanwhile, sizzled like a frying egg in a skillet.

Fuck me.

Fuck me well.

Fuck me really well.

His broad chest made the tank top inadequate for anything other than covering his pecs. His arms, as blessed as they were with well-defined muscles, had nothing on his legs. More specifically, his thighs. Which suggested he did quite a bit of strength training when he wasn't styling his perfect hair.

"Wow. Okay. So you don't pop out of bed in a suit. This is refreshing to see."

And titillating, too. But she'd *never* admit that to him.

He smirked at her. "If you must know, I typically pop out of bed naked. In my experience, clothes tend to restrict your ease of movement when you're...uh...sleeping."

Was she picturing him naked? Of course. But she refused to give him the satisfaction of acknowledging his comment. Pretending not to have heard it, she rushed forward to the sign-in table when another runner relinquished his place.

A woman dressed in athletic wear smiled from her seat behind the table and asked for Mimi's name.

Mimi bent over the table and whispered her given name, the one she didn't want Daniel to hear.

"Found it," the woman said. "Here's your number plate and safety pins. Good luck."

"Thanks."

Mimi shifted to her left and waited for Daniel. In the meantime, she pinned the laminated number plate on the front of her shirt.

"Name, please?" the woman asked Daniel without looking up from her clipboard.

"Daniel Vargas."

The woman's head shot up. "Daniel! What are you doing here?"

Daniel gave the woman a wide smile. "Hey, Beth. Just having a little fun for a good cause. Good to see you."

"Yeah, yeah. Good to see you, too. You headed up to the Spartan Run next week?"

"I wouldn't miss it for the world."

Spartan Run? What were they talking about? Mimi edged closer to the table. "What's the Spartan Run?" she asked them.

"One of the most challenging mud runs out there. Your friend Daniel here came in second last year."

Mimi gave him a sidelong glance. "Did he now?"

Beth nodded. "Sure did. The man's a legend among mud running enthusiasts in this area. Gunning for first place this year, Daniel?"

"I'm certainly going to try."

"Well, this should be a piece of cake for you," Beth added.

"Not sure about that. Thirty obstacles."

Beth laughed. "These obstacles are *nothing* like Spartan. Not even close."

Mimi smiled at them while she seethed inside. He was a mud runner, and he hadn't said a thing. And he'd suckered her into thinking this would be a real challenge for him. If she called him on it, he'd point out that she'd never asked. *The rat.*

She balled her hands into fists and let out a slow breath.

After they'd stepped a few feet away from the sign-in area, she spun around to confront him. "You pretended you knew nothing about mud runs, you cheat!"

"Not so. I asked you about the Dirty Thirty, which I'd never heard of. You assumed everything else."

After hearing the trace of humor in his voice, she stomped off. Exactly what she'd figured he would say. *Whatever.*

"You'll still get your selfie," he called after her.

Grrr. "No, thank you. I don't want it anymore," she shouted over her shoulder.

Minutes later, they stood hip to hip, waiting for the signal to begin the course.

"Are you going to ignore me the entire race?"

She kept her head pointed toward the starting line as she stretched her calves. "Yup."

"C'mon, Mimi." He faced her and bent his knees so that he was eye level with her. "How can I make it up to you?"

"You can stick a handful of mud up your—"

"*Tsk, tsk.*" He straightened to his full height. "I'll tell you what. Let me give you a head start. You can say you beat my time."

"Oh, we're adding a heavy dose of chauvinism to your long list of admirable traits, I see." She raised her hands over her head and then shook them out, loosening her muscles. "No, thanks. I don't need your charity."

He placed his hand on her arm, his brown eyes looking more earnest than she'd ever seen them. "Hey, I didn't mean to offend you. I was just having some fun, but I did it at your expense. Sorry."

What was happening here? Why did she now feel like the death of the party? "Is this some kind of diversionary tactic?"

Before he could respond, the bullhorn sounded and the crowd moved together in one heavy clump. *So much for being off with a bang.*

Daniel held out his hand. "Here, I'll lead you to the front."

She was in danger of being squeezed between two tall men, so she reluctantly took his hand. "This is the only time I'll accept your help, so savor it."

He stroked the underside of her wrist with his thumb. "I will."

She snatched her hand away like she'd touched a hot stove. "Down, boy."

"You want a shot at winning this thing?"

"Why else would I be here?"

"We'll have a better chance of that if we work together."

"Okay, lead the way."

And so he did, pointing out the rocky paths and steering her toward trails that would be easier to traverse. They ran a fifth of a mile before reaching the mud pit. By then, they'd managed to create significant distance between them and the largest group of mud runners.

He turned to her. "The key to this is not to jump in with both feet. The mud at the bottom is like cement. Put one foot in first and get your bearings."

"I've done this before, Daniel."

"I forgot."

Damn proud of her accomplishments thus far, she gave him a satisfied smile. "Came in first place, too. In the women's twenty to twenty-nine category."

"Well, let's do this then."

"Let's."

They sloshed through the mud. Mimi had been careful to wear an extra-long T-shirt, just in case her shorts rode low or her top shifted. Her first mud run had been a different story—and she'd ended up looking like Ms. January in a female mud wrestler calendar. *Never again.*

She'd forgone socks and tied her sneaker laces around her ankles so she wouldn't lose them. No way would she be taking them home, but she planned on dumping them in the donate pile at the end of the race. The mud slid into her sneaks, and she relished the feel of the wet dirt against her skin.

Daniel, meanwhile, rubbed the mud on his arms. "Feels good, right?"

"It does. It was weird the first time I did one of these runs, but now I'm kind of addicted."

"Well, what do you know, we have something in common." He moved forward, brushing his body against hers. Then he ran his muddy finger down the center of her nose. "Now you're ready."

A few runners trudged through the mud, but she didn't care.

"Oh. Game on, Vargas." She scooped a handful of mud and dumped it on his head. But she didn't stop there. Next, she massaged his scalp like she was shampooing his hair. "How does that feel?" she asked.

"Glorious," he said. "Sensual. You're very good at this."

She dropped her hands. "Ugh. You're such a pervert."

He laughed, but his laughter died quickly. "Um, Mimi. We should get going."

"Why? What's wrong?"

She turned to see a group of runners barreling toward the mud pit. "Oh, shit. Let's go."

For the next fifteen minutes, they tackled the obstacles side by side, first getting through the tire course and then crawling under the wire netting. When they reached the climbing wall, Mimi bent at the waist, her lungs burning. *This is hard.* She straightened and shook out her arms and legs. When she peeked at Daniel, he was covered in grime but hardly out of breath.

"Go ahead without me," she told him between breaths. She again leaned over and placed her hands on her knees. *Dammit.* She'd been in better shape for the last race. It figured she'd invite Daniel to the one where she'd embarrass herself. "Go ahead," she repeated. "You can place in the run."

Daniel circled back to her and crouched on one knee, his face level with hers. "I'm not leaving without you, soldier. Get your butt in gear. We're doing this together or not at all."

She burst out laughing. "Okay, okay. No need to be so dramatic."

She rose and let him lead her to the wall. "I'm going to need your help, but if you use this as an excuse to touch my ass, you'll be sorry."

"Um. Have you looked at yourself lately? Believe me, touching your ass is the last thing I want to do right now."

He laughed. And laughed some more. She couldn't help joining him, either.

God, dare she say it? She was having fun with Daniel Vargas.

Cue the zombies, because this *had* to be the apocalypse.

* * *

Daniel hadn't lied when he'd told Mimi touching her ass was the last thing he wanted to do. Because, damn, there were so many other parts of her body he could explore before he got to her backside.

What a tempting picture she made. The mud covered her body, leaving nothing to his imagination. The curve of her breasts, the soft flare of her hips, the flat plane of her stomach—all of it lay before him, a veritable late-night snack run for his eyes.

He wanted her. Badly. But she'd made it clear there'd be no romantic connection between them, so he vowed to enjoy her in whatever way she'd allow. And he was a guy, so right now he was enjoying the view of her ass as she climbed the five-foot wall that separated them from the finish line. He stood ready to help her, but she didn't need it.

She grasped the braided rope and placed the sole of one foot on the wall. As she lifted her arm to grasp another section of rope, the muscles in her toned arms flexed with the exertion. Watching her challenge her body satisfied his very elemental need to admire the beauty of a woman's physique in motion. Faster than he'd expected, she hoisted one leg over the top of the wall, swinging the other leg around before she disappeared from his view.

And when he cleared the wall after her, she stood on the other side, looking dirty, adorable, and pleased with herself.

"What took you so long?" she asked between pants.

"These old legs aren't as spry as they used to be," he said.

Her eyes flew to his thighs. "Those are hardly old legs. You're built like a stallion down there."

He stared at her until her eyes went wide, and he couldn't help chuckling. "You said it. Not me."

She grimaced. "Ugh. My mouth gets me in so much trouble."

He stared at her—again, until her eyes went wide—again.

She brushed the hair off her face and straightened her shorts. "I'm just going to shut up now. C'mon. Let's finish this."

They ran the last one hundred yards, their feet hitting the ground at the same time. Other mud runners had already crossed the finish line, but he didn't care, nor did she if the loud whoop she gave was any indication.

Her flushed cheeks and bright eyes captivated him. If he could guarantee that she'd be standing at the finish line, looking exactly as she did now, he would win every race he entered. Better yet, if he could run each race *with* her, he wouldn't even care about winning.

She raised her hand to high-five him. "That was fanfuckingtastic."

"Agreed," he said as he tried to catch his breath.

They walked in circles, keeping their blood pumping to avoid aches and leg cramps.

A young girl, looking bored in the way tweens had perfected as a rite of passage, stood a few yards from the finish line. "Congratulations on finishing," she said in a monotone voice. "Please turn in your number plate. Hoses to wash off are to your right."

Mimi gave her a cheerful smile. "Thank you."

"Sure," the tween said with a roll of her eyes.

Sparkling personality, that one.

He and Mimi grinned at each other. *Were they thinking the same thing?*

They proceeded to the hose-off area. Eight hoses of various lengths lay on the ground, each connected to a water truck about fifty yards away. Mimi picked up a hose and began to rinse the mud off her body. Slowly, glimpses of her skin emerged. Taking in her compact body, half-dirty and wet, he felt like someone had delivered a roundhouse kick to his head. Was he supposed to be doing something other than enjoying the view?

She whipped the hose in front of her, dousing him with a spray of water. "Hey, are you just going to watch me?"

He swatted at the water as he jumped out of the way. "Hey, yourself. And stop that. I was still catching my breath."

"Right," she said. "And paying way more attention to my cleaning process than yours."

"Maybe I shouldn't admit it, but this is a fantasy of mine. A hot woman covered in mud. It brings me back to the female mud wrestlers I watched on television when I was young."

She wrinkled her nose as she resumed her hose-down. "You're such a dude."

He smirked and bowed. "Thank you."

"Not a compliment, buddy."

"I'm taking it as one anyway."

She doused him with more water. "You would."

He lunged for her, but she dropped the hose and ran away, her laughter coaxing a stupid grin from him.

She'd reduced her frost factor by twenty degrees today, and he intended to capitalize on the opening she'd given him. Dinner this evening would be a first step in that direction.

He caught up with her at the checkout table, where the attendants had stored his and Mimi's personal belongings. After handing in his claim card, he turned to her. "So about dinner. Can I pick you up at seven?"

She held a ponytail holder between her teeth and fussed with her hair. *Is it weird that I want to be that hair band?*

After bending down and pulling her mud-streaked locks into a messy bun, she straightened. "Seven's fine."

"Text me your address when you have a minute," he told her.

She tapped at her phone. "Done."

He glanced at his to confirm that he'd received her text. "Can't wait until tonight."

She cocked her head and narrowed her eyes. "Dinner between acquaintances, right?"

"We just ran a mud race together. I think it's safe to say we're friends."

She turned away and squinted her eyes against the sun, her expression pensive. "Depends on your meaning of *safe*, actually." She didn't wait for a response, jingling her car keys instead. "I'm off to get the mud out of my unmentionables. See you tonight."

"Looking forward to it, Mimi."

She studied his face as she moved in place. And then she grinned—reluctantly, but it was there. "So am I, Daniel."

He watched her go knowing this: He'd found a crack in the seemingly impenetrable wall she'd built around herself. Pumped from the race and a morning in her company, he mentally high-fived himself. Now if he could get her to relax her rules, he might actually have a chance at convincing her to date him. As he made his way to his car, he tried to devise a solution. His steps slowed when a potential fix came to him: Rather than treat her rules as an obstacle, he'd reframe them as an opportunity and convince her to test them. Tonight that fucking wall between them was coming down. But in a rare moment of self-doubt, he wondered if she would bury him in the process.

CHAPTER ELEVEN

Mimi waited for Daniel inside the vestibule of her apartment building. Allowing him to come upstairs didn't seem appropriate, not if she wanted to maintain the last vestiges of her professionalism. She'd dressed the part, too, choosing a simple teal blouse and a black pencil skirt. And as a reminder as much to herself as to Daniel, she'd completed the outfit with her modest *don't*-fuck-me pumps.

Thinking back to their time together this morning, she had to admit that inviting him to the Dirty Thirty might have been a mistake. Initially, she'd figured he'd hate the experience, confirming that he was just like her father. Getting dirty had been one of her dad's pet peeves during her childhood, so she'd assumed Daniel would whine and complain, too. In which case she could safely put him in the "never gonna happen with him" column. But no, Daniel had mucked up her plans.

She'd actually enjoyed hanging out with him.

And he'd been as comfortable in the mud as he typically was in a pristine suit.

The nerve of the man.

A minute before seven o'clock, Daniel eased his car into a rare parking space on her block. He opened the passenger door for her and held her hand as she slipped inside.

She fastened her seat belt and admired the BMW's leather and wood interior. "Very nice. I expected something more James Bond, though, like an Aston Martin."

"Nah. I prefer class over flash."

"Let's not overstate things. It's still flashy, which is why it suits you."

He cocked his head and regarded her with a smile as he eased the car into the driving lane. "So I made a reservation at Co Co. Sala. Ever been?"

"I've been to the chocolate boutique next door but never to the restaurant."

"You're in for a treat then. A chocolate lover's dream."

"And I'm a lover of chocolate."

"And I'm a lover of chocolate lovers."

She stared at him blankly.

"Can I get a pass on that one?" he asked.

She covered her grin with her hand. "Definitely. It was too painful to acknowledge."

"Let's move on then. Is Mimi your real name?"

"No."

"Okay. We're playing twenty questions then. Does your real name start with an M?"

"No."

He tapped at the steering wheel as he drove. "Give me a clue."

"It starts with an A."

"Too easy."

"Har-har. It's Amelia, all right?"

"Amelia. I like it."

"Don't think you're going to use it, Vargas. It won't endear me to you."

"No, I'd never. Amelia is the PR professional who doesn't know how to crack a smile. Mimi is the funny and sassy badass with a judgmental streak."

She twisted her upper body to face him. "I'm *not* judgmental."

"You told me once your father's delusional. Must have picked up the trait from him then."

She laughed. "Touché."

Minutes later, they reached the restaurant. Daniel handed his key to the valet attendant before placing his hand on her lower back and steering her into the building.

"Wait here," he told her once they'd made it inside the vestibule. Then he squeezed past the other guests waiting to be seated and spoke with the hostess.

Mimi's eyes adjusted to the muted lighting as she surveyed the space. Co Co. Sala's interior seduced the senses. The aroma of melted chocolate permeated the air and filled her nostrils. The décor, a combination of fixtures, tables, and booths in reds, blacks, and golds, complemented the sumptuous curtains that separated the sections of the dining room. Candlelit sconces gave the room a soft glow. Everything about the place made her feel warm and cozy—and slightly aroused.

When he returned, Mimi took in his satisfied smile and snorted. "Why'd you decide to bring me here?"

"Why wouldn't I? This place has great food."

"Yes, served on a bed of sex."

"Get your mind out of the gutter, Mimi."

The hostess escorted them past the main dining area to a private room near the restaurant's kitchen. There, she drew back a curtain to reveal a single table in the center of the room. "Your server will be with you shortly."

"We're eating alone?" Mimi asked as he pushed in her chair.

"We are."

"Any particular reason why?"

"Because you're worth my undivided attention."

"Laying it on a little thick for a friendly dinner, don't you think?"

"Yeah. About that—"

She leaned in. "I *knew* it. You have seduction on the brain."

"Can you hear me out before you start making assumptions?"

"Sure," she said.

Their server chose that moment to draw back the curtain. "Good evening," he said as he handed them their menus, each a single page printed on heavy butterscotch cardstock. "My name's Jasper. I'll be your server this evening. May I start you off with a cocktail?"

Daniel picked up the cocktail menu and handed it to her. "For you, I recommend the Fetish."

Mimi read the description and nodded. "You had me at chocolate-infused vodka and strawberry foam. Sounds perfect."

"And you, sir?" Jasper asked.

Daniel took a sip of water. "I'll have the Libido."

Mimi snickered. "Are you sure that's wise? Any more of that could be dangerous."

"Any more of that sauciness and you'll need a bib."

Jasper cleared his throat. "Do you need a few minutes with the menu?"

"Yes," Daniel said.

With Jasper gone, Mimi circled back to Daniel's seductions plans. "So you were about to explain why you chose this place."

"Right. So I've been thinking about your rules, and it occurs to me that I can help you."

Mimi blinked. "You want to help me with my rules." She narrowed her eyes. "How?"

"There's a school of thought on rule-based learning that argues rules aren't really rules unless your adherence to them is tested."

Mimi pressed her lips together to stop herself from smiling. "Is that so? Tell me more."

"The idea is that you can make up rules to live by, but they're meaningless unless you're actually challenged to follow them. Let's take an example. Say you make up a rule that you'll never drive your car over fifty-five miles per hour. Fine. But if your car isn't capable of going over fifty-five miles, your rule has no true meaning."

"Okay. So how does that help me?"

"Well, unless you're tested to break your dating rules, they're pointless. But don't despair. I volunteer to help you test them."

She set aside her menu. "What does testing the rules entail exactly?"

"I try to seduce you. You try to follow your rules. I'm the perfect candidate, too."

"Oh, yeah? Why's that?"

"With me, you can test all three rules: Never date someone you've met through your friends, never date a man who reminds you of your father, and never mix business with pleasure. You have to admit, it's like someone handpicked me for the task."

"You," she said laughing. "*You* handpicked yourself for the task.

And you totally made all that shit up about rule-based learning."

"Sounded good, though, right?"

"It was entertaining, I'll give you that."

And it really was. She couldn't remember having this much fun on any other date. *Wait. Not a date. Dinner with a friend. No, a client. Whatever.*

Jasper returned with their drinks. "Ready to order?"

Mimi picked up the menu. "Sorry. I haven't had a chance to look at it."

"I'll come back in a few minutes."

Daniel watched Jasper leave. "My point remains. I'll try to seduce you. You'll try to resist."

"Because you think you'll make me cave?"

"Because I think you *want* to cave. If it turns out you're able to resist me, then I'll move on. It's a simple proposition. Unless you're not up for the challenge?"

"Hardly. Resisting you is as easy as taking a dirty diaper from a baby."

"Disgusting."

"True."

"Care to test that theory?"

She was strong. She was woman. Hell, she could almost hear herself roar in her head. Plus, once the week was over, she'd prove to him—and more importantly, to herself— that she could resist him. And if she were being honest with herself, she might even admit that she wanted an excuse *not* to resist him. If only for a little while. After all, she was human, wasn't she? *Okay then. Let's do this, Mimi.* "Sure. You have a week."

"A week to convince you to date me?"

Where's the fun in that? "No, a week to convince me to sleep with you."

"My fragile sensibilities can't handle such frank talk, Ms. Pennington."

"Kill it, Vargas."

"Okay. Well, if you're only giving me a week, do you mind if I give you a few menu recommendations?"

"I'd love them."

"Start with the oysters on the half shell."

"Ah. An aphrodisiac. Of course."

"Next you'll want the cocoa-dusted salmon with asparagus tips. And finally, for dessert consider the Latin Love Affair. I typically draw a bright line between Latin and Latino, but tonight, they're close enough."

Mimi hid her face. "Oh, my God, you went there."

"I'm doing my best to make you cave."

"Why?"

"Because you're like no one I've ever met, and I think we would be incredible together."

"Incredible together? But you ditched me in Puerto Rico."

"For a very good reason."

"You don't want to be just another guy in my life, right?"

"Exactly."

In truth, he wasn't. But she could hardly admit that to herself, so telling him was out of the question. "Well, guess what? You got your wish. Now you're my client."

He narrowed his eyes and opened his mouth to respond—to challenge her, she was sure—but Jasper interrupted their conversation.

"Ready to order?" he asked.

Daniel sent her an inquiring look.

"I am," Mimi told Jasper. "I'll start with the oysters on the half shell. Then I'll have the salmon."

Daniel lifted a brow. "I'll have the same."

"Very good," Jasper said. He pivoted and left them alone again.

"Is asparagus an aphrodisiac, too?" she asked.

"It is."

She leaned forward and gave him a wicked grin. "You know what they say about asparagus, right?"

He shook his head. "No. What?"

"It's bad for oral sex. Leaves a bitter taste in your mouth."

He pursed his lips and gave her a conspiratorial wink. "When your dinner arrives, I'll personally remove the asparagus from your plate then."

She fell back in laughter. "That's a good idea. Plus, I hate when they're limp. When they're firm, though? *Mwua.* Perfecto."

"You're messing with me."

Her belly shook as she wiped the tears from her eyes. "I am."

After a brief moment of silence, he cleared his throat. "I want to know more about you, Mimi. Any brothers? Sisters?"

"I'm an only child."

And she was just fine with that. *Really.*

"Tell me about your parents."

There wasn't much to say. "My mother's a doormat. My father's a jerk. The end."

"And I remind you of him?"

Not anymore. Daniel's radar for jerk behavior sometimes malfunctioned, but she suspected he was a good guy at heart. "Now, not as much, but when I first met you, yes. He's a little too perfect on the outside. And he's charming, always the life of the party. But he's lost his moral compass, and he expects everyone, including me, to ignore that fact. I can't."

"Do you see them often?"

She twisted the cloth napkin in her hands. "No. Two, three times a year. My father can't be bothered to be home that often, and my mother...she always seems uncomfortable when I'm around, like she can't think of a thing to say to me. They trot me out every once in a while for important events. I'll be going home soon for one of those."

The truth sounded depressing to her own ears, so he probably felt sorry for her. His face, however, remained impassive.

"Where's home?" he asked.

"Austin."

He tapped his finger against his lips. "Ah."

Her gaze momentarily fixed on the movement, she had to shake her head to continue. *Roar, woman. Roar.* "What about your parents?"

"They live more than half the year in the States and the rest in Puerto Rico. But they're slowly making the transition to living here full-time. The economy is so broken there, they feel they have no other choice."

"Did you grow up here?"

He nodded. "I did."

"And did you grow up with Gracie?"

"Not at all." He chuckled. "Her parents and mine met at the church's Bingo Night a few years ago. They've been inseparable ever since."

"Any other siblings?"

"No. Just the one."

He ran his finger over the rim of his glass, staring at the water in it. If he wanted to share the details of his sister's death, she'd listen. But she wouldn't push.

The murmurs of the patrons in the other room intruded on the quiet moment. His Adam's apple bobbed as he swallowed air. Finally, he spoke. "She committed suicide. My twin." He squeezed his eyes shut and opened them, looking directly at her as though he were drawing strength from the fact that she was there. "My twin...committed...suicide." His voice tripped on the statement, each subsequent word harsher than the one that preceded it.

Mimi struggled to think of an appropriate response. Damn, she was so bad at this. Would a squeeze of his hand be okay here? Or too intimate? And where the hell did all this second-guessing come from? Frustrated with herself, she set aside her misgivings about initiating physical contact, leaned toward him, and set her hand atop his. "I'm so sorry, Daniel."

His eyes, which had been glazed only seconds ago, cleared. "Not your fault obviously. Anyway, I don't talk about it much, but it's come up twice between us, so..."

Jasper swept in with their appetizers, and Daniel rubbed his hands in anticipation. After inspecting his plate, Daniel gave their waiter a broad smile. "Perfect."

If she hadn't been a part of it, she would have seriously questioned whether that difficult exchange had just occurred. But now she knew unimaginable pain remained hidden behind his easy smiles and infectious charm. It made her question the conclusions she'd drawn about him. Made her wonder how much of the man she'd seen in public differed from the man he was in private. Which wasn't helpful to her cause at all.

They spent the remainder of their dinner discussing lighter subjects. His high school years. Her unsuccessful attempts at horseback riding when she was in grade school. They veered into dangerous territory only once, over dessert, when he asked her whether she'd ever been in a serious relationship.

"Never," she said.

"Never?"

"Well, I've had boyfriends. But anything serious? No."

"Their choice or yours?"

She stared at her water glass. "Initially, theirs. After a few false starts, I figured out that I was doomed to be either arm candy or a one-night stand. So I chose to make *them* my one-night stands." When she dared to gauge his reaction, she was surprised not to see any sign of disapproval. "What about you?"

"I had a girlfriend in high school. I convinced myself we'd marry after college. But then she went to California. And we were young and stupid. It's the rare eighteen-year-old who can manage a long-distance relationship."

"Let me guess, you've been collecting notches on your belt ever since."

His expression turned grim. "No more than you, is my guess. But I'm not judging you like you're judging me."

He was right, of course. Nothing like having your hypocrisy shoved in your face across a candlelit table to make you immediately contrite. "Sorry. That was unfair of me."

After taking a sip of his water, he shook his head. "That's *your* pass for the evening. And just for the record, I know how to be with and stay faithful to one person, so I'm not averse to monogamy."

"Yes, well, would you look at the time?" She made a show of inspecting her wrist—which had no watch.

He smirked. Because that's what he always did. That damnable smirk made her want to travel back to the mud run earlier today so she could cover his head in wet dirt again.

He motioned for Jasper's attention.

Jasper, who'd been standing outside the gauzy curtain, rushed to their table. "Sir?"

"We're done, Jasper. I took care of the tab in advance." Daniel reached into his pocket and pulled out his valet ticket. "Could you ask the valet to bring my car around?"

"Certainly, Mr. Vargas. Was everything to your liking, sir? Madam?"

"It was wonderful," Mimi told him.

Daniel's lazy gaze roamed over her face. "Perfect, in fact."

"Careful, Casanova, don't hurt yourself with that smoldering stare."

"Too much?"

"Yep."

He laughed, and she joined him.

But the situation wasn't as funny as she pretended it was. Because he was getting to her. And she really was tempted to cave.

* * *

Mimi smoothed her skirt as she sat in the passenger seat. "I had a nice time."

"Don't sound so surprised."

He stared out the windshield, his gaze following the activity on her block. He'd turned off the engine, and the car's interior lighting had dimmed, leaving his profile visible only by the light of the nearby streetlamps. "Do you ever think about that night?"

Her throat constricted, refusing to help her admit how often she'd thought about it. So she settled for a stripped-down version of the truth. "Yes."

"I do, too." He squinted as he focused on one of her neighbors walking his dog. "I think about it a lot."

Talking about that night was dangerous, especially this close to her home. *Time to go.* "Thanks for a lovely time. I should head in."

"Sure. Let me walk you to your door."

She'd opened the car door and had one foot on the sidewalk before he'd unlatched his seat belt.

She mumbled good night, practically sprinting to her building and then dashing up the steps, keys in hand.

"Mimi, wait," he said behind her.

She fumbled with her keys as she tried to get inside. "Dammit."

His hand closed over hers. "I'll help you."

He fit the key into the lock with ease and swung the building door open for her. "Have a good night."

"You do the same, Daniel."

After she closed the door, all her emotions—good, bad, and definitely not indifferent—rushed out in a tangled mess. She stood in the vestibule, rested her head against the wall, and released the breath she'd been holding. It would have been so easy to ask him in. But she'd only regret it later.

She jumped when he knocked on the door. Wide-eyed, she undid the lock and peeked out. "What is it?"

He stood outside the doorway, a tight expression making his cheekbones more prominent. "I saw you standing there. Are you thinking about it?"

Without much thought, she took a step back, letting him in. "It?"

He crossed the threshold and crowded her with his body. "Us."

"Yes. I was thinking about all the reasons why being with you is a bad idea."

He snaked his hand around her neck and pulled her flush against him. "How many did you come up with?"

"Quite a few."

He caressed her jaw with his fingers and then trailed his thumb across her mouth.

She parted her lips—to say what, she suddenly couldn't recall—and he pressed his own lips against hers, licking his way inside. In a fog, Mimi closed her eyes, her lids weighed down by the intensity of their kiss. "This isn't a good idea," she whispered against his mouth. Her hands had missed the memo, however, and grasped the front of his shirt, drawing him closer. She wanted to lose herself in him, but her brain remained her last defense.

"Are you sure?" he asked. His hands remained at her waist.

"No," she said.

"I was hoping you'd say that." And then he dipped his hands under the edge of her blouse and found her bare skin. One of his fingers skated across her belly, pausing when it reached her belly button. Daniel looked at her, and she arched her back in silent invitation.

He continued to explore her skin delicately, reverently, as though she were made of porcelain and he worried she might break. Though his touch was feather soft, his fingers left a trail of heat wherever they roamed. In her lust-induced state, Mimi imagined that the small vestibule had contracted, urging them into the tiniest space, one where neither of them could move without touching the other. He filled her field of vision, and she saw nothing but him.

With deft hands, he raised her skirt a fraction, giving him access to the area between her thighs. She rose on her toes, the heat from his fingers drawing her to them like a magnet.

Her brain relented. "Please touch me there," she said against his neck. As further encouragement, she widened her stance.

His erection swelled against her stomach, and they both moaned. After tugging her skirt higher, he pressed two fingers against the fabric of her panties and traced a path up her slit. "You're soaked, and you're burning, aren't you?"

She whimpered as he circled her nub, and when he pinched her clit through the lace, she lifted her lips from his collarbone and cried out.

"Let me take you upstairs, Mimi," he whispered against her ear. "I'll make you come over and over again, I promise."

The urgency in his voice cut through the fog. *Whoa, whoa, whoa.* They were groping each other in plain sight of any neighbors who might happen upon them. What the hell had she been thinking?

She pushed his hands out from under her skirt and scrambled to the opposite corner of the vestibule. Her core ached, making the process of righting her clothing a particularly frustrating task. He watched her under heavy-lidded eyes, which no doubt matched her own aroused gaze.

She snapped at him, though she was really just angry with herself. "Did you think you'd make me cave after a single date?"

He gave her a lazy smile that made her picture what he'd look like in the aftermath of fantastic sex. And it *would* be fantastic. She just *knew* it.

"The thought had crossed my mind, yes," he replied.

"Slow your roll, buddy."

"Too much?"

"Definitely."

"You haven't given me much time. Every day is precious when you only have seven."

After lining up the side seams of her skirt, she opened the door and motioned for him to leave. "And now you have six. Make them count."

For a few seconds, his face turned grim, but then he relaxed it, looking as carefree as ever. He chuckled as he waved good-bye, his eyes bright, as though he were eager to meet the challenge.

Tomorrow, though, he'd learn that she didn't plan to make things easy for him.

Oh, he's going to kill me when he finds out.

CHAPTER TWELVE

Fireworks had duped him.

She hadn't responded to his texts on Sunday and now he knew why. Daniel shut his office door and picked up his cell phone. He'd already added her to his favorites. Perhaps it was wishful thinking on his part, but he hoped the gesture would soon be warranted.

Daniel: Called your office and learned you're on a business trip this week.

Mimi: Surprise.

Daniel: Very cute.

Mimi: You said you were looking forward to the challenge. Consider this a challenge.

Daniel: I'd assumed you'd be around for the seduction. Silly me.

Mimi: A smart businessman such as yourself should always engage in a bit of due diligence.

Daniel: Meaning?

Mimi: Meaning you didn't ask the right questions.

Daniel: Fair enough. I have a busy week anyway. Enjoy your trip.

Mimi: OMG, are you pouting?

Daniel: I don't pout.

Mimi: Let me rephrase. Are you doing an impression of someone who pretends not to pout?

He smiled. This was as much fun as having dinner with her.

Daniel: I'm doing an impression of someone who's used to getting his way.

Mimi: It's not a good look for you.

Daniel: No, I guess not. But you're the only who calls me on it.

Mimi: You're welcome.

He chuckled. If Ms. Pennington wanted slow seduction, she'd get it. And he'd work around her contrived obstacles.

Daniel: Good-bye, Mimi.

Mimi: Ciao.

After his first cup of coffee the next morning, he took out his cell phone.

Daniel: What's your favorite color?

Mimi: Good morning to you, too.

Daniel: We don't have time for that. I only have four days left.

Mimi: Yellow. Why?

Daniel: Just curious. Have a great day.

Mimi: You're so weird. Bye.

Daniel: I don't do emojis, but if I did, I'd smiley-face you right now.

Mimi: ☺

The next day he didn't text her—to keep her guessing about what he was up to. Which left him two days to make an impression, and that wasn't enough time.

Daniel: Consider this a request for a one-day extension.

Mimi: I've been meaning to "talk" to you about this. Your texts seem to suggest that I'm going to give in. I hope you realize it's not a foregone conclusion.

Daniel: No worries. If I lose, I lose. The point of this is to test your rules, remember?

Mimi: Oh, yes, my rules. Now I remember. One-day extension granted.

Daniel: Thank you.

The day before she was due to return, he made several phone calls to put his plans into action. He was missing a key piece of information, however.

Daniel: What's your favorite song?

Mimi: Gravity by Sara Bareilles.

Daniel: I don't know that one. I'll have to check it out.

Later that day, after listening to the song on YouTube, he texted her his reaction.

Daniel: Gravity is sad. Anything cheerful on your playlist?

Mimi: You're criticizing my favorite song?

Daniel: No. It's just not appropriate for my purposes.

Mimi: And what exactly are your purposes?

Daniel: You'll see.

Mimi: Kiss.

Daniel: The band?

Mimi: No, the song.

Daniel: By Prince?

Mimi: Yep.

Daniel: Good one. Okay. Last question. Favorite cuisine?

Mimi: Thai food.

Daniel: Got it.

Mimi: What are you planning?

Daniel: What do you mean?

Mimi: I mean, where is this going? My favorite color, favorite song, favorite cuisine. Is there a point to this?

Daniel: Just getting to know you. Why?

Mimi: I thought you were planning something. Never mind.

Daniel: Blue. Queen's Bohemian Rhapsody. Puerto Rican food, of course. In case you were wondering about my favorites.

Mimi: I'm a shit.

Daniel: Hey, don't be so hard on yourself. That's my job.

Mimi: ☺

Daniel: Is any of this working?

Mimi: You no longer remind me of my father.

Daniel: One out of three's not bad. I'll take it. Have a safe trip back. Where are you by the way?

She didn't respond.

Daniel: ?

Mimi: At home.

Daniel: Since when?

Mimi: Since two days ago. I came back early.

Daniel: You didn't tell me.

Mimi: You never asked.

Daniel: I'm coming over.

Mimi: Don't.

Daniel: Okay. ☹

He kept their text exchange open on his screen, waiting for her to respond, but nothing came. *Nice.* He'd finally used a fucking emoji, something he'd once promised himself he'd never do, and she'd ignored it. If the guys ever found out, they'd rib him for days. Only Mimi could bring him to this embarrassing state.

* * *

Mimi tossed her cell phone on the bed and fell face first onto the mattress. It had taken superhuman strength to tell Daniel not to come over. Even now her fingers itched to send him a different text, one in which she told him to run several red lights to get here if he had to. After returning early from her business trip, she'd spent the last two days holed up in her apartment working on an overhaul of another client's publicity strategy. Each day, she'd check her phone for his texts, a welcome break from the work she couldn't focus on. He was *courting* her. And she discovered she liked being courted.

Plus, she couldn't forget the way he'd touched her in the vestibule. He'd known just where to place his hands. With a single caress, all the reasons she shouldn't be with him had receded to the underdeveloped parts of her brain.

She picked up her cell phone and dialed Gracie. "Tell me why I shouldn't be with Daniel," she said when her best friend answered.

"Um…okay. Um…"

"He reminds me of my father?" Mimi prompted.

"He does?"

That one doesn't work anymore, dammit. "Well, not really. What else?"

"Um…oh, I know, he's a client."

Yes, that's it. And she'd never wavered on that point. "Definitely a reason to stay away from him. My professional reputation is at stake here."

"Right. Exactly."

"And even if I were to keep our relationship secret from his partners and the people in my office, *I'd know*."

"Right." Gracie coughed. "Can't have that."

"Yeah. And I met him through you. So there's that, too."

"What does that have to do with anything? Karen met Mark through me."

"Technically, that's not true. Anyway, that's different. They're obviously made for each other. He helps her study, for goodness' sake."

"What's the big deal, Mimi?"

Didn't Gracie get it? "It would be awkward when it didn't work out."

"Isn't it awkward now?"

"I mean awkward for everyone else."

"Don't worry about us, Mimi," she said with a hint of amusement in her voice. "We'll be fine."

"Are you laughing at me?"

"I'd never."

"Bullshit."

"Okay, yes, I was laughing at you, because I don't even know who you are right now. Get a grip, Mimi. He's just a guy."

"Yeah, you're right. Thanks for helping me vent."

"No problem. Bye, babe."

"Bye, *chica*."

This time she placed her phone on her nightstand and settled under the bed covers. Staring up at the ceiling, she puffed up her cheeks and slowly released her breath.

He's just a guy, Gracie had said.

Except that's no longer true.

And that's annoying.

The next day, Mimi returned to the office more determined than ever to keep Daniel at arm's length. Earlier, as she'd soaped herself in the shower, she'd had an epiphany. Daniel thrived on challenges. Starting an architectural firm with three of his classmates and not a lot of experience. Challenge. Competing and winning in mud runs across the state of Maryland. Challenge. Wooing someone who'd initially claimed she didn't want to be wooed. Challenge.

Although his attention might be special to her, it wasn't special to him. A man like Daniel likely pursued women all the time. She couldn't afford to forget that, not when partnership—and the dream of owning her own home—were well within her reach. And she could easily picture the worst of the consequences of acting on her desires. When the relationship had run its course, Daniel wouldn't want to work with her. And then she'd be forced to disclose to the firm that she'd been fired by a client. *Yeah. No. Not happening.*

When she entered Baxter PR's reception area after a midmorning coffee break, the smell of freshly cut flowers tickled her nose. A huge bouquet of yellow lilies sat on the ledge of the reception desk. Gloria, their receptionist, sat behind it, only the tips of her long curly hair visible behind the massive arrangement.

What's your favorite color?

Remembering the innocuous question, Mimi smiled and rose on her toes to smell the flowers. "Let me guess. These are for me."

Gloria popped her head out. "No. These are specifically for the reception area."

Mimi hid her disappointment behind a fake smile as she picked up her messages. "They're lovely."

"Don't worry. Yours are in your office. Good luck getting in there, though."

Mimi's heart thudded in her chest. She didn't bother to ask Gloria what she'd meant, instead jogging to her office to see for herself what Daniel had done.

Oh, shit.

He'd arranged to have her office filled with yellow lilies. They covered her desk, her window ledge, and her floor. She turned sideways and edged her way around the various arrangements, her mouth hanging open at the sheer ridiculousness of his gesture. It must have cost a small fortune. She wracked her brain, trying to recall whether lilies were even in season this time of year.

After rearranging the vases on her desk, she returned a few urgent client calls. She was about to text Daniel when the intercom on her desk buzzed. She parted a cluster of flowers to reach it. "Yes, Gloria."

"You have another delivery." The laughter in Gloria's voice made Mimi clamp down on her lip. *What else is he up to? Thai food maybe?* "Send it back to my office, please."

After opening her office door, Mimi held her belly with one hand and covered her mouth with the other. A short, bald man in a tuxedo waited by a rolling table like the ones hotels used for room service. A silver dome covered a plate that rested on a bright white tablecloth. "Thai food?" she asked the man.

He bowed. "Yes, ma'am. Where shall I set it up?"

Mimi raised a brow and shook her head in amazement. "By the window, please."

She searched her purse for a tip, but the man stopped her. "No need, ma'am. It's all been taken care of."

Mimi slid her chair over to the rolling table and lifted the dome cover. She breathed in the scent of basil and curry, and her mouth watered. Tiny specks of red pepper told her the duck would be spicy, just as she liked it.

Her cell phone buzzed.

Daniel: Good afternoon.

Mimi: Good afternoon. You shouldn't have.

Daniel: Do you like them?

Mimi: Um. I'm allergic to flowers.

Daniel: Shit. That never occurred to me.

Mimi: I'm kidding. I love them. I'm about to start my lunch, too.

Daniel: I hope you enjoy it.

Thirty minutes later, her intercom buzzed again. Mimi pressed the speaker button. "Another delivery?"

Gloria laughed. "Yep."

Mimi walked out to find a woman chatting with Gloria. She wore jeans and a flowy tunic, and she held a guitar case in one hand.

"May I help you?" she asked the woman.

"I've got a singing telegram for you. Do you want me to sing here or somewhere more private?"

"Could you maybe not sing and tell the person who ordered it that you did?"

"Um. Your secret admirer has asked me to record your reaction. I could tell him you declined?"

She had half a mind to do just that, but it seemed too heartless given the trouble he'd gone through. "It's 'Kiss,' right?"

"You got it."

"Okay. Fine. Do it here."

The woman nodded and placed her guitar on the floor. Gloria rose from her chair and rounded her station to get a better view. Next, Mimi's singing telegram set her phone on the reception desk and pointed it in Mimi's direction. "I'm just going to hit Play now, okay?"

Mimi blew a raspberry in the direction of the camera's phone. "Fine."

The woman played a few chords and then went straight into her rendition of Prince's "Kiss." It was a slow and seductive acoustic version, and Mimi blushed when Gloria's gaze flew to her face. Mimi couldn't help shimmying her shoulders to the beat of the infectious tune. At the song's chorus, the singer's raspy voice grew louder, filling the reception area and beyond and drawing the firm's employees out of their offices.

Ian, too. *Shit.* She'd forgotten about that particular member of the audience.

Mimi took in a deep breath and tapped her toe, doing her best to act as though an afternoon serenade were a typical occurrence at Baxter PR. In reality, she wanted the floor to open up and swallow her whole.

Mimi didn't have to look at Ian to know he was considering her. With his head cocked to the side, he stared at her profile. She glanced at him once, then used her peripheral vision to track his movements. Her jaw ached from the fake smile she'd fixed on her face. Eventually, Ian turned his head and focused on the singer. When she finished the song, the ten or so employees that had gathered around the reception desk applauded. A few even whistled.

The woman bowed. To Mimi, she said, "From your secret admirer."

"Thank you," she said in as low a voice as she could manage. "That was lovely."

Mimi smiled for the camera, but her stomach churned as she watched the singer pack up her guitar and collect her phone. Her personal life had no place here, and in the span of a few hours, Daniel's antics had put her personal business on display in the most overt way. Flowers? A catered lunch? A singing telegram? And worse, she felt like a bitch for being upset about it.

Barry, one of the firm's partners, broke up the party. "All right, folks. Play time is over. Let's get back to work."

Barry's directive jostled her back to reality. A relationship with Daniel would be professional suicide, of course. She could imagine it now. Ian would ask, "So who's the secret admirer?" And she'd say, "Remember our new client? My secret admirer's the CEO." And the fact that Ian was in the position to ask that question itself was a problem. No. She wouldn't allow this to go any further.

So she returned to her office and typed out a text to Daniel.

Thank you for the flowers, the lunch, and the song. Everything was perfect, and I really appreciate that you went to all this trouble for me. Still, you haven't changed my mind. I have to do what's best for me. Hope you understand. See you next week.

There. She'd made the right decision.

So why did it feel so wrong?

CHAPTER THIRTEEN

Mimi's angst over her nonrelationship with Daniel continued into the next week. For several days she moped around, unable to shake the feeling that she'd lost a chance to experience something special with him..

And he'd never responded to her text, which compounded her agitation. The silence would be broken soon, however, because she was on her way to the Cambridge Group's offices to prepare the guys for their appearances in a short promotional video for the firm's website.

When she arrived, Felicia wasn't sitting at her desk, but she could see from the reception area that Amar, Jason, and Spencer were already waiting for her in the conference room.

"Hey, guys," she said as she swung open the glass door.

The men greeted her with less enthusiasm than usual.

She took a seat across from Amar, expecting Daniel to take the seat opposite the head of the table. No way would she put herself in his direct line of sight. She pulled her legal pad and a pen from her briefcase and set them on the table. "Is Daniel on his way?"

Spencer looked at Jason. Jason looked at Amar.

"What?" she pressed. "Am I missing something?"

"He's not coming in today," Amar replied.

Mimi smoothed her features, hiding her annoyance and shaking her cross-legged foot instead. "But I cleared this date with Felicia. She keeps his schedule."

Spencer spoke up first. "She's relatively new, Mimi. She didn't know, and his schedule *was* clear for a reason."

"Didn't know what?"

Amar sighed. "He never comes to work on this date."

Mimi took in the men's morose expressions. Even Spencer, the continually happy one among them, wore a frown. *Jesus. She knew of only one meaningful date in Daniel's life that would make him shun the world: the anniversary of his twin sister's death.* "Is today the date his sister died?"

Amar leaned forward. "He told you about Pamela?"

She swallowed. Hard. Amar's surprise all but confirmed that Daniel didn't share this piece of himself with just anyone. And though she felt selfish thinking about it now, she liked being not just anyone to Daniel. "Yes, he told me."

Amar confirmed the answer to her question with a nod. "This is the one day of the year he allows himself to be sad. And he prefers to be alone."

Mimi wiped her clammy hands on the front of her slacks. "Okay. Well, it's not a big deal, really. We can reschedule."

"We could go over our parts now, and then you could follow up with Daniel another day," Jason offered.

"No, I think it makes more sense to wait. Besides, there's something else I have to do."

Amar smiled. "He'll be at home."

Her hands shook as she returned the pen and pad to her briefcase. Was she that obvious, or was Amar that perceptive? Ah, screw it. This wasn't the time to worry about that. Daniel was in pain somewhere. "Would you mind giving me his address?"

Jason cleared his throat. "I'm not sure that's a good idea, Mimi. He—"

"I'll write it down for you," Amar said.

Jason glared at Amar, who shrugged halfheartedly.

Any other time, she might have used diplomacy to navigate around Jason's objection, but her mind was focused on Daniel and how he must be feeling today. Amar handed her a Post-it with Daniel's address written on it. Murmuring her apologies, she rushed out of the conference room thinking about nothing but Daniel. She had to see him.

* * *

Mimi dropped her grocery bags on the stoop of Daniel's townhouse in Georgetown. After pressing his doorbell, she wrung her hands. As she waited for him to answer, she admired his street. Rows and rows of homes, each distinct from the next, lined both sides; a mix of trees—beech, maybe—shaded Daniel's side of the block.

She stood motionless and listened. Quiet. It blanketed the street like a protective veil, giving the neighborhood a serene quality. For a few seconds she could even forget that she was standing in the nation's capital, a place known for its movers and shakers. She'd never considered this historic area of the city for a future home because it was too pricey, but she certainly understood its appeal.

Engrossed in her observations, Mimi took a few minutes to realize Daniel hadn't responded to the doorbell. *Maybe he isn't home?* If Daniel had adopted an annual ritual on the anniversary of his sister's death, though, she doubted it involved interacting with the outside world. She rang the doorbell again, this time pressing on it continuously. If annoying him got him to answer, she'd happily oblige.

Then a thought occurred to her. *What if he loses himself in sex as part of his ritual?* She let go of the buzzer and embarrassment flooded her senses. Her cheeks warmed, and her hands wouldn't stop shaking. She blinked her eyes furiously as though doing so would bring clarity to her muddled state. *What am I doing here?* An even more frightening thought entered her mind: *I don't want him to be with someone else.*

She scooped up the grocery bags by their handles and rushed down the stairs. But the rough unlatching of a deadbolt stopped her before her feet hit the pavement. *Shit.*

She turned and swallowed, readying herself to apologize for the disruption. Daniel's body filled the doorway, and she took her first good look at the man she'd come to visit.

Fuck a duck.

She'd seen him in athletic gear, yes. She'd even caught glimpses of his naked chest that night in Puerto Rico. But nothing had prepared her for the sight of Daniel in low-riding jeans—and nothing else—with the sun shining on him as though he were its god.

"Mimi?" he asked, his brows knitted in confusion.

His garbled voice made her wonder if he'd seriously forgotten how he knew her. This was a bad idea. If she hadn't known that before, she certainly knew it now. His face bore no traces of the charm he'd used to disarm her countless times before. Dark circles surrounded his eyes, and he already sported a five o'clock shadow. His current appearance simply didn't mesh with the picture of him she'd filed in her brain.

God. She'd intruded into his personal space, and she had no right to be here. "Sorry. I…the guys told me where to find you…but this was a bad idea. I'll go."

"No, wait," he said. "Is everything okay?"

"I should be asking you that, right?"

He lifted his arm and raked his fingers through his hair. So much activity accompanied the single movement that she didn't know where to look first. Muscles flexed everywhere—his biceps, his chest, and his stomach fought for her attention. She wanted to clap and tell him to do it again. She was a terrible, terrible person.

He straightened. "I'm fine. Did you want to come in?"

"I'll stay a few minutes, if that's okay?"

He opened the door to let her pass. "I'm not the best company today, but sure, come in."

To say that her first impression of his home did not jibe with his public persona would have been an understatement. A grand staircase, in rich cherry wood, greeted her from the entrance. Down a long hall filled with period details and hardwood floors, she glimpsed a modern kitchen. To her right, a living area with a large fireplace and a massive couch drew her eye. A bow window in the back corner created the perfect nook for reading. "This is gorgeous, Daniel."

"Thanks," he said behind her.

She turned to him, trying to gauge whether he was irritated by her unexpected visit. More than anything, he appeared wary. "Did you decorate it yourself?" she asked.

"Nah." His gaze fell on the bow window. "Someone did it for me." He pointed to the bags in her hands. "What do you have there?"

"Oh. These," she said, raising her bags to chest height. "These are the makings of the best ice cream sundae you'll ever have. Oh, and margaritas if you're into them."

"Going for all the major food groups, huh?"

"There's no such thing as a wrong time to eat ice cream—or drink margaritas, for that matter." She lowered the bags. "If you're not up for them, maybe I could just stow the ice cream in your freezer until I leave?"

"No, no," he said with a smile, the first one she'd seen since she'd interrupted his plans. "I want to taste the best sundae I'll ever have."

She gave him a wide smile before her gaze dropped to his chest. *Yup. Still bare.* "Lead the way."

He smirked. "Let me throw on a shirt first. Feel free to make yourself comfortable in my kitchen."

"*Mi casa es su casa?*"

He scrunched his face playfully. "Wow. Your Spanish accent's awful. We'll have to work on that."

Seeing the smile on his face, she knew then her decision to come had been the right one. But she had to remember why she was here: to comfort him. Nothing more.

Hear that, brain? Nothing more.

CHAPTER FOURTEEN

Daniel climbed the stairs in quick steps, and when he disappeared from view, Mimi took her groceries into the kitchen. To her surprise, he kept the pantry well stocked and the drawers organized. She found the perfect bowls for the sundaes and began laying out the contents of the recipe she'd perfected in grad school: brownies, vanilla ice cream, strawberries, fudge sauce, and Godiva Liqueur. She did a body roll in anticipation of eating the sinful dessert.

She'd just begun to mash the bottom layer of brownies into two small bowls when Daniel walked in.

His face was damp, like he'd just splashed water on it. "I'm going to have diabetes after eating that."

"You'll eat it and love it. No junk food haters allowed, okay?"

"Okay," he said as he sat on the stool in front of the counter. "Is there anything I can do to help?"

"No, just watch the magic happen."

He swiped a slice of strawberry and dropped it into his mouth. "So is this a favorite recipe from your childhood?"

"God, no. My mother didn't cook or bake."

"Who did?"

"We had a live-in housekeeper who basically ran the house. She cooked and cleaned. Read bedtime stories to me, too."

When the sundaes were done, she held out a bowl for him. "Is it okay to take these into the living room, or are you a stickler about food there?"

"I'm not a stickler about much, and that is definitely not a pet peeve of mine."

They plopped onto the couch at the same time, smiling at each other.

He ate a spoonful and closed his eyes briefly, savoring the taste. "It's good," he said as he dug his spoon into the bowl for a second mouthful. "It's really good."

She moved the contents of her sundae around in the bowl as she worked up the nerve to explain why she'd come. "Okay, so I'm just going to say this. The guys told me it's the anniversary of Pamela's death"—he shuddered at her verbal reminder—"so I just wanted to make sure you were okay, and maybe cheer you up. And saying it out loud makes me feel stupid because ice cream sundaes and margaritas aren't going to change what happened, but I don't know…"

Daniel's eyes cleared. "It's fine, Mimi. Really sweet of you."

The knot in her stomach unfurled. "Do you want to talk about it?"

"Not really."

"Can I ask you something?"

"If I say no, will you let it go?"

"Yes."

"Then, yes, you can ask me something."

"Why do you take the day off? What does it accomplish?"

He set the bowl on the coffee table, laced his hands together on his lap, and said nothing. The silence stretched beyond a minute, until he drew a deep breath and answered her. "The day she died was the worst day of my life. Think about that for a sec. People throw around that phrase all the time. But that day? That *was* the worst day of my life. And I relive it each year, because I can't just forget her, right? It seems wrong not to take time to remember her. So I do, but I don't trust myself to be around people when I do."

"What do you think will happen? In public, I mean."

"I don't know. I've never tested myself. Maybe I'll flip out. Maybe I'll get angry and say something really hurtful to someone. No matter what, I won't be the Daniel people know and love."

"Is that such a bad thing? Not being the Daniel people know and love? It's like you don't allow yourself to be human. People hurt. People cry. People grieve. How are you different?"

"I'm not. But I have parents who hurt, who cry, who grieve. I have to be strong for them. Our family's been through enough already. And since my sister killed herself after a long bout with depression that she kept hidden from me, it's hard to get upset about much."

She covered his hand with hers. "Other than her death."

He squeezed his eyes shut. "Right. Other than her death."

"Are you angry with her?"

"God, I hate that question."

"Sorry. You don't have to answer that. I think I'm being counterproductive."

"No, you're not. You're the first person I've talked to about this. My parents certainly don't want to talk about it. For years, they just tried to smother me without really acknowledging that she was gone. I think they were worried I might hurt myself."

He dropped his head and plucked the sofa cushion with his fingers. "I hate that question because the answer is yes. You know, if I'm being one hundred percent honest with myself, I'd have to say I resent her." He looked up at her then. "Isn't that fucked up? I'm the one who lived, and I resent her for dying. I'm a selfish, egotistical bastard."

"Why do you resent her?"

"Because she didn't confide in me. I was her fucking twin." He pounded his chest as he said it, and she jerked back in response, wanting to give him the space to release everything he'd been holding back for God knows how long.

"Why didn't she tell me how she was feeling?" he continued, his voice so strained she could feel the ache in her own bones. "And she left me to pick up the pieces. To watch my parents grieve for her. Even though I was twenty-six, it was a lot to handle."

She shifted to her right, creating some distance between them, and then she patted her lap. "Come. Put your head here. I think you need it."

His chest collapsed, as though he'd finally lost the battle to appear invincible in her eyes, or maybe it wasn't as much a battle lost as it was a layer shed. He'd let her see him at what he considered his worst. To her, that showed strength, not weakness.

Slowly, he lowered his head to her lap. With only his profile visible, one would never know the pain he held inside. But he'd shared his pain with her, and the intimacy of their conversation humbled her.

"My sister would have liked you," he whispered. "All that strength and vulnerability in one package. You two are kindred spirits."

Her heart banged against her chest. Once again, he'd delved

beneath her exterior and thought about her as a person, not an object. Not many men had bothered to even try, and certainly none had touched her heart the way he did. In fact, she couldn't remember the last time she'd had a meaningful conversation with a man that didn't involve her job or his fumbling attempts to get her into bed.

She massaged his scalp as she thought about what he'd told her.

After several minutes of quiet, she felt a tear drop onto her thigh. Her hand in his hair froze. Not knowing what else to do, she continued to weave her fingers through his hair until his even breathing signaled that he'd fallen asleep.

Her heart ached for Daniel. For his sister. Also for herself, because despite her best efforts not to be drawn to him, she wanted more from him than was wise. What exactly constituted more, she had no clue. But she wanted it.

And it was bound to end in a disaster.

* * *

Mimi blinked her eyes open and checked her watch. Over the course of two hours, they'd rearranged their bodies on the couch, fitting themselves into an intimate embrace while they slept. Daniel lay in front of her, his entire length stretched out on the couch. Mimi lay behind him with her arm across his stomach.

His even breathing nearly lulled her back to sleep, but the reminder that she'd come here on impulse forced her awake. This midday excursion hadn't been planned, and she hadn't told anyone at the office not to expect her to return before the end of the day.

But she couldn't help herself. Before she could think better of it, she pressed her body into Daniel's, enjoying the feel of her breasts against his back. Needing more, she brushed her fingers against his stomach. The heady combination of hard muscle and soft skin there momentarily drugged her senses.

Then reality returned. *Oh, my God.* She was molesting him.

Disgusted with herself, she drew back, causing him to stir.

Eyes closed, he moaned and stretched, and she could feel his muscles flexing against her skin.

Pure torture.

"Hey," he said as he sat up, his eyes sleepy and his voice soft.

"Hey," she said as she righted her clothing. "I have to get back to the office."

He scanned the room and settled his gaze on the cable box's digital clock. "It's almost four o'clock."

"I can still get some work done. Besides, I didn't let anyone know I'd be gone this long."

He rubbed the back of his head. "Right. I'm sorry I screwed up your day."

"You didn't screw up my day. Far from it." She grabbed her purse off the sofa table. "We'll have to reschedule the practice run for the video."

"Mimi."

"Yeah?"

"Stay. I'd like you to."

"Why?"

"Because for the first time in…because you helped me get through the day. And I just don't want you to leave."

Staying would complicate their situation, but leaving didn't seem like a viable option. She set her purse back down. The room compressed her on all sides, leaving a narrow opening that led straight to him. "I don't want to leave, either."

He patted the sofa cushion. "Then come back here."

She sat next to him and settled her hands together between her knees. Though she made no outward movements, inside she was a jumbled mess. Nervous energy circled around her belly as though someone were beating it with a whisk.

She *wanted* the right to touch him, but she didn't know how to make that happen. Never before had she felt this out of touch with her own power to seduce a man. She'd followed the script many times: a breathy laugh here and a seductive wink there. None of it seemed right under the circumstances. Talking, though. *That* she could handle.

She turned to him and flicked her hair away from her face. "You made fun of my Spanish accent earlier, and I realized I haven't heard you speak it much. Tell me something."

He didn't answer her immediately, their breathing the only sound in the room. Then he faced her. *"Quiero que seas mío."*

"What does that mean?"

"I want you to be mine."

She could pretend that he was merely translating the words for her, but she knew differently. She saw it in the intensity of his gaze. In the way his eyes focused on every part of her face and ultimately rested on her mouth. He was telling her what he wanted her to know.

He'd shared the deepest part of himself with her today, telling her things he'd never told anyone else. He hadn't cared about appearing perfect in her eyes. He'd just been real. She didn't know how to describe their relationship, but if this is what she could expect from being his, she wanted it—for as long as she could have it.

She bit the corner of her lip, realized what she was doing, and relaxed her mouth. "How would one respond to that? How do you say, 'I want to be yours' in Spanish?"

"*Quiero ser tuya.*"

He was so wonderfully male. With his hair in disarray, his eyes puffy, and his stubble more pronounced than just two hours ago, he looked sexier to her than she'd thought possible. *This* was the man she ached for. The man underneath the slick exterior and practiced charm. And *this* man wanted her. His expression, at once languid and intense, broadcast his desire like the brightest of billboards.

She climbed into his lap and faced him on the couch, her knees pressed against his hips.

She stroked his cheek, imagining how the hair on his jawline would feel against her thighs. "*Quiero ser tuya.*"

He placed his hands on her waist and squeezed. His voice was rough when he responded, "Say it again."

Before she said anything, he closed his eyes, as though he wanted to focus on the words and nothing else.

She took a deep breath, readying herself to repeat the phrase with more confidence and less hesitation. Given what he'd shared with her earlier, he deserved this bit of honesty, even if it scared her to be so open with him. She leaned over to whisper the words in his ear. "*Quiero ser tuya.*"

He shifted, drawing her closer and grinding his body against hers. "Do you?"

That small movement set off a chain reaction in her. Her core pulsed. Her stomach contracted. Her nipples beaded. At that moment, her body wasn't her own. Whatever he asked of her, she'd give it to him—willingly. "God, yes. I want to be yours."

With a speed that startled her, he snaked his hand under her hair and pulled her torso toward his. "You sure?"

"Right now, very sure. But I can't make any promises about tomorrow."

"That's good enough for me—for now."

She didn't want to think about what "for now" meant, so she trailed her fingers to the top button of her blouse.

"Not yet," he said.

She'd always preferred sex a little rough and raw, a tug of war between two bodies thrashing, scraping, and biting, two people wrestling with each other until they both reached orgasm. Maybe it was because she didn't have to think beyond the passion in the moment. Didn't have to wonder what came next, because, for her, next rarely came—by design.

But Daniel's plan involved a slower and more tortuous pace.

She dropped her hands, and he pressed his face against her chest, breathing in her scent. He opened his mouth, moving it over the outline of her breasts through the silk fabric. The pressure of his lips, the soft rub of the material against her nipples, the feel of his erection growing inside his jeans, all of it, made her anxious to touch him. She raked her fingers over his shoulders, but he redirected her hands onto her thighs. Then he sat back and watched her, a possessive gleam in his eyes. "I want to watch you unbutton your blouse for me. More slowly this time."

Those words, the realization that she could please him by slowing down, had the effect he'd undoubtedly sought: Her core tightened under the strain of knowing that her release wouldn't come soon.

Rather than fret about it, she vowed to savor each moment before she reached her peak. She undid the buttons, drawing the process out as he'd asked. Then she trailed her fingers over her puckered nipples, her gaze never leaving his. Dropping her hands to her thighs, she left the blouse hanging open on her shoulders.

He glanced between her face and her breasts. Then he slid his hands under the fabric and undid her bra. Each time his hands touched an expanse of her skin, she burned. Burned for him. Burned for what he made her feel.

With the greatest of care, he removed her bra and blouse, placing them beside him. "You're beautiful. I'm sure you've been told that a million times before, but it's true. It's not just your body, though. It's you. Your personality. Your sassy mouth. The way you pretend not to care about anyone and yet fret about everyone, including me."

"I've got nice tits, too, right?"

"And it's that," he said as caressed her cheek. "The way you fight so hard not to feel anything. It makes me want to consume you, to get closer to you than anyone else, so I can force you to admit that you care. I *know* you care."

She didn't just hear the intensity of his voice, she felt it, too. Thick with emotion, it wrapped itself around her, his words settling into the one place she'd kept hidden from other men: her heart. Over time, he'd bared himself to her, making himself vulnerable along the way. And all he'd asked for in return was a chance. Pretending she didn't care was no longer possible. "Of course I care. It's why I'm here."

"But in the morning, you'll call it a mistake, or an aberration. Something not to be repeated."

She felt more exposed now than she did seconds ago. Still, she resisted the urge to throw her blouse back on. "What is this, Daniel? What do you want me to say?"

"I don't want you to say anything. I just want you to leave yourself open to me. Let me in."

She didn't want to think about tomorrow. Doing so would mean she'd have to acknowledge the potential consequences of being with him. She opened her mouth to tell him just that, but she made the mistake of returning his stare and all she could think about was having him inside her.

Eyes still focused on his, she reached down and flicked open the button of his jeans. With a smile, she tugged on his zipper and then worked her hand inside his underwear. She sucked in a breath, overcome by the feel of him, his warmth, his girth, the smoothness of his cock in her grip.

She could lose herself in his brown eyes, in the pleasure she saw there.

He closed his hand over hers, guiding her to stroke him. Faster. Tighter. "You're trying to distract me."

"Is it working?"

"Hell yes, it's working."

The strain in his features confirmed his words. Without any warning, he grabbed her ass and rose from the sofa. "Wrap your legs around me. We're going upstairs."

She released his cock, cuddled into him, and held on for the ride. "What are you going to do to me there?"

"Fuck you senseless."

Yes, please.

CHAPTER FIFTEEN

Daniel hadn't been joking; he did indeed intend to fuck Mimi senseless. But first he had a few memories to make. She was going to push him away in the morning, so he needed to relish every minute she spent in his arms.

Once they reached his bedroom, she slid down his body and stood before him. He dropped to his knees and helped her slip off her slacks and panties, his hands kneading her ass and hips as he did so.

"You're beautiful here, too," he whispered as he brushed his fingers against her center. "I love it bare like this."

When he looked up, her smiling face greeted him.

"Such a flatterer," she said.

"Get on the bed, Mimi."

She twisted her body and took in her surroundings before sliding backward onto the bed. He didn't join her. Not yet. Instead, he walked to the right side of the bed. "Lie down."

She did as he asked. For a few seconds, he enjoyed the sight of her complying with his instructions without protest. When it came to Mimi, that phenomenon rarely occurred. And he liked that about her.

Although her mouth wasn't moving, her body certainly was. As he scanned every inch of her, she squirmed, her breasts jiggling in a perfect reenactment of his wettest dream. She carried those pert tits really well. And her slim waist and soft hips completed the ensemble, his very own violin to play with all night.

She licked her lips, drawing his gaze to them. Tense with need, he shucked off his jeans and boxer briefs in seconds, climbed onto the bed, and kneeled by her face. Stroking his dick in slow succession, he stared at her lovely mouth. "I want to feel your lips around my cock. Will you do that?"

She moaned, turned on her side, and parted her lips in answer. He guided himself into her mouth and nearly came right then. Then she slid her arm through his thighs and grabbed his ass for balance.

Fuck, fuck, fuck.

He pumped his dick into her mouth, and she widened to take all of him. *Por dios.* The sight of her, her blond hair fanned around her face while she sucked him off, sent every nerve ending in his body to the edge. The need to touch her was just as urgent as his need to breathe.

"Put your knees up, Mimi. Open for me."

Still sucking him, she shifted and opened her legs. He caressed her thighs and reached their apex. She was so fucking wet, and the silky feel of her on his fingers made his dick expand even more. Her eyes flew open and widened in surprise when he sank two digits into her. With a moan, she closed her eyes again and squeezed his ass, never interrupting her rhythm.

"That's it, Mimi. It feels so fucking good."

He twisted his fingers inside her and hooked them as he pulled out. She let go of his cock and dropped her head back. "Yes, yes, yes. Do that again."

"You like that?"

"Yes. *Please.* Do it again."

The desperation in her voice made him feel ten feet tall, but the night wouldn't be complete until he heard the sound of her orgasm. He climbed over her and covered her with his body. "Anything you want, *preciosa.*" Then he kissed her, tasting himself on her tongue.

He lifted himself off her, holding himself in a plank position. "Scoot back."

She shimmied up the bed and threw her hands above her head.

He lowered himself and slid down her body, his damp skin brushing against hers, and ultimately settled his torso between her legs, his face inches from her mound. "You want my fingers inside you again?"

"Yes."

"What about my mouth?"

"That, too, yes."

He slid two fingers inside her and settled his thumb over her clit. Then he covered her mound with his mouth and licked up her slit as he hooked his finger inside her.

She pressed her legs against his shoulders and lifted her ass off the bed. "Please don't stop, Daniel. Don't stop. Don't."

The way she said his name. Perfect. The way she begged for more. Insanely arousing. Her taste. He wasn't sure he'd ever want to stop. He couldn't wrap his head around all the ways he wanted to have her.

He quickened his pace as he slid his fingers in and out of her, and she bucked against him. Her responsiveness was such a turn-on he rubbed his cock against the mattress, mimicking the friction he'd feel when he buried himself in her. A poor substitute, he knew, but his body was on fire for her.

And she was burning for him, too. As he lapped at her, she alternated between moaning and murmuring her encouragement. "Right there, yes, right there, right there."

For several minutes, he sucked and nipped at her, enjoying the way she writhed against his mouth.

After she let out a small cry, her legs shook around his ears, melding with the tremors going through his own body. "I'm going to come, Daniel,"

He closed his mouth over her clit and sucked her until she screamed her release.

Panting, she raised her torso off the bed and pulled him to lay flush against her. "I want you now."

"Let me get a condom."

She blinked several times and nodded. "Of course."

He reached over and grabbed a condom in the top drawer of his nightstand. He'd never sheathed himself so fast. The desire to sink into her was all he could think about.

He lifted her arms above her head and guided his dick to her entrance. "I want this to be good for you. Tell me what you need, and I'll give it to you. Okay?"

"Believe me, I'll tell you if it isn't good for me."

In answer, he pushed inside her, amazed by the way she stretched to accommodate him. She gasped in his ear.

He raised his head. "You're so fucking tight. Are you okay?"

She squeezed her eyes closed and licked her lips. "I'm okay. It feels good. Really, really good."

He grasped one of her hands, lacing his fingers through hers, and filled her with slow strokes. She was wrapped around his cock like a tight leather glove, her hold on him firm but malleable. He couldn't get enough of it, of her. "Look at me, Mimi."

She opened her eyes—and closed his heart off for anyone else. This woman was his. Somehow he'd make sure of it. But she was definitely going to fight him first. And he looked forward to her inevitable defeat.

"Don't go getting serious on me, Daniel."

"Too late," he said with a thrust that wrung a cry from her beautiful lips.

Then he proceeded to fuck her senseless.

* * *

Mimi awoke with the sun in her face and Daniel's hand on her waist.

Not a bad way to greet the day.

She disentangled herself from him and padded barefoot and bare-assed to the bathroom that adjoined Daniel's bedroom. After using the restroom, she eyed herself in the mirror and yelped. He'd marked her with whisker burns along her jaw, her neck, and her chest. Whisker burns between her thighs would have been just fine, but these were a different story. Hopefully they'd fade over the weekend.

She scanned the bathroom. Neat and tidy. Just like Daniel. On the surface, at least.

The frameless shower beckoned to her. She could picture herself under the square, shoulder-width rainfall showerhead. Oh, and the shower had three rows of side jets along the wall, one of those rows perfectly positioned for an incredibly stimulating experience. No way was she going to pass on the opportunity to try that.

She opened the glass door, stepped in, and stared at the panel of buttons and dials. Okay, this actually made sense. The dials and buttons matched the positions and sizes of the showerhead and jets. After flicking a few buttons, a cascade of water fell on her head. *Perfect.* She smoothed back her hair and soaped herself with Daniel's body wash. She might end up smelling like eau de man, but the pleasure of sliding her hands over her soapy skin was worth it.

She blinked her eyes and lowered the overhead shower's pressure. Next, she fiddled with the side jets, setting them to maximum pressure and aiming one of them between her legs. The massaging jets of water pulsed against her clit. *Oh, shit.* Good didn't even begin to describe the sensation.

She jumped when she heard a tap on the shower door. She turned and found Daniel standing there wearing a wicked grin and nothing else.

"Need any help?" he asked.

"No, I'm good. Your shower's taking very good care of me."

"You didn't even take it out on a date. What kind of hussy do you think my shower is?"

She couldn't help laughing. "All I did was step in and it started working on me. What can I say? Your shower's a slut."

He stepped back and leaned against the bathroom counter. "Don't let me stop you. I'll just watch."

She braced her hands above the shower panel and let the stream of water hit her core. "Damn, this is incredible. With a shower like this, who needs a man? How much did this set you back?"

He snickered.

She looked at him over her shoulder. "You know, I could be persuaded to replace the jets with something more stimulating."

His cock jumped at the suggestion, and he fisted it. And oh, wow, watching it lengthen and thicken went right up there as one of the most erotic sights she'd ever witnessed.

"You want me inside you?" he asked as he stroked his very thick and very long erection.

"Yes." She spied the condom packet resting on the counter. "I see you came prepared, too."

"Believe me, this was all about your safety."

She raised a brow. "How so?"

"I figured even if you didn't want to have sex with me, we could share a shower, and I didn't want you to slip and find yourself impaled on my dick unexpectedly. Most home accidents happen in the bathroom, I've heard."

She shook her head in mock amazement. "I admire that you're always forward thinking." After licking her lips, she crooked a finger at him and opened the shower door. "Now get over here so I can be impaled."

He reached the stall in a single stride. Mesmerized by the purpose in his dark brown eyes, she felt for the wall behind her, bracing for the impact of his body against hers. He stepped in and stood under the spray, but he didn't touch her. The water saturated his dark brown hair, making it appear black as coal, and droplets dotted his nose and lips. The man tempted her like no other man before him. She placed her hands on his shoulders, her breasts skating over his torso, and angled her face to kiss him. He swooped down and captured her mouth, cupping her ass and grinding against her.

She slid her hands from his shoulders and fondled his balls.

"Ah, baby," he said against her mouth. "I don't want anyone else's hands on me. Just yours. Can you feel how much I want you?"

She whimpered into him. "Yes, I feel it."

Then he spun her around. "Place your hands on the wall."

She placed her hands at shoulder height. He stepped closer, so close his dick grazed her ass. He covered her hands with his own and slid them higher up the wall, stretching her so that the small of her back ached from the angle. She forgot that mild discomfort when he swiped his finger along her slit, testing her wetness.

"You're ready," he whispered in her ear.

It wasn't a question but a statement. She answered it anyway. "Yes, I'm ready."

He bent his knees against the backs of hers and rubbed his cock against her folds. "I'll try to last, but morning wood isn't always reliable."

She twisted her neck and looked him in the eyes. "I believe in you, champ."

He smiled, and her heart clamored to escape her chest.

Then he filled her to the hilt, a rough entry that sent tingles up her spine and through her core. She gasped from the force of it, and he responded by placing one of his digits in her mouth. She sucked it in tandem with his thrusts as the shower heads pounded water over their bodies.

He chanted his approval in her ear, his voice gruff, needy, and deliciously low. "You feel like everything I've ever wanted, and I don't want to stop. Tell me this pussy is mine, baby."

"It's yours, Daniel. It's yours. Over and over, whenever you want it, it's yours."

The vow seemed to flip a switch in him. He grabbed her thighs and pressed his chest against her back, bending her from behind. And then his morning wood made a liar out of him, showing her just how reliable it could be. Like a man possessed, he stroked her over and over, until their bodies shook from the exertion, the delicious friction causing them to cuss and shout.

He snaked his hand around her waist and massaged her clit, the steam, their lust, and the water having a dizzying effect on her. "I'm going to come, Daniel."

"Let go, baby. I'll be right there with you."

"Oh, yes, yes, yes, yes," she chanted.

The orgasm jolted her, rippling through her body, the pleasure so intense she squeezed her eyes shut and saw spots when she opened them. As promised, Daniel joined her, hitting his peak as she descended from hers.

"You're amazing," he whispered in her ear. "And I can't get enough of you. But you should know one thing."

She struggled to form words, her mouth, dry and swollen. "What is it?"

"I'm sending you this month's water bill."

She wanted her laugh to be genuine, but it wasn't. Because she was worried about what came next.

* * *

After their "shower," they walked to a neighborhood café for coffee and pastries. Daniel could tell Mimi wanted to broach a subject and didn't know how to begin. She kept picking at her nails as they walked back to his place. And when he tried to engage her in conversation, he had to repeat himself before she would respond.

He stopped her on the sidewalk in front of his home. "Say what you need to say."

Her eyes widened.

The skittishness he saw in her eyes twisted his gut. He'd slay dragons for her. Shield her against anyone or anything that would cause her pain. But the possibility that *he* might be the reason for her distress damn near broke his heart.

"Sorry. I'm a bit distracted."

He led her up the steps, sat on the stoop railing, and sandwiched her between his legs. "Talk to me."

With her eyes squinting against the sun's rays, she blew out a breath and placed her hands on his shoulders. "We have to talk about the guys."

"What about them?"

She looked down at him, her expression serious. "I don't want them to know about us."

"Okay."

She drew back and furrowed her brows. "That's it? Okay?"

"Sure, I understand. For now."

She pushed against his shoulders with the tips of her fingers. "Will you stop with the 'for now' business?"

"Look, I'm just glad you're willing to admit there's an 'us.' If at some point it makes sense to tell them, then we will."

"And if there's never such a point, we won't."

He nuzzled her chest. "I'm guessing there will be."

"I'm guessing there won't be."

He drew back and looked up at her. *Fuck this.* He wasn't going to pretend he was okay with her flippant attitude. That's not how this worked. Not given how he felt about her. "Can you stop with the 'I'm tough as shit and I'm going to pretend this doesn't matter' act? If you're not going to give us a chance, what's the point?"

She gave him a wry smile. "Good sex?"

He clenched his jaw and blew out a long breath. "I can get that elsewhere."

Her mouth fell open and she eased out of his embrace. "Nice. There's the Daniel we all know and love."

He tugged her back to him. "You'd like to tell yourself that, wouldn't you? Haven't I convinced you yet I'm not the guy you thought I was? If you don't know the real me by now, it's because you don't *want* to."

She stepped away from him and rubbed her arms as she paced on his stoop.

"You know I'm right. That guy scares the shit out of you, doesn't he? I've *never* pretended not to want you, sure, but you've never looked closely enough to realize that this has *always* been about more than just getting you in my bed. That scares the shit out of me, too. Because you have the capacity to break my heart, and if that happened, I'm not sure I'd recover. So either stop trying to fuck this up from the outset or move on without me."

She chewed on her bottom lip as she scanned his face. "I liked you better when you were just trying to get into my pants."

He stood and faced her. "I haven't changed. I still want in your pants." He placed his hand over her heart. "But I want in here, too. I let you in. Now it's up to you to do the same."

He held his breath as several seconds of silence passed. Then she rose on her toes and pressed a soft kiss to his forehead. That tiny show of affection would be enough to last him a few weeks. It meant that much.

Stepping closer into his embrace, she cradled the sides of his face. "Okay."

"What do you mean 'okay'?"

"I want to give this a chance."

"You're worrying me."

She pushed against his chest with a laugh. "Why?"

"Because you gave up too easily, and *nothing* about you is easy. What gives?"

"I'm trying, okay? But we need to establish some ground rules."

He groaned and raised his face to the sky. "Here we go with the rules again. You know, for someone who's so footloose and fancy free, your obsession with rules is unsettling."

She poked him in the chest. "Work is different. That's why this is important."

"Okay, what are the rules?"

"We don't tell anyone about us unless and until I'm ready to."

He wasn't surprised by the request. "Fine."

"That includes the guys," she said.

"For the record, I think we should tell them now, but sure, if we must."

"And if we…if we don't work out, we'll both do our best to not let it affect our professional relationship."

"Yeah, sure."

She poked him in the chest again. "Are you taking this seriously or not?"

He hunched over and grabbed her finger. "Yes, yes. I am. What else?"

"No special treatment at the office. If you think I'm screwing up somehow, tell me, okay? No holding back."

"That's a given. The question is, can you handle that?"

She scoffed. "Of course I can."

Yeah. We'll see about that.

CHAPTER SIXTEEN

It was official: She was whipped.

After spending a weekend in Daniel's bed, she'd returned to work with a goofy grin and the worst case of horniness she'd ever experienced. *Who knew interval training could lead a man to initiate such inventive sex positions? Shaun T deserved a raise, that's for sure.*

And she couldn't stop thinking about Daniel. The male orgasm had always fascinated her, but Daniel's face when he hit his peak was something altogether different, and a joy to watch. He squeezed his eyes shut and bit into his lower lip, slowly sliding his teeth up until he released it. *So freaking hot.*

She hid her face from Nina's prying eyes during the Monday morning meeting by doodling on her pad, until she caught herself drawing pictures of her and Daniel in the various sex positions they'd tried. Nina kicked her under the table, glanced at Mimi's pad, and gave her a "what the hell are you doing?" look. Mimi quickly turned the page and straightened in her seat. Right. This was neither the time nor the place for her to think about Daniel. Not in that way at least.

Ian wasted a few minutes of the meeting berating one of their team members. And then, as he usually did, he turned his attention to Mimi. "What's going on with the new client? The Cambridge Group, is it?"

Mimi cleared her throat and tried to keep any sign of emotion off her face. "It's going well. They're due to appear on a panel at Harvard in a few weeks, and they've asked me to join them."

"On their dime?"

"Yes, they've agreed to pay for it. It's just a day trip anyway."

"Will there be press?"

"Yes. The student paper and a local. I'm scheduled to meet with reps from both."

"Good. Anything else in the works, or are you planning to rest on your laurels now that you've managed to snag a single client?"

Wow. Asshole. "Um. No. I've got a meeting with a potential client this Friday. An interior design firm looking to publicize its work in a unique way."

Ian didn't loosen his tight expression. If anything, he appeared more annoyed than before. "Good. Do your best to make that happen."

Because what? Without that gem of advice, she'd do her very worst to ensure she didn't get the client? Moron. "Of course."

Ian ended the meeting, and she scurried out the door.

Nina called after her as Mimi rushed down the hall. "Ms. Pennington, may I have a word?"

Mimi kept walking and called behind her, "Can't, Ms. Matthews. I've got an appointment."

"Bullshit," Nina said.

Mimi stopped, spun around, and waited for Nina to catch up with her. "What do you want to know?"

Nina circled her and sniffed the air. "Damn, woman. Why do you smell like you spritzed *eau du good sex* all over you?"

Mimi grabbed Nina's arm and pulled her into Mimi's office. Once the door was closed, she said, "First of all, I showered, okay? But if you're referring to my unmistakable well-fucked glow, then yes, you are correct, I had sex all weekend."

Nina waggled her eyebrows. "Oooo, more gossip. Yes!"

"A lady never gossips."

Nina placed her hand across her forehead as though she were searching for something beyond the proverbial horizon. "Lady? What lady?"

Mimi bumped Nina with her shoulder. "No details for you."

And that was unlike her. Because she'd often shared her exploits with Gracie and Nina without a second thought—Karen, too, when Mimi could get her to lift her head out of her medical school books. So why the need to keep her relationship with Daniel private? She could claim that he was different because he was a client, making it inappropriate to discuss their relationship with a coworker. But Nina was part of her inner circle, so that couldn't be the reason.

Special.

He's special, you idiot.

There. That's not so awful to admit, right?

Breathe. It'll be okay.

Nina gave her a dirty look. "Fine. If you want to be tight-lipped about it, don't expect me to divulge my freakiness." After she threw open the door, Nina added, "And you're going to miss some good stuff."

"I'll take you to lunch tomorrow to make it up to you," Mimi called after her.

Nina huffed. "Why not today?"

"I have plans."

Nina gave her a dismissive wave as she walked down the hall. "Whatever. And you'll have to do better than lunch to make it up to me. Hope he's worth it."

Yeah, he is.

And that scared the shit out of her.

* * *

Daniel made a few adjustments to the PowerPoint presentation and checked his watch. The girls from Brigham Middle School would be here any minute now. He stood and paced his office, running through the schedule for the few hours they'd spend at the firm.

He wanted to make the day interesting for the girls. Though only in its second year, the shadowing program meant a lot to him. In a way, the girls' visit kept him connected to his sister. Before her death, she'd worked as a math teacher at the school.

His speakerphone buzzed. "Yes, Felicia."

"Mimi Pennington's here to see you."

It took him several seconds to process what Felicia had said.

Mimi? Here? In the middle of the day?

He grinned, but when he realized the implications of her presence minutes before the girls were due to arrive, his grin faded.

"Send her back, Felicia." He quickly took his seat and placed a few reports in front of him, sifting through them for good measure.

She peeked her head in. "Hey."

His body went still at the sight of her. He'd made love to this woman last night, and he wanted her again. But he couldn't tempt himself, not when 15 thirteen-year-olds were due to show up soon. "Hey. This is a surprise."

She stood at the threshold of his office. "May I close the door?"

"Actually, we're expecting visitors and Felicia's going to buzz me in a minute."

She wrinkled her nose. "Okay. Well, I guess this is a bad time. I have a meeting across the street at one, so I thought I'd pop in for a few minutes to say hi."

He couldn't leave her with the impression that he didn't want her here. That wasn't anywhere near the truth. "Close the door a sec."

She shut the door and stood in front of it. "Is everything okay?"

"Yeah, everything's fine. Any other time, this visit would go a lot differently. But if I so much as touch your hand, I'll want to devour you. And I'm really trying not to get hard before my meeting."

Her eyes widened, and her mouth went slack. *Fuck. Not that.*

She advanced a step.

"Stay back, Mimi. Please."

She snickered. "Oh, this is hilarious."

He leaned forward and spoke in as low a voice as he could manage while being confident she could hear him. "If you like me just a tiny bit, please sashay your ass out of this office and return tomorrow."

She backed up and slung her purse over her shoulder. "Fine. I suppose we'll talk later."

"Damn right we will."

She gave him a wave. "*Ciao.*"

His speakerphone buzzed. "Are they here, Felicia?" he asked as he watched Mimi saunter out the door.

"They're here," Felicia replied.

"Did you let the guys know?"

"Yes, they're on their way to the conference room."

"Fantastic," he said as he rubbed his hands together.

He looked down at his crotch. *And no boner. Even better.*

* * *

After Mimi left the restroom, she glimpsed Daniel and the rest of the architects shuffling to the conference room. A group of young girls in school uniforms giggled and walked ahead of them. *Hmmm. What's that about?*

Mimi walked over to the reception area. Thumbing her finger at the conference room, she asked, "What's going on in the conference room, Felicia?"

"Oh, this is STEM day. Science, technology, engineering, and math."

Mimi hid her impatience. "Yes, I know what STEM stands for. I meant, what are the guys doing in there?"

"Oh, a group of girls from Brigham Middle School visit each year. The guys talk to them about how STEM relates to architecture. It's part of a district-wide initiative to get more girls involved in science and math. Then the guys take them to lunch."

Wow, that's impressive.

And wait. This was a photo op if ever there were one.

She didn't carry a digital camera, so her iPhone would have to do. With a sheepish grin, she tiptoed into the conference room and sat in a chair in the corner. The men stood in front of a large projector screen while Daniel sat at the head of the table tapping on a laptop computer.

They were going around the room introducing themselves.

Poised to take a photograph of the group, she jumped when Daniel called her name. Only the top of his head and his eyes were visible behind the laptop screen.

She raised her chin. "Yes?"

"No photographs."

"Oh, I'm just going to take a few for the website. You won't even notice me."

Daniel straightened. "Mimi, I'm not asking, I'm telling you. No pictures."

She'd never heard him speak to anyone that way, his voice taut and his words clipped. They might as well have been strangers. *All righty then*. That was not what she'd expected from this impromptu outing. Served her right for showing up unannounced. "Fine." She tossed her phone back in her purse and stood. "Sorry to interrupt."

With too many sets of eyes watching her, she walked out the door and didn't stop until she'd reached the bank of elevators outside the office. She didn't wave good-bye to Felicia, either. *How embarrassing*.

She straightened at the sound of the elevator's ding. Before she could escape, though, Daniel swung open the glass door to the office.

"Mimi, wait," he said as he jogged toward her.

She turned and the elevator doors closed behind her. "Daniel, you're busy. Don't worry about me. We'll talk later." She smiled to show him that she was fine, though it would be more apt to say his outburst had confused her.

"I just want to explain. The girls. They come each year, and this isn't about bringing business to the firm. It's about giving back, and I don't want to use what we do with them as a marketing tool."

"Of course. That's fine. I should have run it by you anyway. I didn't know the firm did this, so I just figured I'd take a couple of shots and contact the girls' parents for waivers later."

"Let's not, okay?"

"Okay."

"I'll explain later." He jerked a thumb toward the office. "For now, though, I've got to get back in there."

"Sure, sure."

Ask and ye shall receive, right? Well, she'd asked him to treat her no differently than anyone else when they were in the office. But being on the receiving end of that? Quite frankly, it sucked.

CHAPTER SEVENTEEN

After the girls from Brigham left the firm, Daniel attended a marathon meeting to deal with a longtime client's request to change the blueprints Daniel had drafted months ago. Despite his annoyance with the eleventh-hour revisions, he'd smiled through the conversation, never letting on that the additional work could have been avoided had the client agreed to Daniel's initial suggestions.

After walking the client out, he returned to his office and texted Mimi.

Daniel: I've been working nonstop. This is the first chance I've had to get in touch with you. Can I see you?

Mimi: Sure. Come on over.

Her text gave him no insight into her mood. But if she was truly pissed, he reasoned, she wouldn't have replied at all.

Twenty minutes later, he arrived at her doorstep, pressed the buzzer for her apartment, and texted her to let her know he was downstairs. Through the intercom, she simply said, "Come on up," and buzzed him in. Again he wondered what could be going on in that head of hers.

After climbing the flight of stairs to her apartment, he found the door to her apartment ajar. "Mimi?"

She sat at the small desk adjacent to her kitchen, her gaze glued to her laptop computer. "I'll just be a minute. A client just called me in a panic looking for talking points for an upcoming interview."

He nodded. "Take your time."

Meanwhile, he took a visual tour of her apartment. Bold colors—a mix of orange and red hues—covered the walls. Mimi's furnishings, a hodgepodge of unique items reflecting her eclectic taste, lacked any pairs. In the corner, a lime green bookcase with irregular edges held as many magazines as it did books. If one were to stage a play based on a Dr. Seuss book, Mimi's living room would serve as the perfect set.

"Okay," she said as she rose from her chair. "All done."

He turned in her direction and his brain short-circuited as he watched her approach. Damn. The silk sleepshirt she wore skimmed the tops of her thighs, and her breasts bounced as she sauntered over.

Explaining his behavior at the office had been his priority in coming here, but he doubted he'd be able to string two intelligent sentences together when she was dressed like that. And she was doing that sexy move with her tongue, where she pressed it against the corner of her mouth.

The room warmed by ten degrees when her hand flicked open the top button of her shirt. He swallowed and licked his lips. "Should I explain now or later?"

Another flick of a button. "*Definitely* later."

His gaze narrowed and he gave her a wolfish grin. That's what she did to him. Summoned his baser instincts whenever he could sense her arousal.

She gave him a coy smile in return. "My, what big…eyes you have."

"The better to devour your beautiful body with."

She stood before him and closed her eyes as she placed a hand on her neck and trailed it down the center of her shirt. Yet another flick of a button, and the smooth expanse of skin at her belly peeked through the opening in the fabric.

He placed his hands on her shoulders and slipped the shirt off, letting it drop to the ground. Backing up to get a better view of her, he slipped his own jacket off and loosened his tie. "You're almost perfect, but you still have too many clothes on."

Her eyes twinkling in amusement, she slid her panties down her legs and tossed them behind her. "Done. Now you."

"My clothes stay on."

"Why?"

"Because I don't think I can waste any time taking them off. I want my mouth on you now."

She shrugged. "Do what you must."

He bridged the distance between them, spun her around, and moved her hair off her shoulder. Being inside her would come later, but the anticipation of it made his hands tremble. He rested his lips against the silky skin behind her ear, taking in the faint scent of vanilla.

She shivered.

"Cold?" he asked.

"So, so hot," she whispered.

He snaked his hand around her waist and fanned his fingers over her belly. "You're so fucking soft. I could suck on your skin all day."

She rubbed her ass against his crotch. "That can be arranged."

Smiling, he trailed his lips over one shoulder, then across the back of her neck and along her other shoulder. As he nuzzled her, he massaged her scalp with one hand, eliciting a low moan from her.

Wanting his mouth on hers, he turned her head to the side and brought their lips together. He ended the kiss with a gentle tug on her bottom lip, then he descended to her neck and nipped at it. She giggled under his assault, and he smiled against her skin. She made him happy. Full stop.

With his knees, he nudged her forward. "Kneel on the couch and don't turn around."

She did as he asked, and then he guided her hands to grasp the back of the couch. "Stay just like that, please."

Her body swayed, evidencing her agitation. He loved that she was strung tight for him, that she was waiting for him to bring her pleasure. "You're awfully quiet. I'm not used to this."

"Enjoy it now. It won't last."

The humor in her voice touched him on some level he wasn't ready to acknowledge. If she knew how much he craved her, she'd have a weapon whose blunt force could wipe him out with one strike. Better to keep it to himself for now.

He undid the top two buttons of his shirt as he rounded the couch. Her eyes widened at her first full sight of him in several minutes. He toed off his shoes and slipped off his socks, and then he used his arms to lift himself over the sofa back.

She snickered. "Show off."

He slid his body in the space between her outstretched arms, gliding under her and landing on the floor with her pussy inches from his mouth.

"Shit," she whispered. "You're so freakin' agile."

"Comes in handy, no?"

"Yes, yes, yes."

"Now here's what I need you to do," he said as he massaged her ass. "You listening?"

"Yes, yes, I'm listening." Her voice tightened on the last word. "What do you need me to do?"

"Nothing. Just enjoy."

She whimpered and his cock hardened at the sound.

He pressed openmouthed kisses on the insides of her thighs as he breathed her in. The smell of her arousal drew his lips closer to her mound, his brain commanding him to taste her. With a firm hold on her ass, he centered her above his mouth and licked his way up her slit, until he reached her swollen clit and grazed it with his teeth.

Her head fell forward, her hair creating an intimate space where he could focus on her pussy and nothing else. Over and over he licked and sucked, pulling her close and steadying her with his face when she threatened to collapse under the onslaught.

"Daniel, that feels so fucking good, you have no idea."

Her unbridled encouragement fed his lust, turning on his beast-mode switch. His lazy strokes turned feral, and her cries grew louder. Once he'd established a rhythm, she circled her hips against him and grasped his hair with one hand, controlling the pleasure his mouth provided.

Her lips parted on a gasp when he captured her nub. "Yes, Daniel. I'm going to come. I'm so close. Lick me and don't stop."

So he didn't, and seconds later, she tightened her thighs against his face and cried out. He continued to lick her as she came down from the high, and she whimpered in protest.

She rose off him in a languid stupor as he wiped his face.

"Too much?" he asked.

She stood on shaky legs and lowered herself to the floor, straddling him in one smooth move. "Too perfect." She stared into his eyes as she unbuckled his belt and pulled it out of his pant loops. "Now you."

"Now us."

She unzipped his slacks. "Now us."

He lifted his ass off the floor and helped her tug his pants and briefs to the middle of his thighs. She stroked his cock, her soft hands assertive and strong and fisting him perfectly.

"Fuck, woman. That feels incredible."

He could feel the pressure building in the base of his dick already, but it was way too soon for that. Tugging her chest closer to his, he spoke against her neck. "Slow down, baby. I don't want to come yet."

He pulled a condom from his pocket and handed it to her. She quickly dispensed with the packaging and rolled the latex over him. Then she positioned her pussy over his cock. Leaning forward, she pressed her lips against his and sank down.

They rocked together for what seemed like ages, content to be connected without a quick ending. He toyed with her breasts as he sucked on her skin, and she alternated between caressing and grabbing his shoulders each time she came down on his dick.

Had he ever experienced pleasure this intense? Only with her. Unable to take her slow torture any longer, he cupped her ass and lifted her up and down his length until they both came with a shout.

She collapsed against him and wrapped hers arms around his neck. "Well, hello there."

Only then did he remember he had an explanation to give her.

* * *

Mimi faced Daniel as they lay on the couch. He'd propped his elbow and rested his head on his hand. With his other hand, he drew lazy circles on her back. As far as she was concerned, this was where they'd be sleeping tonight. If he chose to stay, that is. She wanted him to, though she wasn't sure how to ask without sounding silly.

"We should talk about what went down at the office," he said. "I need to explain."

She stiffened at the memory of how he'd called her out in front of everyone. On the way home, she'd twisted and tortured the moment until it barely resembled the original. That wasn't fair to him, particularly because she'd asked him to treat her no differently than he would anyone else he worked with. So she was curious to hear his explanation, but she'd already decided not to get upset about it. "Okay. Explain."

"Pamela was a teacher at Brigham."

It all clicked into place with that single statement. "The girls are your connection to her."

"In a way, yes. They weren't her students, but she taught at that school. So when they come, I feel like I'm honoring her. Remembering my sister even though my parents refuse to talk about her. And when you tried to take a photo, it felt like a violation even though I know that's not what you intended."

She shook her head. "Definitely not what I'd intended."

"I'm sorry I raised my voice."

She gave him a wicked grin. "It kind of turned me on. It's such a rare thing."

He stopped stroking her back and peered at her. "It didn't turn you on."

She sighed. "You're right. It didn't."

He pulled her closer and she reveled in his warmth. His body's capacity to calm her was as effective as its capacity to excite her. Moments ago she'd ground herself against his powerful thighs and met him thrust for thrust. Now she lay wrapped in his arms, feeling safe and protected with his hard chest pressed against her breasts.

"It won't happen again," he murmured against her hair.

She appreciated the promise, though she didn't need it. It was enough that they'd been able to talk about his reaction. His feelings about his sister's death were complicated and still raw, even after all these years, and she wanted to give him a safe space to discuss them. "Have you ever thought of naming a scholarship after Pamela? You talked about wanting to honor her, and that would be one way to do it."

"Never thought of that."

"You could award a college scholarship to one of the girls at Brigham. Or some other scholarship depending on the student's needs."

He stared at a point behind her, his face pensive, and then he gave her a soft peck on her lips. "I like the idea of that. I'll definitely look into it, but I wouldn't want to publicize it."

"That's your call, of course." She kissed one of his biceps and rested her head on it. "Thanks for sharing with me."

He cradled her face and brought his lips to hers. "Thanks for being you."

Fuck it. I'm going for it. She tamped down the butterflies in her belly and gave him a saucy smile. "Care to retire to my boudoir?"

"Are you asking me to stay the night?"

"I am."

He rose from the couch and pulled her up against him. "For the chance to sink into you first thing in the morning, the answer is hell yes."

With that out the way, she crouched on the floor and began to gather their discarded clothes in a pile.

He rounded the couch in search of his socks and shoes. "Can I take you to an early dinner Saturday? I have plans in the evening."

"I'd love to go to dinner with you, but I have my own plans Saturday. I scheduled a spa day and then I'm meeting the girls for dinner. We'll end the night at Decadence. We could meet there."

"The one in Georgetown?"

"That's the one."

"Who are you going with?"

"Let's see. Gracie and Ethan. Karen and Mark. Oh, and my friend from work, Nina."

"Not a good idea, I don't think, given that I'm your…"

She stopped searching for her thong. "My what?"

"Your dirty secret," he whispered. In his normal voice, he said, "Plus, I promised Amar I'd hang out with him."

"Why don't you bring him with you? It'll be fun."

He cocked his head. "Because he's your client, and because you don't want any of the guys to know we're together, remember?"

She stopped gathering her clothes and stood in the middle of the room. "Yes, I remember." She glanced at him once and then resumed her search for her underwear. "Found it," she said, twirling her thong in the air. "I have an idea about that, though."

"Should I be scared?"

She dropped her underwear on top of the pile and snuggled into his chest. "No, you shouldn't be scared. Bring Amar to Decadence anyway. You and I will be cordial. You can watch me on the dance floor. I won't dance with anyone, I promise. And it'll be this sexy secret between us. You'll know that I'll be in your bed by the end of the night."

"And when some jackass makes a move on you, I'm supposed to do what? Watch and do nothing? No, thank you. As tempting as that offer is, and yes, I'm being sarcastic here, I think I'll pass."

She pouted. "I understand. And now that I've said it out loud, it does seem like a stupid idea. I'd kiss you, but my foot is lodged in my throat."

He kissed her anyway. "You're forgiven." When he pulled back, he pinned her with an intense stare and a salacious grin. Placing her hand on his cock, he said, "Dislodge the foot. I have plans for your throat tonight."

She should have been happy that he was so understanding, but she couldn't ignore the obvious: He wasn't going to Decadence because she didn't want anyone to know about them. And though her feelings for him were growing each day, she couldn't shut off the part of her brain that told her their relationship could sour at any moment. So no, she wasn't ready to tell anyone about them. Not yet. And maybe never.

CHAPTER EIGHTEEN

After a grueling remainder of the week, Saturday could not have come soon enough for Mimi. Club Decadence was just the antidote she needed to put it all behind her, but she wasn't having as good a time as she'd expected.

She took a sip of her cocktail and placed the glass on the table. "I need to check my makeup. It feels like it's sliding off my face."

Karen rose from her spot next to Mark. "Do you want me to come with you?"

"Nah. I'm fine. Only one drink to my name tonight. Be back in five."

She squeezed her way through the throng and grimaced when the bottoms of her shoes met a patch of sticky fluid on the dance floor. Great. Now she had to clean up her favorite stilettos, too. She grumbled the entire way to the bathroom, unsure why her brain exploded at even the most minor inconvenience.

After patting her face with a napkin—yes, her makeup had in fact glided off her face—she wiped the bottoms of her shoes and readjusted her boobs in the pushup bra that revealed not only Victoria's secrets, but hers, too.

Hearing the thump of the infectious bass beat playing on the dance floor, she rushed out of the restroom and slammed into a body.

"Fuck. I'm so—"

"Horny?"

"Daniel," she exclaimed. "What are you doing here?"

It was a rhetorical question, really. Seeing him brightened her mood in a way no spa treatment or booty-shaking song could. Now she knew her pissy attitude stemmed from his absence.

What a picture he made, too. He wore charcoal slacks and a dark blue shirt, a pair of onyx cufflinks and a stainless steel watch his only accessories. Had she once thought he was arrogant? Yes. Not anymore, though. He was confident, but he didn't consider himself the center of the universe, and he treated the people around him with kindness and respect. She *liked* him as a person, and she liked him even more as her boyfriend.

He wrapped his hands around her waist and tugged her close. "Changed my mind."

She peered up at him in the dim hall, enjoying the way their bodies melded together, the top of her head aligned with his broad chest. "Checking up on me?"

"Hardly. More like I just wanted to see you, and I knew exactly where you'd be."

"Where's Amar?" she asked.

"He's out there somewhere, nursing his ex-girlfriend wounds with gin."

"And you came to find me."

"Of course."

Standing on her toes, she reached up and pulled him down for a kiss. The soft meeting of their mouths quickly turned fiery, until he tugged on her lower lip and she moaned.

His mouth traveled across her cheek and landed on her ear, where he licked the outer shell. Grabbing her ass, he pulled her against his crotch. "I want to fuck you so badly right now."

"I want to be fucked by you so badly right now."

He scanned the area. "Go back in there and take off your underwear."

Her mouth parted on a soft "oh." The directive quickened her pulse and weakened her knees. She didn't need an explanation or further instructions. Leaving him without another word, she rushed into a stall and pulled down her thong, stepping out of it with an awkward hop. When she emerged from the restroom, Daniel was leaning against the wall, his eyes heavy with arousal.

He held out his hand. "Give it to me."

Mimi placed her thong in his hand and watched him slip it in his pants pocket. Then he pulled her down a narrow hall to their right.

"Look," she said, her voice laced with excitement. "There's an exit sign. That might be a stairwell."

He tugged her toward the door.

She jerked herself out of his grasp. "Wait. What if an alarm sounds or something?"

He bridged the distance she'd created between them and pulled her flush against him. "That's a risk I'm willing to take. In thirty seconds, I can slide into you and very quickly after that I can make you come hard. Really, really hard. Do you want that?"

She grasped his upper arms, spun him around, and gave him a gentle shove. "What are you waiting for then? Stop dragging your feet."

He chuckled as he stumbled forward.

The stairwell was dimly lit, and she had no idea where it led.

Daniel kissed her forehead and held out his hand. "Let's go up. We might have better luck there."

They climbed the steps two at a time, her stilettos no match for her horniness. At the landing, he guided her to face the wall and lifted her dress to the waist. His arm snaked over her belly and his fingers zeroed in on her clit.

"Soaked. Christ, Mimi. I want that all over my cock."

The clang of his belt buckle and a crinkling sound told her that his hands were busy ensuring that would happen soon.

"Bend over a little, baby," he said in her ear.

Together, the command and the warmth of his breath against her skin made a direct hit on her clit, and the pulsing pleasure his words had evoked ran through her. She leaned over, turned her face to the side, and placed her cheek against the wall. If he didn't enter her soon, she'd cry. Big fat ugly tears for the suppressed sex hormones raging through her body.

Another shift of his legs and she felt his cock thump against her ass. Seconds later, he drove into her, and her mouth hung open as his cock filled her to the hilt.

He slipped a hand under her hair and grasped the back of her neck for purchase. His big fingers massaged her neck and he ground into her. She met each of his thrusts by backing into him, tightening herself against him, feeling the veins of his cock sliding against her walls. The feel of him was delicious. So good, in fact, that if someone came upon them in the stairwell right then, Mimi wasn't sure she'd want him to stop.

Their moans echoed in the cavernous space until the orgasm ripped into her and forced out a sharp cry.

Behind her, Daniel chanted as his body shook against her. "Fuck, fuck, fuck."

As she caught her breath, he nibbled on her neck, prolonging the fuzziness in her head. Too bad they couldn't stay like this a little longer. "Back that wood up, Vargas."

He chuckled as he pulled out of her and handed her his kerchief. "Damn, Mimi. I wish you could have seen my dick when I pulled it out of my briefs. It sprang out like a fucking jack-in-the-box. Hell, it almost scared me."

She cackled as she wiped between her legs. "You are so made for me."

The next thing she knew, he'd pressed her against the wall once more, his expression serious. "Damn right I am."

Oh, this man. This man who knew how to push her buttons. This man who saw through her façade. This man who'd let her see through his. The same man who knew how to call her out on her shit when she wasn't acting right. She didn't just *like* him; she was falling in love with him. And she didn't know how to process any of it.

They walked down the stairs hand in hand and separated when they reached the door. After she'd freshened up in the restroom, she stepped out into the hall. He again straightened from his position against the wall.

"All set?" he asked.

"Ready."

"How do you want to play this? Tell them you ran into me?"

She nodded. "Sure, that sounds good." But it didn't *feel* good. He deserved better than to be her dirty secret. She deserved better than a quickie in the stairwell. Actually, if they dated in the open, she'd still want that quickie, so she set aside that issue. They *were* dating, and she wanted to share that with her friends.

They wove their way through the crowded dance floor and found the table where her friends were sitting. Butterflies tickled her stomach as she considered the group. Ethan was nuzzling Gracie's neck. They'd become the quintessential "get a room" couple, especially now that Gracie was expecting. Karen, for her part, sat on Mark's lap, sipping a drink and bobbing her head to the song playing through the club's speakers. Her boyfriend drummed his fingers on the table, a nervous glint in his eyes.

Nina tapped at her phone.

Karen was the first to notice them. "Did you fall into the toilet?"

"Um, no. I ran into Daniel."

Nina looked up and set her phone on the cocktail table. "Whoa," she said with a smirk. "You're flushed. Again. You sure you're okay?"

Mimi went for quick and virtually painless, hoping it would be like ripping off a Band-Aid. "I'm fine. And if you'd guessed that Daniel and I just had sex in the stairwell, you would be right."

Every head at the table whipped in her direction. Then Nina slammed her hand on the cocktail table as she fell over in laughter. Daniel dropped his head and covered his face.

Mimi gave them jazz hands. "Surprise. Daniel and I are dating."

* * *

After Mimi's announcement, the women formed a circle around her, banishing the men to the perimeter.

Ethan slapped his shoulder. "Welcome to my world, Daniel. Get used to it."

He liked the sound of that. Liked the idea of being Mimi's plus one.

Ethan peered at him. "So you and Mimi, huh?"

"That's right. She's incredible."

"And a spitfire."

He chuckled. "Believe me, I know."

Ethan stared at Mark and waved a hand in front of his face. "You with us, man?"

Mark rubbed the back of his neck. "Yeah, I'm here. Just got something on my mind."

Ethan surveyed Mark's face, turned in Karen's direction, and grinned. "You're going to ask her to marry you tonight, am I right?"

Mark gave him a relieved smile. "You're right."

Before Daniel could think better of it, he asked, "Why here?"

Ethan answered for him. "They met here."

Daniel nodded. "Ah. Good luck then."

Mark took a big gulp of his beer, strode to Karen, and pulled her out of the circle. He whispered something in her ear that made her smile. Seconds later, they were gone.

Mimi sidled up to him and whispered in his ear. "Are you mad at me?"

He drew back and scrunched his eyebrows. "Why would I be mad at you?"

"I didn't warn you about the big reveal."

"Mimi, you come with a perpetual warning. Nothing you say or do could surprise me."

He and Mimi chatted with Ethan for a few minutes until a loud squeal made him jerk. He shoved Mimi behind him before he realized that the commotion had been caused by Gracie and Karen, who were jumping and hugging each other, while Mark watched the celebration.

Mimi ran to the women and joined the circle, after which another round of cheers erupted.

Amar joined him and clinked his beer bottle against Daniel's. "What did I miss?"

He nodded his head in Karen's direction. "That's Gracie's sister, Karen, she's dating that guy over there, Mark. I think he just proposed. Something about them meeting here."

"Nice."

"I'll introduce you when everyone settles down." He scrubbed his face. "And Mimi just told them we're dating."

Amar chuckled. "Not surprised."

Daniel raised an eyebrow. "You're not?"

"Not at all," Amar said after taking a swig of beer. "Who spends ten thousand dollars to pull a joke on someone? Maybe someone out there does, but that person is not you, my friend. So, yeah, I had my suspicions." Amar's gaze traveled over Mimi's body. "That's how she dresses outside work, huh?"

Daniel clenched his jaw and hands simultaneously. "If you value your teeth, let that be the last question you ask about her appearance."

Amar held up a hand. "Relax, D, or this is going to get real awkward real fast. Have you thought about that?"

"It'll be fine so long as no one gets out of line."

"Look, this isn't a surprise to me, but I can't say the same for Jason and Spencer. She's our publicist."

"She's a public relations rep."

"Too hard to say. And you know what the hell I mean, so stop focusing on the shit that doesn't matter. Figure out how you're going to explain to the guys that we hired the woman you're dating. And more importantly than that, figure out how to convince them it isn't going to pose a problem for our business."

All along he'd been focused on convincing Mimi that they should date. He hadn't given a single thought to whether the guys would have their own concerns about the relationship. Once again, he couldn't see the forest for his dick. But now he had to answer for it.

* * *

The partners of the Cambridge Group always met on Tuesdays, because meeting on a Monday, their least favorite day of the week, would end with a brawl.

Daniel opened with the most pressing topic on his mind. "So I wanted to talk to you guys about Mimi."

Jason's head whipped up, his attention on his newspaper diverted by her name. He narrowed his eyes. "What about her?"

"I'm just going to say this. We're together."

Spencer laughed. "You sly dog. I *knew* it."

Amar joined in Spencer's laughter.

Jason, however, pinched his brows and pursed his lips. "Am I the only one who didn't get the memo?"

Spencer cocked his head. "Memo? All you had to do was look at those two and see that they were seconds away from going at it."

Daniel gritted his teeth. "Shut up, Spence."

"No disrespect, D. Just telling you what I saw. Anyway, is that all?"

Jason pushed back his chair. "Is that all? Doesn't anyone see there's a potential conflict of interest here?"

Amar tossed his pen on the table. "All right. Let's discuss."

Jason stood, his lips pressed together in a firm line. Taking an audible breath, he grabbed the back of his neck and paced. "She's going to be distracted by you. We won't feel comfortable complaining about her performance. And what if it doesn't work out between you two? Then she doesn't want to work with us, and we're out a publicist."

Daniel cracked a knuckle before he responded to Jason's concerns. "One, she's a professional. We're not going to make out in front of you guys, if that's what you're worried about. The relationship happens outside this office. Two, she's asked me to treat her no differently than I would any other professional we work with. I'd expect the same of you. And three, my relationship with Mimi will work, so your last concern is neither here nor there."

Spencer made a hissing sound. "Damn. You're a cocky son of a bitch."

"No. Just confident in our relationship." He turned to Jason. "Look, I get it. You have concerns. I hear you. But keep an open mind. If it's not working, we'll revisit, okay?"

"Fine with me," Spencer said.

Amar drummed the table. "Same here."

Jason's nostrils flared. "Fine."

Daniel relaxed for the first time since the meeting had started. "Great. It'll work. You'll see."

His confidence stemmed more from his wishful thinking than his conviction. It had to work. There was no other option, because if it didn't, he'd be faced with an impossible choice: to put either Mimi or his business with the guys first.

CHAPTER NINETEEN

The more time he spent with Mimi, the more Daniel resolved never to choose between her and his work. She was adorable in every way, with or without her social filter, and he couldn't get enough of her.

Looking at her now, with her hair in sexy disarray as she stared at the mess they'd made on the floor, he could imagine spending many nights like this one with her, years from now. The scary question was: Could she?

Mimi huffed. "Tell me again why we're doing this?"

Daniel held his laughter in check. Mimi sat on the floor beside him with several hundred Lego pieces scattered around her. And she wore nothing but one of his T-shirts, which dwarfed her frame. He leaned over and kissed her on the cheek. "You're dating an architect. The minute you said you hated Legos, it became my personal mission to make you love them."

"I'm not saying there's anything wrong with Legos. They've just never been my thing."

"Well, they're my thing, okay? So just give it a shot."

"But did you have to get a kit with a million pieces? One of these is going to find its way up my ass. In fact, I think I'm sitting on one now."

"This is a basic kit, Mimi. I spared you the one with a thousand pieces."

"How considerate of you. What are we making anyway?"

"A replica of the Eiffel Tower. Give me the ones you just put behind you."

"Is that supposed to be a substitute for the real thing in Paris, because if it is, I have to say, it's a poor one." She sorted the pieces, throwing a few behind her as though she'd deemed them unnecessary.

"You've ever been?"

"No, but I'd love to go one day."

"Amar and I visited Paris our first summer after starting grad school. Kind of a required trip for an architectural student." Behind her, the pile of discarded pieces grew. "Give me the pieces you keep throwing back there."

She feigned innocence. "What? What pieces?"

"I'm looking right at them."

"I have no idea what you're talking about."

He lunged for her, tickling her until she toppled over and curled into a ball.

Shielding her face, she shrieked with laughter. "Ow, ow, ow. Is this some twisted game, Daniel? These things hurt."

He stood and pulled her out of the pile. "I can see I'm not going to be able to make you love Legos tonight. So why I don't just make love to you instead?"

She cuddled into him. "Well, that's the best idea you've had all day."

"Have I told you lately that I like you?"

"You have. And for the record, I like you, too."

He stepped back and pinned her with his gaze. "A lot, Mimi. I like you a lot."

She gave him a shy smile. "I like you a lot, too."

And that was enough for him—for now.

* * *

Later, they lay in bed, Mimi's head resting on his chest. He enjoyed the silence and the warmth of her body. This, just this, gave him a sense of peace he hadn't experienced in a long time. She absently trailed a finger along his chest as he toyed with a lock of her hair.

She took a long breath and blew out. "I want to ask you something, and you should really feel free to say no."

He grinned. "And you make your living pitching people?" Of course she wouldn't let that comment go without a response, but he hadn't expected a physical one. "Ow. Dammit, Mimi. Plucking my chest hair is low even for you."

She raised her head and gave him a fire-breathing dragon stare. "*Even* for me?"

He pushed her head back onto his chest. "Kidding. Please continue."

"I'm wondering if…if you'd be willing join me for the awards dinner for my father. In Austin. I mean, my plan is to spend a few days with my mother, but maybe you could join me the evening of the dinner and then we could return together. I just thought it might be nice to have a friend there."

"A friend?"

"My boyfriend."

"I'd be meeting your parents."

"Yes. But given how absent they've been in my life, you shouldn't view this as a big deal. It's not a grand statement, okay? Also not a big deal if you don't want to go. I'd understand."

He raised his shoulder to get her to lift her head. When he was sure she was focused on his face, he peered at her. "Just answer one question. Do you want me there?"

God, he wished she'd just admit it. No bullshit. No explanations or disclaimers. But with Mimi, he never knew when he'd get the unadulterated truth about her feelings for him.

"Yes."

Ah, damn. This time she didn't disappoint. He loved this woman, and he trusted that she'd come to love him, too. *Baby steps, it is.* He pressed his lips against her forehead. "If you want me there, then that's where I'll be."

* * *

Okay. Maybe he shouldn't have come to Austin.

Less than an hour in Mimi's parents' presence had been enough to confirm Mimi's succinct description: Her father was a jerk, and her mother was a doormat.

Mimi's father, Richard, gave off an air of charm and sophistication that drew people to him. Throughout the evening, people stopped by his table, and he received them like a king holding court.

He had little to say to his wife and daughter, however, and Mimi, for her part, handled his inattentiveness as though it were expected, rarely bothering even to look in his direction.

Daniel tried to engage Mimi's mother, Gayle, in conversation, but her eagle-eyed gaze didn't stray from her husband, particularly when another woman was in the vicinity, and the few questions he'd asked her were met with half-baked responses that underscored her distracted state.

When the waitstaff served dinner, Mimi's parents were forced to engage in some semblance of conversation with each other for the benefit of the guests at the table. By the time dessert arrived, Richard appeared exhausted from the exercise, fidgeting with his watch and glancing at his phone at regular intervals. As Richard ate his pie, he turned his attention to his daughter, his gaze traveling between Daniel and Mimi.

Daniel gave Mimi a reassuring smile, and Mimi returned it with a less effusive one of her own.

The fork in Richard's hands sliced through the air as he spoke. "How's the job, Mimi?"

After Richard had addressed her, Mimi's fork hovered in the air as though she were shocked that her father had deigned to speak with her. A few seconds later, she set the fork down and wiped her mouth with her napkin. "My career's going well. I'm poised to make partner in the next few months, or so I've been told."

"Not a sure thing until it actually happens, so don't go gettin' cocky on me. In business, decisions can change from one day to the next."

"Yes, I'm aware." She took a sip of her water, her hand trembling as she lowered the glass to the table.

What a jackass. The man saw his daughter once, maybe twice, a year, and he couldn't find the heart to praise her obvious success. Daniel studied Mimi. Her gaze darted everywhere, and she shimmied her shoulders to the eighties music playing in the background. Her father might be incapable of showing his support, but Daniel had no problem filling the void. "Mimi's phenomenal at what she does, Richard. I have no doubt she'll make partner."

She stopped shimmying her shoulders and covered his hand with hers. He winked at her, and she smiled.

"How did you two meet, by the way?" Richard asked. "I don't think Mimi mentioned it."

"Through work," was all she said.

Her father must have sensed a story because he leaned in and pressed for more information. "You work in the same office?"

"No," Mimi said through tight lips. "I work with his architectural firm."

Richard choked on his laughter. "Oh, he's a client then."

Mimi's mother attempted to intercede. "Richard, let it go."

He held up his hands. "What? I'm just making friendly conversation." To Mimi, he said, "Well done, my dear. Well done."

What would be the point in responding to this man's bullshit? The woman beside him was all he cared about. He stood and held out his hand to her. "Nobody puts Mimi in a corner," he announced.

She looked up at him, her eyes glinting with humor. "Did you just quote *Dirty Dancing*?"

"A loose interpretation." He gave her a pleading look. "You have to take my hand so I don't look like an idiot."

She rose and took his hand, her eyes twinkling. "We can look like idiots together."

He swept her onto the dance floor.

She giggled. "Are you going to perform Patrick Swayze's solo now?"

"Who's Patrick Swayze?"

After opening and closing her mouth, she shook her head. "Never mind. How do you even know about that movie?"

"Pamela used to rave about it."

"I think that's the first time you've mentioned your sister's name in casual conversation. That's definitely progress."

She was right. He'd voiced Pamela's name without the usual tightness in his throat that made it hard to swallow. And he discovered something else: Talking about her made it easier to absorb that she was gone.

"Yeah. She was always going on about a remake in the works. And that line became her battle cry when someone pissed her off. She tried to get me to watch the movie, but I wisely declined."

Mimi stopped swaying and pulled back. "Wisely? That movie has endured for decades. There's a reason."

"Let me guess? Patrick Swayze and dirty dancing."

"Might have something to do with it."

The music slowed and he pulled her closer. "You okay?"

"I'm fine."

"What was that about back there?"

"My father being a dick. Exhibit A."

"Why did he say 'well done'?"

"The story isn't a short one, and I'm not sure this is the right time or place."

"He upset you, so I'd say this is exactly the right time and place. And I have nothing else to do but focus on you."

The jazz band switched to an up-tempo song.

Mimi dropped her head. "He'll be getting his award soon."

"Do you care?"

She didn't hesitate to answer him. "Not at all. I'm here because my mother asked me to be."

"Then let's go outside."

She linked her arms with his, and they strolled to the hotel's courtyard, looking as though they were nothing more than a couple enjoying a lovely evening. But Daniel knew better. Because Mimi was quiet, and she hadn't made a dirty joke the entire evening.

They walked the hotel grounds as she talked.

"In all my adult years, I confided in my father once. I'd just graduated from college and had my first full-time job in a law office. A friend from college had hooked me up with a short-term gig working for her father's firm. I was so clueless that I didn't recognize the signs that another lawyer there wasn't really trying to mentor me but wanted to have sex with me."

Daniel's heart thumped wildly in his chest. He hoped this wasn't going where he thought it was going. "Did he hurt you?"

She shook her head. "No, nothing like that. I'd been assigned to help him prepare for a trial. It involved lots of long nights in the firm conference room with take-out food strewn everywhere. I was excited to be helping on the case. Everyone on the team working together. And then one night he sat next to me as I highlighted witness statements. Everyone else had gone home. And the next thing I knew, his hand was on my thigh."

Daniel squeezed her hand. "What did you do?"

"I froze. That hand on my thigh made no sense, and I think I was hoping it would go away and I'd never have to deal with it again. But it didn't go away, and that fucking hand reached under my skirt, until I shoved it away."

They reached a bench and he guided her to sit. "Did the guy give you any trouble?"

"No, he backed off but not before telling me I'd been sending him mixed signals. My skirts were short. My cleavage practically in his face all day. He said, and I quote, 'You have to know any red-blooded male is going to respond to those signals.'"

"What a dick."

"He was. But you know, in a way he was right, too. I hadn't put much thought into how I presented myself at work."

Daniel now understood the impetus for the complete transformation she made in her appearance when she was in a professional setting. "No, he wasn't right in any way. He was, and likely still is, just a dick." She smiled, but it didn't reach her eyes, and his heart hurt for her. "Did you report him?"

She dropped her head as she shook it. "No. I just wanted to be done with the whole experience."

He lifted her chin. "This is me you're talking to. Don't ever be embarrassed about this with me."

She nodded, her eyes glistening with unshed tears. "Okay."

"So I gather you told your father about it?"

A line appeared between her brows, and she pressed her lips together. "I did. He asked me lots of questions. What had I been wearing? Had I made any sexually suggestive jokes around the guy? Did I flirt? On and on and on. And I wracked my brain trying to figure out what went wrong. Maybe I had flirted. Maybe I'd smiled too much. Maybe my makeup was more than was appropriate for the office. I mean, we all know there's a difference between what you wear in a social setting and what you wear in a professional setting, right?"

"Is that what your father led you to believe?"

"No. My father's point was slightly different. He wanted to give me a dose of reality. Said my looks would always be a factor in the workplace, whether it was because people would assume I was a dumb blonde, or because men would make unwanted advances. My father has some sick theory that you should use your physical assets to get ahead in life. He claims that's how my mom caught him. She was his secretary. What a cliché, right? I told him he was sexist for suggesting that, and even more fucked up for suggesting that to his own daughter, but he laughed it off."

Daniel didn't even know where to begin. There was so much shit to unpack here. But Mimi wasn't done.

"What a message to send to your daughter, huh? Need a job? Flirt with the guy who's interviewing you. Need a promotion? Screw your client." She wrung her hands as she dropped her head. "Which I'm doing, actually, so yeah, I proved him right."

Whoa. He wasn't in a courtyard, he was standing on a minefield, and he had a feeling that he'd be fucked no matter which direction he stepped. "I don't recall having a particularly easy time convincing you to date me, so I'd say you did the exact opposite of what your father expected of you."

"But it doesn't change the position I've put myself in. As much as I want things to work out between us, I'd be an idiot if I didn't recognize the potential consequences. And if anyone knows the hazards of putting a man before their career, it's me."

"What do you mean?"

"You met my mom. That's the hazard. She just lives in his shadow, and she's trapped. So she takes his bullshit and his affairs, puts his interests before hers. There's no way I'm letting that happen to me."

"Of course you aren't. Is it even a question in your mind?"

He'd expected to see fiery determination in her gaze, but she looked at him with sad eyes instead. "No question in my mind."

A part of him appreciated her honesty. Another part of him understood the silent message: If forced to, she'd choose her career over him any day.

He could tell her that he loved her. That he couldn't imagine a life without her. That they'd figure it out no matter what. And he opened his mouth to tell her just that, but he stopped himself, because those sad eyes told him she didn't feel the same. Maybe she never would. And that was a possibility he was just going to have to deal with. So he took the easy route. Holding her in his arms, he said, "Let's just take it one day at a time, okay?"

She nodded and rested her head against his chest. "That's exactly what I needed to hear."

But it wasn't exactly what he'd wanted to say.

CHAPTER TWENTY

The Department of Architecture was holding its panel on the future of the industry in Gund Hall, a building that itself fascinated Mimi in a way it never would have before she and Daniel began dating. One side of the hall resembled an ordinary office building. The other side, however, jutted into the air, a transparent roof stacked on top of a triangle of windows that let in tons of natural light.

After a brief call to the office, Mimi strolled through the courtyard, imagining Daniel as a grad student staring up at the sky as he studied in this hall. Being here connected her to him in a way that transcended their physical relationship.

She slipped into the auditorium and took a seat in the last row. The event had been organized in a question-and-answer format, with one mic set up in the middle of the two main aisles so that attendees could ask the panelists questions. A member of the audience stood at the mic as Spencer responded to his query.

Mimi, meanwhile, focused on Daniel. He'd dressed the part of the successful businessman, choosing a tailored navy suit and a slim burgundy silk tie. But for once his hair wasn't perfectly styled and instead bore evidence that someone—Mimi to be exact—had run her fingers through it minutes before he took the stage. It had been a quiet moment, away from the eyes of his partners, and she'd ruffled his hair to make the point that he was perfect in all his imperfections.

The angry voice of a young woman interrupted her introspection.

"Well, that may be, but as I see it, the Cambridge Group exemplifies the problem female architects face in this industry. C'mon. Four guys who met at GSD and years later opened up their own firm. And said firm has no female architects? Was there not a single female classmate who could have been part of this venture?"

The young woman wore a Harvard sweatshirt and jeans and kept her arms crossed as she spoke.

Daniel jumped in to address the woman while Mimi made her way to the mic. If the exchange became contentious, she'd be in place to step in. Hopefully, she wouldn't have to.

"The Cambridge Group is sensitive to the issue of gender parity," Daniel said. "It's something we're working to address in the coming months."

The woman leaned into the mic. "How?"

Daniel exuded confidence, his expression calm despite the woman's brusque tone. "I can tell you that this issue is foremost in our minds. Once the firm is ready to hire an architect, you can be sure that every qualified candidate will be given a fair shot at a position, and the firm certainly will advertise for the position far and wide, including encouraging female candidates to apply."

Mimi blew out a soft breath. He was handling the woman's question with poise and tact. Still, she should have anticipated someone in the audience taking issue with the composition of the firm. Hadn't Daniel mentioned that a women's group on campus had already complained about it to the career counseling office? At a minimum she should have prepared the owners for a question like the one the woman had posed to them. But if she were being honest with herself, she hadn't prepared for the panel with her usual thoroughness. Typically, she overcompensated when dealing with new clients. But she'd taken a more relaxed approach to her dealings with this client, probably because she was dating its CEO.

Now positioned in front of the mic, Mimi said, "I'll also add that apart from what Mr. Vargas has mentioned, the firm itself mentors young women in the D.C. area in the hopes that they'll be part of the next crop of architects in the industry. So much so that the firm is considering a scholarship in the name of one of the founder's family members. So you see the firm is aware and being proactive on this front."

The dean of the school, with a microphone of his own, interjected. "Perhaps this issue can be explored further during the reception. In the meantime, I'm interested in hearing about your experiences immediately after leaving the Graduate School of Design."

Mimi returned to her seat as Amar tackled the question. The rest of the panel passed in a blur. She picked at her fingers while she surveyed the owners' faces. Each wore flat expressions, one more placid than the previous one, but she suspected they were pissed that an event meant to raise the firm's profile might undermine it instead. And she couldn't blame them if that were the case.

Thirty minutes later, the dean thanked the panelists and asked the audience to join him in applauding the group.

Afterward, the men stormed into the anteroom.

When Mimi shut the door, Jason rounded on her. "What the hell was that?" he said in a tight voice.

"Okay, that was unfortunate, but I think we handled it well."

Jason barked out a harsh laugh and clenched his jaw. "Well? That was embarrassing." He glared at her and Daniel. "Why the hell did you even dignify her question with a response?"

"Because that's our job," Mimi replied.

Jason's eyes flashed with anger. "No, your *job* is to make us look good, and we ended up looking ridiculous."

Spencer squeezed himself between them and poked at Jason's chest. "Chill out. It's not her fault the woman asked the question. Plus, it was a fair one."

"Yeah, but she should have given us the heads-up about it. Talking points about this issue would have been nice." He gave Daniel a sidelong stare. "But I guess you've got other things on your mind."

"Shut the fuck up, Jason. This isn't the time or place."

Jason's eyes bulged. "Oh, it isn't? Well, tell me when's the right time and place to discuss it. Or are you so caught up that you're incapable of criticizing her when she does a poor job?"

Daniel's face settled into stone and he positioned his body within inches of Jason's. "We're not having this conversation right now because you're acting like an asshole. Show her some respect."

Jason took one step forward, meeting Daniel's piercing stare with his own. "Or what?"

Mimi pulled Daniel back by his suit jacket. "Let me remind you, gentlemen, that you need to make an appearance at the reception. This is a snag, that's all. Go out there and don't be shy about discussing your views on gender diversity. Now's not the time to be tight lipped about all the wonderful things you *are* doing. I'll find the reporters from the student paper and the *Cambridge Gazette* and reinforce what you're saying out there. Okay?"

"Okay," Amar said.

Spencer shook his head in exasperation. "Yeah, fine."

Jason stormed out of the room, and Amar and Spencer followed him.

Daniel stroked her arm. "You okay?"

She stepped back. "I'm fine. Let's focus on the reception." She walked to the door and opened it. "After you."

An hour later, they waited in front of Gund Hall for the car service that would take them to the airport. Mimi checked her e-mails because she didn't know what to say or do to ease the awkwardness in the air.

When the black town car pulled up, she turned to Spencer. "Where's Jason?"

Spencer sighed. "He decided to take a later flight."

"Because he's pissed at me?"

"He's just pissed, Mimi. He's the hothead of the bunch."

Daniel gritted his teeth. "He's the baby of the bunch. Fuck him."

Mimi let Daniel lead her into the car. She was too exhausted by the day's events to do anything but climb into it and sit quietly. A client had never been this angry with her. Not even close. And she couldn't help pinning the blame on her relationship with Daniel. She could rationalize it all she wanted, and maybe Jason was being a dick, too, but he was being a dick because of her relationship with Daniel.

She snuck a glance at Daniel and her stomach twisted. His face was set in a permanent scowl, and he bore no resemblance to the fun and carefree man he usually portrayed to the world. Worse than that, he was pissed at one of his closest friends—because of her.

When they reached the airport, Amar and Spencer claimed to want to pick up some food before their flight, giving her and Daniel a few minutes alone. As they progressed through security, Daniel reached for her at various points, but she moved out of his grasp each time.

His eyes narrowed and he clenched his jaw. "Talk to me."

"Just give me a little space, okay? My head's a mess right now."

He backed up. "Fine. I'll leave you to yourself."

* * *

They reached the departure gate well before their scheduled flight. Which meant there was just enough time for him to figure out how messed up Mimi's head was.

They found seats facing the floor-to-ceiling window, giving them a view of their airplane being prepped for the flight.

He squeezed her hand. "Talk to me. Tell me what you're thinking."

She rubbed her temples. "Let's not do this here, Daniel."

He ground his jaw, hating the fucking wall he could see being re-built in front of his eyes. "Do what here?"

"Oh, c'mon, Daniel. We just dealt with a shitload of tension back there, and you're the only person who won't acknowledge that I'm the cause of it."

"You're blowing this out of proportion. Jason's been in a crappy mood lately, and it's got nothing to do with you."

"Don't pin all this on Jason. Amar and Spencer weren't happy with me, either. They're just being diplomatic about it."

"If they have any complaints about your performance, they're bullshit excuses for our weakness as a firm."

"That's just it, Daniel. It doesn't really matter whether their complaints are well founded. What matters is that they're concerned about how my relationship with you affects my work. And if you weren't so concerned about maintaining the status quo, you'd see that I broke your confidence."

"Broke my confidence? How?"

"I mentioned the scholarship when you specifically asked me not to. That was a conversation we had *on my couch*, Daniel, and I used it to dodge a publicity gaffe. I can't keep all of this straight in my head, and it's affecting my job."

He lowered his voice. "So what are our options?"

She shook her head slowly. "There are none, unfortunately. Getting this account was a big deal for me, but if I hadn't gotten it, I could have proved myself by landing another one. Several even. But losing an account is a big red flag, and I can't let that happen when the partners are evaluating me for partnership. And what would I say? That I'm dating my client, and his colleagues were upset about it? I'd be mortified."

His jaw tightened. Mortified? Did he mean that little to her? "So this is about your embarrassment?"

Her lower lip trembled as she explained. "This is about my credibility, Daniel. You have to understand. I just put a down payment on a home, Daniel. I *need* this. I have to make partner, and if I lose this account, that's not going to happen."

He stared at her, knowing she'd been predicting this moment all along. "Yet you have no problem losing me."

"I don't *want* to lose you, Daniel. But sometimes we can't always get everything we want. Sometimes the puzzle pieces don't fit the way we'd like them to."

Could she hear herself? Probably not, since her very existence depended on believing all that bullshit was true. But no one deserved the crap she was dishing out, not even him. "Did you rip that off a Hallmark card?"

She blinked back tears. "Let's not do this, okay? I want us to be able to work together. And when we started this, you promised you wouldn't make things difficult for me if we decided to part ways."

He cocked his head and surveyed her from head to toe. No matter how much he wanted them to be together, he couldn't fight their battles alone. "Yeah. I'll keep my promise. You had priorities way before you met me, right?" He stood and smiled. "We're fine, Mimi. I'm going to grab a cup of coffee before the flight."

He wasn't fine, though. His heart felt disengaged from all the veins and arteries pumping blood into it.

Is that why they called it a broken heart?

CHAPTER TWENTY-ONE

Mimi pulled into Gracie's driveway and dropped her head onto the steering wheel. After gathering her composure, she trudged up the walkway and rang the doorbell. *Breathe in. Breathe out. Smile. Pretend everything's okay.*

With worry in her eyes, Gracie opened the door and ushered her in. "I didn't know."

"Know what?"

"Daniel's coming over," she whispered.

Mimi's head pounded. *No, no, no.* "Why?"

Gracie looked heavenward. "Ethan got the bright idea to enter a mud run and Daniel's helping him train. Mark, too."

"Midlife crisis?"

"More like moving-to-suburbia crisis."

Mimi placed her bag on the entryway table and dropped onto Gracie's couch. "Perfect. I'll just be over here dying."

Gracie stood at the window and peeked through the blinds. "Have you seen him lately?"

"Not even once. I went to their office to meet with Spencer for a magazine interview, but I didn't see him, and I certainly didn't go out of my way to find him. Plus things are quieting down now that we've overhauled the website and rolled out the new brand strategy. So yeah, I won't have to see him *unless he happens to be at my best friend's house.*" She shook her head in disgust. "Why didn't I stick to the fucking rules?"

"Because you love him?"

"Maybe."

"Probably."

"Possibly."

Mimi fell over and rested her head against the sofa's armrest. "You look beautiful, Gracie. Pregnancy does wondrous things to your ta-tas."

Gracie cupped her breasts. "I know, right?" She flicked her gaze upstairs. *He loves them*, she mouthed.

"He better. And he better love them when they're flapping around like a collapsed soufflé, too."

Gracie stuck her middle finger up at her.

The crunch of the gravel alerted them to someone's arrival. Gracie peeked through the blinds again. "It's just Mark and Karen."

A minute later, Karen walked through the door and straight to the morning table. She dropped her purse onto it and pulled out a stack of books.

Mimi, Gracie, and Mark watched her in silence.

Finally, she looked up. "Shit. Sorry." She crossed the living room and hugged Gracie. "*Lo siento, hermana.* I have a big test on Monday."

Gracie held her chin. "Nothing to be sorry for. Do you want something to eat?"

"No, I'm fine. Hey, Mimi."

Mimi lifted her head. "Hey, Karen."

Karen, Gracie, and Mark exchanged worried looks.

"Uh-oh," Karen said. "What's going on?"

"She broke up with Daniel," Gracie explained.

Mimi punched a pillow into submission before she placed it behind her back. "My current state has nothing to do with that."

Gracie huffed. "Hmm. Okay. Denial. Stage one."

Mark backed away from them. "I'm going to grab a glass of water. Leave you to discuss...stuff."

Karen flared her nostrils. "You do that."

Ethan came barreling down the stairs. "What's up, Mark?"

Ethan and Mark exchanged an intricate handshake that left Mimi's head reeling.

But then she focused on Ethan's athletic gear, which bore the unmistakable crispness of clothing that had recently been removed from a shopping bag.

Mimi snorted. "There's a price tag on your shorts."

Ethan reached the bottom step and stopped. "Where?" he asked as he twisted his torso to look for the tag.

"Ha. Just kidding."

Ethan's mouth twitched. "Mud running is a different animal than cross-country. I had to make sure I was properly outfitted."

"To borrow Gracie's words, 'Hmm. Okay. Denial. Stage one.'"

Gracie barked out a laugh.

And then the doorbell rang. They all turned their heads to watch Mimi's reaction.

She grimaced. "Is someone going to get that?"

Gracie rushed to answer the door. And Mimi sprang from the

couch and headed toward the back of the house. "I need a drink of water."

She picked at her nails as she paced the kitchen. *I'm not ready for this.* Straining to hear Daniel's voice, she moved closer to the kitchen's entryway. She felt short of breath, overwhelmed by the possibility of seeing him in the flesh without her professional armor to protect her. Maybe he'd leave with Ethan and Mark, and they wouldn't have to say a word to each other.

He peeked his head into the kitchen, and Mimi jumped. *Nope. No such luck.*

"Oh, hey, Daniel."

He smiled. "Hey, Mimi. They told me you were in here getting a drink."

"Yeah." She looked around her as though a glass would magically appear in her hands. "Drank it already."

The corners of his eyes crinkled. "They're acting weird in there. I told them we're fine, but they seemed skeptical. We *are* fine, right?"

If fine meant that she wanted to pull him into the pantry and ravage him, yeah, they were fine. And if fine meant that she'd be touching herself tonight with an image of him in her head, yep, they were fine. And if fine meant that seeing him made her heart crumple like discarded paper, then yes, they were super. "Yes. Everything's cool."

He nodded. "Great." A flash of emotion, a second of regret perhaps, flickered in his eyes, and then it disappeared so quickly she couldn't trust that she'd actually seen it. "It's good to see you."

Her throat tightened under the pressure of having to talk to him. After clearing it, she forced the words out. "It's good to see you, too."

She wanted to turn away, before he could see the tears that

threatened to fall, but he reached out and touched her wrist. "Listen, I"—he paused and took a deep breath—"I do miss you, but I also want what's best for you. So do what you need to do, okay?"

Though she was sure he'd meant to make her feel better, his words pelted her, compounding her pain. She managed to give him a ridiculous answer. "Okay."

From the living room, Mark whistled. "Yo, Daniel. Ready to go?"

"Yeah, I'm coming," he said, his gaze never leaving hers. "Take care. I'm sure we'll be talking soon. You'll be prepping me for the interview in *Architectural Digest*, right?"

"Right."

But she wished she could say more. So much more.

I miss you.

I made a mistake.

I don't know what I'm doing, and I wish we could go back to the way things were.

She told him none of that, of course. He didn't deserve to bear the brunt of her confusion.

"Take care, Daniel."

"Take care, Fireworks."

When the front door clicked shut, she released the breath she'd been holding. Screw the water. She needed alcohol.

* * *

When Mimi rejoined Gracie and Karen, the sisters were sitting on opposite ends of the couch. "I made a margarita for me and virgin margaritas for you guys."

Gracie shook her head in wonder. "Made yourself comfortable in my kitchen, did you?"

Karen squished her brows together. "Why virgin for me?"

"Gracie's pregnant so she gets no part of this. And you get a virgin because you're studying. We can't have you hungover before a test."

"You sound like Mark."

Gracie took a sip of her virgin margarita. "Speaking of which, was it just me or was there some pissed-off vibe going on between you two?"

Karen gulped her drink. "This needs alcohol," she said to Mimi. To Gracie, she said, "It wasn't just you. He thinks I'm not taking care of myself. I study too hard. I'm not eating enough. On and on. Blah, blah, blah. We had words."

"Give him a break. He loves you."

"He needs to give me a break. He's stressing me out."

Mimi set her drink on the coffee table and tucked her legs under her. "See? This is why you keep the apartment. If he pisses you off, you have somewhere to go to clear your head."

"Yeah, well, I'm giving up the apartment."

"What? Why?"

"Um. We're engaged to be married, Mimi. And I never stay at my place anyway."

"But you're not getting married immediately, right?"

"No, we're not, but that's beside the point. I'm ready to share my life with him."

"Do you have some money stashed away at least? For a rainy day?"

Karen scowled at her, something she'd never done before. "Mimi, what is with you? I have friends and family, and I'm studying to be a doctor. I think it's highly unlikely I'll need to keep my apartment as protection against a failed relationship."

Mimi threw back her head and took the last sip of her drink like a shot. "No, you should *own* a place, not rent it."

Karen scrunched her face. "No, I should work things out with my boyfriend, not live my life protecting myself against the worst that could happen. You should try it sometime."

Mimi glowered at Karen. *No. She. Did. Not.* "What's that supposed to mean, Karen?"

Gracie injected herself into the fray. "Ladies, relax." She placed her hand on her belly. "The baby doesn't like tension."

Karen groaned, rose from the couch, and plopped onto the chair. "Sorry, Mimi. I'm tired and stressed, and it's none of my business. Forget I said anything."

Except she couldn't forget it. Not easily, at least. Because for the first time, she realized that preparing for the possibility that a relationship would end before it even began was exhausting. although she wasn't happy, she was safe. And that's what mattered.

Right?

CHAPTER TWENTY-TWO

Ian knocked on her office door and walked in without waiting for an invitation. *What an asshole.*

"Are you free tomorrow evening?" he asked.

Sadly, she had nothing to do. Two weeks ago, she would have declined, claiming a conflict but knowing she had plans to be with Daniel. Now, however, she spent the bulk of her day going from one work crisis to the next, volunteering for assignments that would force her to stay late in the office. By the time she made it home, she was exhausted and could do nothing more than collapse on her bed for a fitful sleep. Reducing the number of hours she was awake and idle meant she didn't have to think about how much she missed Daniel. Although spending an evening in Ian's presence was never an appealing prospect, it was still better than moping at home. "Yes, I'm free. Why?"

"A potential client to reel in." He mimicked catching a fish on a hook. "A few drinks and a good meal, and this deal will be as good as done. Figured you could join us. Regale him with stories of your upbringing in Austin. He's originally from Texas."

She forced a smile. "Not that many interesting stories to share, but sure I can join you. What time?"

"Seven p.m. at Ruth's Chris Steakhouse."

"I'll meet you there. Send me the client info."

"Will do." He turned to leave but spun around before he reached her door. "Oh, and the guy's a little conservative. I'm thinking a skirt might be more appropriate attire."

What. The. Fuck? *Please tell me he didn't just say that.* Her legs bounced as she tried to formulate a sensible explanation for Ian's comment. "Excuse me? You're going to tell the client to wear a skirt?"

"That's cute, Mimi. No, I'm suggesting that *you* should wear a skirt."

She said nothing, because whatever she'd say surely would get her fired.

Ian straightened and fidgeted with his cuff links. His narrow gaze searched her face as though he were trying to gauge her mood. "Oh, c'mon, flashing a little leg never hurts."

Her entire body turned hot. She opened her mouth to rip into him, but then she stopped herself. What would that accomplish? The damage was done. And going off on Ian wouldn't help her bid to make partner. "I have work to do, Ian."

She registered his shaky laughter as he turned to leave.

"Such a conscientious employee. See you tomorrow."

With Ian gone, Mimi searched for a piece of chocolate in her desk. When she couldn't find anything, she slammed the drawer shut and went to find Nina. Seconds later, Mimi stormed into her friend's office and paced.

"Damn, woman. What's got you so fired up?"

"Ian."

"Yeah. That'll do it."

"Do you have any idea what he just said to me?"

"Nope."

Mimi blew out a harsh breath, ruffling her bangs. "The fucking prick invited me to join him for a client dinner and suggested that I wear a skirt because, and I quote, 'flashing a little leg never hurts.'"

"Oh, the little shit. Did you tell him to kiss your ass?"

Mimi stopped pacing. "Of course not."

"So what did you say?"

"I said nothing."

"I don't get it. You're a firecracker in every aspect of your life except here. What exactly are you accomplishing by taking his shit?"

"Look, you know what we have to face here. So I've tried to lay low until I get that promotion. Then I won't be under his thumb anymore."

"And you'll have lost yourself in the process. You say nothing when he acts like a jerk. You dress as though you're Amish. News flash. I'm pretty sure Ian knows you have a vagina no matter what you wear. And that's not going to magically change when you become a partner."

"My choice of work attire has nothing to do with this."

"It doesn't? Let me ask you this. If Ian were to make a sexist comment about the length of my skirts, would you think I had it coming? Would you think I'd asked for it by not dressing like you do? Because that's what it sounds like. He's the asshole, not me, not you. But you're playing into his bullshit. Mimi, there's always going to be an Ian. A boss, a colleague, a client."

"I've just had to fight the dumb blonde stereotype my whole life."

"And I've encountered all kinds of stereotypes my whole life. I can change my clothes all I want, but I can't change the color of my skin, nor do I want to. So I deal with it. Because they're the problem, not me."

Mimi collapsed into the chair facing Nina's desk. She'd spent most of her professional career downplaying her sexuality, desperate to achieve success without her femininity inviting harassment or sabotaging her advancement. All because success guaranteed her independence. Guaranteed that she would be okay if someone hurt her. And where had that gotten her? In the exact place she'd been running from. Her relentless pursuit of freedom had actually become her cage. Now she felt stupid and small. Ridiculously naïve, too. "I'm an idiot."

"Stop."

"No, really. How can I be so self-aware in certain aspects of my life and such a nitwit in others?"

Nina stood and rounded her desk. "Oh, I wasn't disagreeing with you. I just want to be closer to you for this talk." After taking Mimi's hand, she sat next to her. "Okay. You were saying you're an idiot. Continue."

"I'm a mess."

"Yes. Yes, you are."

The corners of Mimi's mouth quirked up despite her best efforts not to crack a smile. But the lighthearted feeling dissipated when she remembered how she'd treated Daniel. "Oh, God. I rejected Daniel like he was an inconvenience, because he threatened the sham of a professional life I'd developed over the years. And all because I wanted to protect myself against the very thing I'm dealing with now anyway. I was always preparing for the worst. And because of that, I threw away the best thing that's ever happened to me. How could I have been so stupid?"

"Listen here, sweetie. Men and women have been acting stupid around each other since time immemorial. The thing is, it's only a problem if you don't fix it."

"So I wear my nicest pair of slacks to this dinner, and if Ian says anything about it, I tell him to kiss my ass."

Nina nodded. "Right."

"And I make sure HR knows about Ian's asinine comments."

Nina tapped her nose. "Exactly."

"And I go after my man."

"Yup."

"And who gives a shit if that screws up my chances for partnership, right?"

"It won't. You'll make sure of it."

Mimi contemplated how that would play out. It could blow up in her face, but it was a chance she was willing to take. She'd start over somewhere else if necessary. It would probably mean she'd have to wait a few more years for partnership, but the sacrifice would be worth it. If given the choice between keeping her job and loving Daniel, she'd choose Daniel every time. "I'll try not to botch this, at least. And listen, to make this work, I'll need a favor."

Nina nodded. "Anything." Then she raised her index finger in the air. "Within reason."

"It'll mean more work for you."

"As I said, anything—within reason."

"Your unconditional support warms my heart."

"Do you want my help or not?"

Mimi smiled. "I do. So here's what I'm thinking…"

* * *

Ian was already sitting at their table when Mimi arrived at Ruth's Chris. He rose and glanced at her lower body.

She held her breath, wondering if they were going to come to blows this early in the evening, but he said nothing about her pantsuit.

"Mr. Burke's running late," he explained as he sat down again. "Which isn't a bad thing necessarily. It'll give us a few minutes to talk before he arrives."

A server filled her water glass, and she thanked him. Pulling out her phone, she pulled up the Google search she'd run on Jackson Burke. "I agree. I have some ideas."

As usual, Ian gave her a dismissive wave. "Let's table your ideas and talk about the e-mail you sent to the partners this afternoon."

Shit. She hadn't anticipated that he'd want to talk about it before their meeting with Burke. "What do you want to talk about exactly?"

"The unprofessionalism of it all, frankly. You've been dating one of our clients? Hardly demonstrates that you've got the firm's interests in the forefront of your mind."

Mimi's cheeks flushed, but she refused to cower anymore. "It's not what I would have wanted, yes, but I'm trying to deal with the situation as professionally as possible."

"By suggesting that Nina replace you as the main client contact while you get credit for the account as a supervising partner? You have *cojones*, lady."

She curled her lip, no longer caring whether she pissed him off. "More than you do, I'd say. Is that why you have a problem with me, Ian? Because my balls are bigger than yours?"

"Watch it, Mimi."

She leaned forward. "No, *you* watch it. I've worked at Baxter for seven years and you've been an ass for six point nine of them. Say what you want about my professionalism in this one instance in seven years, but you *can't* say I don't know how to do my job."

"Don't try to convince me. You won't get my vote."

"That's fine. Luckily for me there are four other partners who aren't out to tank my career."

They glared at each other until Jackson Burke arrived seconds later. *Thank fuck*. She'd do her job and get as far away from Ian as possible.

Ian stood, pasted on a smile, and gave Burke a firm handshake. "Good to see you again, Jackson."

Mimi rose as Ian made the introductions. "This is Mimi Pennington. One of our senior associates. Mimi, this is Jackson Burke."

Jackson was around her father's age. The sides of his thick hair were graying, and he sported a small paunch that suggested he had an affinity for beer. "A pleasure to meet you, Ms. Pennington," he said with a tight smile.

"Call me, Mimi."

Their server returned and handed them their menus. "Good evening, all. Can I start anyone off with a cocktail?"

Jackson spoke first. "A Founder's Reserve Whiskey for me. Neat. Mimi? Ian?"

Since she had no more fucks to give, she asked for what she really wanted. "I think I'll live a little tonight. A Lemon Drop, please."

Jackson beamed at her. "Well, all right."

Ian closed his menu. "A glass of Chardonnay for me."

Mimi made a snoozing sound and waggled her eyebrows at Burke. "As you can see, he's the life of the party."

Jackson roared with laughter, and Mimi nearly jumped out of her skin. The man was a bear in human clothing. Ian used his menu to hide his grimace from Burke. Mimi simply smiled at him.

They made small talk until their drinks arrived. After their server had taken their orders, Jackson set his elbows on the table and leaned forward. "I'm not going to bullshit you. I have half a mind not to hire any PR firm at all. I just don't think you can help our situation."

Ian's eyes widened, obviously surprised by Burke's imminent defection.

She'd done some preliminary research on Burke's business that afternoon. He owned a dozen pet boarding kennels in Virginia and had come under fire recently for having substandard accommodations for his clients' pets. Simply put, pet owners worried that their beloved animals wouldn't be treated well at one of his kennels.

Burke's solemn expression suggested he'd given up on trying to resuscitate the business. "I started my company because I love animals, but I can't be everywhere at one time, and the business is bigger than I'd ever intended. It might be time to sell it."

Mimi had a few ideas, though. "Mr. Burke—"

"Call me Jackson."

"Jackson, I've taken a look at the press you've gotten, and I understand your concerns. I've been at Baxter for seven years, and we've always operated on three pillars: show, tell, or bury. You might be inclined to think the right strategy is to bury this story, but I think the opposite might be true."

Ian cleared his throat. "I'll take it from here, Mimi."

She gnashed her teeth and leaned back.

"Now hold on a minute," Jackson said. "I'd like to hear what she has to say. She's piqued my interest."

Ian's face turned crimson. "Of course. Go ahead, Mimi."

She sat up and folded her hands on the table. "Well, it's clear that some of your potential customers don't have confidence in your kennels, but if you were responsive to those concerns, they might give you another shot. Let's face it. In the social media age, negative reviews get around fast, and customers will go elsewhere if there's a better alternative."

Jackson closed his eyes. "Are you trying to cheer me up here?"

Now that she knew Jackson's troubles stemmed from mismanagement rather than malice, she *wanted* to help him. She gave him a lopsided grin. "So if customers will go elsewhere if there's a better alternative, *be* the better alternative."

"How do I do that if they won't bring their pets to my kennels?"

"Bring them *into* your kennels, that's how. I've seen stories about childcare centers that allow parents to monitor their children while they're at work. From behind their computers, they can check in to see how their kids are doing." She leaned in. "Do that for pets."

Jackson rubbed his jaw. "Sounds expensive."

"Charge for it, then. It's an added expense for the owners, for sure, but the fact that you're even willing to provide the service will bring nonsubscribers in. And then we sell the heck out of that service in the press, explaining how it came about and what you're willing to do to address clients' concerns. Pet lovers will eat it up. And you'll have a way to monitor your staff. I'm sure there are a host of issues you'll want to consider, but that's one idea."

Their food arrived, and Jackson dug into his steak with enthusiasm. In between chews, he said, "You've given me a lot to think about, and you've shown creativity. That alone makes me want to hire your firm."

Ian the deadwood chimed in then. "We'd love to have your business, Jackson."

Jackson swallowed. "I think that can be arranged. I have just one condition."

Ian gave him a shit-eating grin. "What's that?"

"I'd like Mimi to run the account."

This time Mimi beamed. "I'd love to, Jackson."

"Think that can be arranged, Ian?" Jackson asked.

Ian's face fell for a second, but he regrouped quickly and faked a smile. "Sure, Jackson. Whatever you want."

Mimi, meanwhile, was laughing inside. *Take that, jackass.*

CHAPTER TWENTY-THREE

Daniel rubbed his jaw and winced at its rough texture. He couldn't remember the last time he'd gone this long without shaving. And the dark circles under his eyes he'd spied in the bathroom mirror this morning matched his dark mood. As Mimi would have put it, he was a fucking mess.

Two weeks.

Two weeks since she'd broken his heart.

Two weeks since he'd felt whole.

He'd get beyond it. He was better than most at rising out of the ashes and finding a way to channel his hurt into something productive. He'd do it again. Just not today apparently.

The ding of his computer alerted him to a new e-mail. No surprise there. The firm's business had increased fourfold since Mimi had rebranded their website and client communications. Knowing that their recent successes were largely her doing seemed cruel in the extreme. Everywhere he looked, she was there. Even the mock-up of

their new client brochure that sat on his desk awaiting his approval
had been her idea.

He swiveled in his chair and his stomach dropped at the sight
of Mimi's name. The subject read: *"Potential New Personnel on
Board."*

What the hell does that mean?

He clicked on the e-mail, which she'd addressed to the Cambridge Group partners. It read:

Gentlemen,

In light of your firm's continuing needs, I've proposed to the
partnership that Nina Walker, another senior associate at the
firm, serve as your primary contact going forward. Nina is one
of Baxter's finest publicists, and I have complete confidence
in her ability to assist you with any public relations projects. I
would serve in a supervisory role but would not handle any day-
to-day concerns. The partners have indicated a willingness to
accept my proposal, but as you might imagine, they're interested in your feedback and obviously would not move forward
should you have an objection. I'd like to meet with the members
of the firm at your respective conveniences to discuss the matter and to give you an opportunity to meet Nina. Please let me
know whether you are amenable.

Best,
Mimi Pennington

Fuck. He shoved his chair back, and a stack of papers on his desk
went flying through the air before landing all over the floor. He

stood and paced his office, his steps so heavy he'd probably get a noise complaint from the tenants of the office below.

So now she wanted nothing to do with the firm? Was she that desperate to avoid him? Where was the ultraprofessional woman who wouldn't back away from a challenge? Hiding from him obviously. He'd never been the kind of man to throw objects in frustration, but today he considered doing just that.

His cell phone vibrated on his desk. It was from a number he'd committed to memory.

Mimi: Check your e-mail again.

He didn't want to. A short note explaining herself would only anger him more.

Buzz.

Mimi: Please.

She couldn't have known that he hadn't opened the e-mail yet. But she knew him. That alone made him curious to read her explanation.

He opened his e-mail account and saw the second e-mail with the subject line "Operation Grovel." This one had an attachment: an audio file. He tapped the Play icon, and the sounds of "Bohemian Rhapsody" filled his office.

Then his speakerphone buzzed, and he couldn't hold back his smile. "Yes, Felicia?"

"You have a special delivery, Daniel."

He jumped up. "I'll be right there."

A bouquet of blue orchids rested on the ledge of the reception desk. His heart thudded in his chest. He grabbed the flower-filled vase and spun around. "Anything else?"

Felicia glanced at him and dropped her head. "That's it."

He returned to his office and placed the flowers on the side table by the window. His phone buzzed again.

Mimi: Is any of this working?

Daniel: Depends on your goal.

Mimi: I'm trying to orchestrate a reconciliation.

Daniel: Where's the Puerto Rican food?

Mimi: OMG. It's hard to find Puerto Rican food in D.C. Who do I have to bone to find it? I'm on it, though.

He threw back his head and laughed. Only Mimi would describe sex as boning in a text.

Daniel: You better not bone anyone but me. Just come see me.

Mimi: Will do.

He paced his office while he waited for her. Ten torturous minutes passed. She'd come back to him, and he couldn't wait to hold her in his arms again.

What the hell is taking her so long?

After smoothing his hands on his slacks, he hit the speakerphone.

"Yes, Daniel?" Felicia asked.

"When Mimi arrives, send her straight back."

"You got it," Felicia said in a singsong voice.

A few minutes later, Mimi herself peeked into his office with a smile that made his chest ache. Her presence alone tilted his world back into place.

He strode across the room and pulled her inside. After closing the door, he pushed her against it, and her purse landed on the floor with a thud. With his arm bent above her, he used his other hand to caress her cheek. "God, I've missed you."

She threw her arms around his neck. "I've missed you, too.

And I'm going to grovel, I swear, but first I need to kiss you."

He lifted her, and she locked her legs around his waist. And then she gave him the sweetest, softest mind-blowing kiss, and he was done. He'd listen to whatever groveling she needed to get out of her system, but she was back in his arms and that was all that mattered to him.

She slid down his body and guided him to sit on his desk. He cataloged her features, what she wore, and the wary expression on her face.

She took a deep breath and blew out slowly. "You had every right to be mad at me."

He reached out and threaded his fingers through hers. "Mimi, I was never mad at you. I was sad for us."

Her eyes watered. "I gave up on us too easily. I know that now. I was so afraid to risk my heart that I hid behind my concerns about my independence and my career. For years, I've focused on protecting myself against being hurt. So long as I had my independence and my career, I'd always land on my feet when someone disappointed me. But you never disappointed me, not once, and the hurt I experienced when I turned you away was worse than anything I've ever felt before. I should have fought for us, but I didn't, and I should have realized sooner how much you mean to me."

"How much do I mean to you, Fireworks?"

"I can't imagine my life without you."

He pulled her close. "And now you won't have to."

She stared back at him with glossy eyes. "God, I love you."

"I love you, too, Mimi. Everything else, we'll figure out as we go."

And he meant it. Because no one else understood him the way she did. No one else dug deep enough to find the real man underneath the layers he'd developed over the years. She'd gotten under his skin from the beginning, and that's exactly where he wanted her to be.

With her face burrowed in his neck, and his arms wrapped around her, he felt whole again. The silent moment didn't last long, however.

She pulled back and snapped her fingers. "So I know I bombed on the Puerto Rican food, but I'd like to make it up to you."

He smiled. "Oh yeah. How?"

"Well, if you're not doing anything this weekend, I'd like to take you to Virginia," she said with a mischievous glint in her eyes. "I found a spa where we can take a mud bath and get *very dirty* together. We might even be able to reenact your teenage fantasies and mud wrestle."

He chuckled. "Damn, woman, you are made for me."

She tugged on his tie, rose on her toes, and kissed him hard. When they separated, she winked at him. "Damn right I am."

Did you miss Gracie and Ethan's love story?

An excerpt from the first book in Mia Sosa's The Suits Undone series, *Unbuttoning the CEO*, follows.

CHAPTER ONE

Ethan Hill couldn't have imagined a more craptastic morning.

He stood next to his lawyer in a dim and musty courtroom in the nation's capital. The dreary atmosphere made his stomach churn. And the gluten-free muffin his assistant had given him earlier wasn't helping matters. Now that he thought about it, what the hell was wrong with gluten anyway?

Judge Monroe, a regal woman with a crop of silver hair and flawless skin, peered at him over her tortoiseshell-framed glasses and cleared her throat. "Mr. Hill, as I'm sure you're aware, a reckless driving conviction carries the possibility of a one-year jail sentence. It's not my penalty of choice, but given that you've accumulated five speeding tickets in as many months, a fine won't do."

Jail? Was she seriously considering jail? Ethan's heart raced, and his knees threatened to buckle. He even considered running through the Lamaze breathing his sister Emily had practiced in preparation for the birth of his niece. *Hee-hee-hooo. Hee-hee-hooo.*

Judge Monroe clasped her hands and leaned forward. "Your company's support of charities is to be commended. But in my view, a man who claims such *devotion* to charitable endeavors ought to spend time serving the community rather than throwing money at it. I'm sentencing you to community service."

Ethan's heart slowed to a gallop. Given a choice between jail and a couple of weeks of community service, he'd pick community service any day. "Thank you, Judge Monroe."

"Hold on, Mr. Hill. You might not want to thank me just yet."

Ethan's stomach twisted, ending its protest with a loud gurgle. *Damn you, gluten-free muffin.*

Judge Monroe scribbled on a legal pad. Ethan couldn't see what she wrote, but the hard strokes of her pen suggested she wanted to stick a figurative foot up his butt. Ethan mentally prepared himself to bend over.

After a few seconds, the judge looked up and smirked. Or was that a snort? Dammit, he wasn't sure.

"Mr. Hill, I'm sentencing you to two hundred hours of community service, to be completed with one charitable organization over the course of the next six months. Choose a charity that could benefit from your technical skills. And have your lawyer inform my clerk of the charity you've selected."

Ethan swiped a hand down his face. The sentence was outrageous. He calculated the hours in his head, figuring he'd have to spend just under eight hours a week for the next twenty-six weeks to fulfill the sentence. He doubted he could manage to do that on top of his eighty-hour workweek, but he didn't appear to have a choice.

His lawyer, a buddy from college with stellar credentials and a ruddy, cherubic face, leaned his stocky frame toward Ethan and whispered in his ear. "You got off easy, pal. Judge Monroe tends to take creativity to a new level when she's pissed. She must have gotten laid last night."

Ethan's gaze darted to the judge, whose tight expression made him wonder whether she'd heard his lawyer's quip. He'd dealt with intimidating businessmen twice her size, but when her bespectacled gaze landed on his face, Ethan barely suppressed the urge to squirm.

She took a deep breath. "Mr. Hill, use this sentence as an opportunity to think about your choices. Self-destructive behavior is one thing. Behavior that endangers others is quite another. And be prepared to take the bus for the next several months. What you do after that is up to you, but if you get another speeding ticket, this court will impose the maximum penalty. Got it?"

"Got it, Your Honor."

Judge Monroe nodded. "Court is adjourned."

The slam of her gavel against the bench might as well have been a slap upside his head. As he watched the judge exit the courtroom, Ethan vowed never to speed again. He couldn't afford to go to jail. Not again anyway.

* * *

Back at the office, Ethan's first task was to update the company's board about his legal situation. Two years ago, the board had taken a chance on him. He'd be wise not to alienate any of its members, especially when those members had hired him based on his vow that his reckless days were over.

He'd just begun to type an e-mail to the board when Mark Lansing, the company's CFO, waltzed into his office. Mark also served as his personal pain in the ass. And though he hesitated to tell Mark this, Ethan considered the man his best friend.

"Well, well," Mark said. "If it isn't Dale Earnhardt, Jr., in the flesh."

"Very funny. This time, I'm screwed."

Mark rubbed his hands together as he sat down. He didn't bother to hide his wide grin. "What happened?"

"She gave me community service. Two hundred hours of it."

Mark scrunched his brows and whistled. "That's harsh."

"Harsh or not, the sentence stands."

"How long do you have?"

"Six months. I get to pick the organization, but it has to be the right fit for my technical skills, whatever that means. And I'm going to use my first name there."

He hadn't used his first name since he'd left home to attend college at Penn. Sure, he wasn't a household name, but thanks to Google, anyone could easily discover his role in the corporation. If all went according to plan, no one at the organization would know he was the CEO of a multimillion-dollar communications company. And no one would know about his unflattering past. *How refreshing*.

Mark tapped his lips with a single finger. "And by first name, do you mean you plan to go in under the radar?"

Exactly. If no one knew who he was, the board could pretend it never happened. "Right. Something on your mind, Mark?"

Mark's gaze shifted around the room as he tapped his hands on Ethan's desk. His eyes were bright. Too bright. "Give me a minute. I'll be right back." Before Ethan could stop him, Mark shot out of the chair and left the office.

Ethan turned back to his computer. He'd just finished the e-mail to the board when Mark returned and dropped a section of the day's newspaper on his desk.

"Check that out," Mark said.

Ethan sighed, the steady throb at his temples making him more irritable than usual. "What am I looking for?"

"C-2. Flip the page."

Ethan turned the page. The headline of the full-page article read, LEARN TO NET TEACHES STUDENTS AND SENIORS HOW TO SURF THE WEB.

A photograph of a woman and two young boys accompanied the article. The boys sat in front of a computer and the woman stood behind them, her arms draped over their shoulders. Her dark, wavy hair fell against her cheeks, and her brown eyes gleamed with excitement. He scanned the first paragraph, searching for her name.

Graciela Ramirez.

A dozen images hit him at once. All of them involved Ms. Ramirez in a compromising position. With him. He looked up at Mark, who studied his reaction to the photograph. Ethan shrugged and tossed the newspaper on the ever-increasing pile of untouched papers on his desk. "I'll read it later. I need to get this e-mail out to the board."

Mark smirked. "Okay, sure. It's too bad, though."

"What's too bad?"

"She's engaged."

If he'd had a gun pointed to his head, Ethan would have been hard-pressed to explain why he was disappointed by that knowledge. "How do you know?"

Mark smiled. "It says so in the article you're going to read as soon as I leave." With his smile still in place, Mark sauntered through the door and saluted Ethan before he closed it.

When the door clicked shut, Ethan dove for the paper and placed the page in front of him. According to the article, Ms. Ramirez had been promoted from program manager to director three months ago.

The mission of Learn to Net—or LTN, as she referred to it in the article—was to serve individuals without regular access to computers, educating them about online research libraries, online job applications, social media websites, and other resources on the Web.

He read further, looking for information about Ms. Ramirez's engagement. Finding none, he gritted his teeth, speed-dialed Mark, and placed the phone in speaker mode.

Mark answered after the first ring. "What?"

"It doesn't say she's engaged."

Mark chuckled. "No, it doesn't. But you'd only know that if you read the entire article in the few minutes since I left your office. You're so predictable that I can predict when you're trying not to be predictable."

"Is she engaged or not?"

"I have no clue," Mark said.

"Do you know anything else about her?"

"Nope."

Ethan threw his head back against his chair. "I'm surrounded by people who are useless to me."

"You're wrong. I listen. Aren't you the man who whined about wanting to meet someone without the baggage of your pseudo-celebrity status getting in the way? Here's your chance, *Nic*."

"Your craftiness scares even me."

Mark snorted. "One day, you'll thank me. I'm hanging up now."

"No, wait."

"Is this about the company?" Mark asked.

"Yes."

"Good, because I'm not inclined to provide any more advice about your miserable love life."

"Mark, shut the hell up already. This is about the computer systems upgrade."

"What about it?"

"Where are the old computers going?"

"I don't know. The IT department handles recycling and donations."

"Have the old computers donated to Learn to Net, but arrange for them to be donated anonymously."

"I'd love to, but I can't."

"Why not?"

"No low-key donations, remember? Board policy. All charitable donations are to be publicized within an inch of their lives. The gift of corporate giving comes with shameless promotion of the company."

Of course. Ethan had recommended that policy. From a business perspective, it made sense. Now, it seemed cold. Manipulative. "I remember. Never mind."

"Anything else?"

"No, that's all," Ethan said. Then he disconnected the call.

Rather than e-mail the board, Ethan browsed LTN's website. It was a legitimate charitable organization, with locations in New York and D.C. Given his company's interests in Internet communications, Ethan's decision to complete his community service hours with the organization was a no-brainer. His choice to serve there had nothing to do with its director. *Yeah. Right.*

Ethan squeezed his stress ball, a constant companion since he'd become the company's CEO. He hoped he wouldn't regret the decision to work with LTN. The court had ordered him to serve the community. And he would. Pretending to be someone else. At an organization with an attractive woman at its helm. *What could go wrong?*

* * *

Gracie Ramirez sat at her desk and reread the letter she'd received from Nathan Dempsey, a lawyer at a prestigious law firm near DuPont Circle. Two weeks ago, she'd agreed to host a man who'd been sentenced to community service for reckless driving. Nicholas E. Hill. Sounded plain enough. Mr. Hill's lawyer had assured her that his client posed no threat to her or LTN's members, and he'd even provided a statement attesting to Mr. Hill's criminal record. According to that record, the man only possessed a lead foot, but given LTN's limited resources, she would have been crazy not to accept the free help that went along with that foot.

With her morning to-do list set, she turned to her computer to work on LTN's annual report. Her fingers hovered over the keyboard, however, and she dropped her head. She had yet to tackle the worst part—the organization's woeful lack of funding.

Uh-uh. There'd be no pity party for her. She was going to stay positive. She refused to dwell on the fact that she'd inherited a mess of an organization, one that hadn't made a serious effort to solicit donations to ensure a steady cash flow. Still, if she didn't secure funding soon, the doors of the D.C. location would close by the end of the fiscal year. And Gracie would return to New York, where her father would greet her with open arms and a smug expression.

She'd accepted failure in her love life, but failure in her professional life was *not* an option.

A rap on her door jolted her out of her thoughts. Gracie grimaced when she saw Daniel Vargas standing at the threshold. His family, like hers, lived in New York. Somehow he'd finagled his way onto LTN's board. As a result, she'd come to think of him as her father's spy.

Daniel swept into her office and assumed a stance that reminded her of a soldier at attention: feet wide apart, chest out, and hands behind his back. "*Hola, Graciela, esta todo bien?*"

"At ease, Mr. Vargas. Everything's fine. What can I do for you?"

"I was wondering if you're available for lunch."

Gracie was thankful she had a good excuse today to turn him down. "I can't, Daniel. I have someone coming in soon. For community service. I have to give him a tour of the facility and get him started on a couple of projects."

"Fine. Another time, then."

Daniel was a prominent architect in the city, and almost universally regarded as a catch. Daniel himself thought he was a catch. Just another reason she considered him an arrogant and eligible man who simply happened to draw excellent architectural plans.

Gracie opened a drawer and reached for her purse, an excuse to avoid his gaze as she turned him down for the fifth time. "Daniel, we've been over this before. It's not going to happen. I just don't think of you that way. And your role on the board presents a clear conflict of interest." She peeked at him to gauge whether any of her spiel was sinking in.

His chest caved in at her words, but then it puffed back out. "I'm a patient man, Graciela. You will come to your senses. And when you do, I'll resign from the board. It's that easy."

Gracie's mouth gaped. Did he think the casual way in which he treated his position on the board somehow endeared him to her? Not in this lifetime. "I've got a lot of work to do, Daniel. Was there anything else?"

Wise enough to take the hint, he cut a corner and pivoted toward the door. "No, no. I'll catch up with you some other time."

She waved him off, dismissing him and his perfectly styled hair.

With Daniel gone, she swiveled her chair toward her computer screen and returned to the annual report. Thirty minutes later, her office phone buzzed and the voice of her assistant, Brenda, filled the room. "Gracie, Nicholas Hill is here to see you." After that announcement, Brenda's voice lowered to a whisper. "He's hot, Gracie. I think I'm going to head to the bathroom to sort myself out."

Gracie rolled her eyes. Brenda was a smart and efficient assistant, but she had either no ability or no desire to filter her inappropriate thoughts, which meant she shared them with Gracie—often.

"I'll be right out," Gracie said.

She straightened in her chair and twisted her neck from side to side to ease the tightness in her shoulders. Checking her reflection in the mirror near her door, she licked her lips and swept her hair away from her face. Before she reached the reception area, she took a deep breath and pasted on a welcoming smile.

Brenda came into view first. Gracie resisted the urge to laugh when her assistant fanned herself. *Focus, Gracie. Focus.*

Nicholas Hill stood with his back to her, giving Gracie a few seconds to glance at her feet to be sure her hem wasn't tucked into a shoe. Distracted by her wardrobe check, she gave him her typical perfunctory greeting as she held out her hand. "Welcome, Mr. Hill. My name is Graciela Ramirez, the director of Learn to Net. Call me Gracie. It's a pleasure to meet—"

When Nicholas Hill's warm hand grasped hers, she looked up at him and her mouth stopped moving. Brenda's assessment of his appearance was trite, but Gracie had to admit the description was spot on. This man—*her ward for two hundred hours*—rendered her speechless.

Taking in the twinkle in his green eyes and the lopsided grin that emphasized his full lips, Gracie wanted to stuff him in a box, slap a bow on it, and set it under the Christmas tree. What the hell? So unlike her. And unsettling. Frankly, she needed a minute to collect herself, because he was too much to absorb at once.

"Hello, Gracie. This isn't the best of circumstances, but it's a pleasure to meet you. And call me . . ." He paused. "Call me Nic."

Nic's deep voice filled the space as his fingers lingered on hers. Her gaze dropped to their clasped hands, a joining more intimate than it should have been in this context. He snatched his hand away, maybe in recognition of that fact, and ran it through his tousled, dark brown hair. Gracie's fingers itched to touch those locks, because she knew they'd be just as soft as they promised. Returning her gaze to his face, she suppressed a sigh.

Wait. She had to remember why he was here. He was a reckless driver, and that was a bad thing. *Bad, bad, bad.* But she couldn't help wondering whether he was reckless in more pleasurable ways. *Yum, yum, yum.*

Ugh. Get it together, Gracie. He's just a man, and you're a smart, capable professional who has an important nonprofit to run, she reminded herself.

She cleared her throat and willed herself to settle down. "I'll show you around and then we can head back to my office to discuss the projects I'd like your help with. Sound good?"

"Sounds great," he said. "Lead the way."

Gracie hesitated. It was a truth universally acknowledged that a man in possession of a pair of eyes would check out a woman's butt upon meeting her. Hoping to divert him from checking out said butt, she walked beside him and pointed out the framed awards that hung on the walls.

She was sure he was no stranger to women who came undone in his presence, and she didn't want to be the latest poor soul to join them. She tried. She did. But when she closed her eyes for the briefest of moments, she imagined Nic's lips pressed against her neck as he held her in his arms. *Do not think of him in that way. Do not think of him in that way.*

Saving LTN was her highest priority. She couldn't afford to be distracted by any man. So it should have been no surprise that Nic was distraction personified. Somewhere the gods were laughing at her. Six months. She could ignore him for that long, right? *Right.*

About the Author

Mia Sosa was born and raised in New York City. She attended the University of Pennsylvania, where she earned her bachelor's degree in communications and met her own romance hero, her husband. She once dreamed of being a professional singer, but then she discovered she would have to perform onstage to realize that dream and decided to take the law school admissions test instead. A graduate of Yale Law School, Mia practiced First Amendment and media law in the nation's capital for ten years before returning to her creative roots. Now, she spends most of her days writing contemporary romances about smart women and the complicated men who love them. Okay, let's be real here: She wears PJs all day and watches more reality television than a network television censor—all in the name of research, of course. Mia lives in Maryland with her husband and two daughters and is still on the hunt for the perfect karaoke bar.

You can learn more at:
MiaSosa.com
Twitter @MiaSosaRomance
Facebook.com/MiaSosa.Author

CPSIA information can be obtained
at www.ICGtesting.com
Printed in the USA
BVOW08s1915280717
490463BV00001B/47/P